PENGUIN BOOKS

COLD DOG SOUP

Stephen Dobyns is the author of twelve novels and seven books of poetry. His fiction includes *The Two Deaths of Señora Puccini* and a series of detective novels featuring Charlie Bradshaw of Saratoga Springs, all published by Penguin Books. His most recent collection of poems is *Body Traffic* and is also available from Penguin. Mr. Dobyns is a professor of English at Syracuse University.

COLD DOG SOUP

Stephen Dobyns

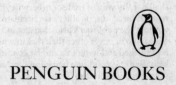

PENGUIN BOOKS

PENGUIN BOOKS
Published by the Penguin Group
Viking Penguin, a division of Penguin Books USA Inc.,
375 Hudson Street, New York, New York 10014, U.S.A.
Penguin Books Ltd, 27 Wrights Lane,
London W8 5TZ, England
Penguin Books Australia Ltd, Ringwood,
Victoria, Australia
Penguin Books Canada Ltd, 2801 John Street,
Markham, Ontario, Canada L3R 1B4
Penguin Books (N.Z.) Ltd, 182–190 Wairau Road,
Auckland 10, New Zealand

Penguin Books Ltd, Registered Offices:
Harmondsworth, Middlesex, England

First published in the United States of America by
Viking Penguin Inc., 1985
Published in Penguin Books 1991

10 9 8 7 6 5 4 3 2 1

PUBLISHER'S NOTE
This is a work of fiction. Names, characters, places, and incidents
either are the product of the author's imagination or are used
fictitiously, and any resemblance to actual persons, living or dead,
events, or locales is entirely coincidental.

THE LIBRARY OF CONGRESS HAS CATALOGUED THE HARDCOVER AS FOLLOWS:
Dobyns, Stephen, 1941–
Cold dog soup.
I. Title.
PS3554.O2C58   1985   813'.54   85–10604
ISBN 0–670–80840–7
ISBN 0 14 01.2155 2

Printed in the United States of America

FOR JAMES COURTNEY HOBLOCK

COLD DOG SOUP

CHAPTER ONE

As Latchmer took hold of the knob of the front door of the apartment house, the doorman on the other side smartly yanked it open. Latchmer had waited a shade too long in letting go and consequently was pulled into the lobby with some force. In his right hand, he carried a potted begonia with pink flowers. The pot itself was wrapped with green tinfoil. Normally, it would have been easy enough to recover his balance, but just inside the door were three descending steps. These he met with a half stumble and half skip.

The walls of the lobby were lined with mirrors, presenting Latchmer with the opportunity to see himself in flight. Standing still, he was an agreeable looking man in a three-piece brown corduroy suit. Before leaving his apartment half an hour before, he had studied himself in the hall mirror and decided that he bore his thirty-five years with reasonable dignity. Tall and thin, he reminded himself of a diplomat or the maitre d' of a really good restaurant. But no man off a dance floor looks his best while doing irregular pirouettes.

The doorman stood by the entrance and stared at Latchmer with a flat, expressionless face. He wore a maroon uniform and appeared to be Indian or Pakistani. The mirrored walls made it seem to Latchmer that he was surrounded by a crowd of dark-skinned men who watched but did not judge. To be so encircled made Latchmer feel primitive and tribal.

He did not fall. With great effort, Latchmer managed to keep both legs more or less perpendicular, and, after half a dozen circles of decreasing speed, be bumped softly against the wall next to the elevator.

"One hundred percent, I thought you were going down," said the doorman. He sounded sympathetic, yet disappointed.

"Just lucky, I guess," said Latchmer. Glancing again at the mirror, he saw that his brown hair had become slightly mussed. Licking two fingers, he smoothed it back in place.

"You are visiting a resident?" asked the doorman.

"Sarah Hughes."

"She is expecting?"

"I'm having dinner with her and her mother." Latchmer looked at his watch. It was just seven.

"Floor eight, first door on the left," said the doorman. "Once within the elevator, please push the button reading eight."

Latchmer entered the elevator and pushed the button. For a moment, he and the doorman stared at each other. Then the sliding doors snipped their exchanged look like scissors snipping a taut string. The walls of the elevator were also lined with mirrors, which gave Latchmer the chance to observe himself as he was borne upward. He picked several dead leaves off the begonia. It seemed his whole day had been surrounded by mirrors, that mirrors had italicized each important event.

Latchmer had met Sarah Hughes only that Saturday morning, although he had been noticing her for several weeks. Both were members of a health club on West End Avenue. Latchmer went there each day after work to spend forty-five minutes pitting his muscles against the

Nautilus machines. Often, through a glass wall, he could see Sarah Hughes practicing gymnastics. She was tall, thin, and reminded Latchmer of a canoe. Being tall, thin, and canoelike himself, it had occurred to him that he found her attractive simply because she resembled him. She always wore a bright red leotard with the word *Ready* printed across the front in black letters. Latchmer had no idea what the word meant, but it created a sort of hollow feeling in the pit of his stomach.

Latchmer liked the way that Sarah Hughes could bend over backward and touch her head to the floor, making her look like a croquet hoop. He liked the way she could stretch out her legs in one straight line on the canvas mat, then lie on her stomach rocking back and forth on her pelvis. She had very long and very straight blond hair the color of wheat. Sometimes it would be braided and pinned up on the back of her head. Sometimes it would be loose, hanging like a wheat-colored waterfall. Latchmer would have sexual fantasies in which he saw himself lying beneath its golden tumble while she worked on her pelvis. "Ready," he would say to himself, "I'm ready." Her leotard had long sleeves and on her right hand she always wore a gray glove. Mirrors covered the three walls of the gymnastics room, and Latchmer wondered if he wasn't attracted to Sarah Hughes just by her multiplicity.

That week at work had been especially busy for Latchmer and he had missed several days of beneficial exercise. Consequently, on Saturday morning he had spent a solid hour with the Nautilus machines, imagining he was catching up. Afterward, he changed into his bathing suit and went down to the whirlpool bath which was in the same room or recreation space as the club's small swimming pool. The bath was eight feet by six feet and full of hot, bubbling turquoise water. Sometimes as many as twelve people were crowded into it. But on this morning it was occupied only by Sarah Hughes. Her hair was piled in a precarious blond tower above her head, while her shoulders rose above the surface of the water like, Latchmer thought, a tropical island. Latchmer took a place on the shelf directly across from her. She looked up and smiled.

"Doesn't it hurt your back to keep bending over like that?" he had asked.

"It did at first, but now my body is like rubber. Of course, I have to keep working at it." She had a high, clear voice which reminded Latchmer of the sound made when you run your finger around the rim of a wine glass. As she sat, she kept massaging her upper right arm with the thumb and bent forefinger of her left, working her hand up and down along the bone.

"Pull a muscle?" Latchmer asked. He was always pulling muscles and was prepared to be sympathetic.

"I'm smoothing the bone."

"Pardon me?" It seemed to Latchmer that Sarah's teeth were too large, making her face appear somewhat carnivorous.

"I'm trying to make my bones smooth. Normally bones are rough and a little bumpy. Even the connective tissue can have lumps."

"I've never thought of that," said Latchmer. "And you can get rid of it?"

"Sure, just by massaging. The connective tissue is like gelatine and by rubbing it long enough, you can turn it into liquid, then you can start smoothing it out. Also, once it's liquid, you can start working on the bone. All it takes is a lot of rubbing. I've got a girlfriend who's just finished smoothing all her bones on her entire body, even her toes."

She spoke easily and Latchmer thought she was probably used to giving instructions. Perhaps she was a teacher or even a tour guide.

"It must take some time," Latchmer said. Here too the walls and ceiling were lined with mirrors so that while Latchmer watched Sarah's face, he could also see both profiles, the back and top of her head and watch himself watching her. He even became momentarily uncertain as to whether she was the focus of his attention or if he was more interested in watching himself watching her.

"It took her years," she said. "I've only been at it for six months, since October, but I've already finished my left arm." She stretched it out toward Latchmer across the bubbling water. "Feel."

Latchmer ran his fingers across her wet forearm. "Smooth," he said.

Sarah smiled and withdrew her arm. "Just imagine when my whole body is like that."

"It shows a lot of dedication."

"Not really, but it gives me something to do during the evening news or at a movie or even on a bus. I like to keep busy."

They had continued to talk. It turned out that she worked for IBM while he worked for Xerox. They found this a significant coincidence. Latchmer explained he had only lived in New York for six weeks, having moved from Rochester in the middle of February. He had lived in Rochester all his life and as yet hadn't met many New Yorkers.

"That's why I joined the health club or at least that was one of the reasons—just to meet people."

Sarah had gone back to smoothing the bones of her upper right forearm. "Most of them are gay or have diseases," she said.

"I always thought Rochester was full of opportunity," said Latchmer, "but even in Rochester there weren't so many choices. In New York, the sky's the limit."

They talked for ten more minutes and toward the end of that time, Sarah invited him to her apartment for dinner. She lived with her mother on West End near Eighty-ninth Street.

"It's hard to move into the city and not know anyone," she said. "We've only lived here a short time ourselves. You'll like my mother, she's very advanced."

As Latchmer wondered whether this meant she had leftist leanings or was simply old, he felt Sarah brush her feet against his at the bottom of the whirlpool bath. He looked into her face and imagined he saw sexual interest. It was as if she was listening to a conversation in another room: a sort of concentrated yet unfocused attention.

"I'll be glad to come," he said. On the other side of the swimming pool a group of ten men in matching black Speedo bathing suits were doing synchronized calisthenics in front of a mirror.

A few minutes later, Sarah had gotten up to leave the whirlpool bath. Her figure reminded Latchmer of the dolls collected by his niece—dolls that came with miniature backyard barbecues, Winnebagos, and kidney-shaped swimming pools. As Sarah reached for her towel hanging over a railing near the wall, Latchmer saw that her right hand was missing. It appeared to have been cut off cleanly at the wrist. At that moment, he seemed to see the reflection of the wrist in half of the room's mirrors. It made her right forearm look like a small white club— one hundred small white clubs scattered over the walls and ceiling, punctuating the deep kneebends of the group on the other side of the pool. Then she covered it with her red towel, waved to him, and disappeared down the stairs to the women's spa area.

That evening, Latchmer had dressed in his dark brown corduroy suit with vest, his ecru oxford cloth shirt, his dark brown tie with overlapping red and yellow stars, and his dark brown penny loafers which he wore without coins of any kind. Latchmer lived with three roommates in a five-room apartment on 109th between Broadway and Riverside Drive. All three of his roommates were trying to get started as pharmacists and one was Lebanese. Christian or Moslem, Latchmer had never asked which.

He had bought the potted begonia on Broadway and chose a begonia because it seemed the least showy and pretentious. Then he walked back to Riverside Drive. It was a warm spring day at the beginning of April and the warmth of the season made him nostalgic for Rochester. By walking along Riverside Drive and looking out at the river, he was able to shed a bit of the claustrophobia he still felt in the city. Dogs ran frantically from tree to tree sniffing out squirrels. People were roller skating. Down by the Henry Hudson Parkway a crowd of men and women in loose white suits and colored belts were practicing karate in two straight lines. Whenever they jabbed or lunged, they would shout in unison. The noise drifted up to Latchmer as a violent whisper. A red tug pulling two black barges moved slowly northward, while on the farther shore New Jersey lay beneath the lowering sun as if it had cornered the market on tranquility. Above the river a skywriter wound back and forth shooting out little puffs of white cloud in order to complete its sentence.

It was a small yellow airplane and completely silent under the drone from the parkway. Latchmer stopped to watch it. The plane wrote its message in great block letters of the sort a child first learns in school. So far it had written: "Beware the coming of," and as Latchmer craned back his head, the plane spat out "the," left a space, then spat out "d-r-a-g-o-n." "Beware the coming of the dragon." Latchmer felt both thrilled and let down. He assumed it referred to a new kung fu movie. Already the first letters of the sentence were being blown away as the plane disappeared over New Jersey. Latchmer continued along Riverside Drive. Perhaps, he thought, "dragon" referred to some new car or motorcycle or sports team or dance or hair style. Maybe the message was meant for him alone. It had been a strange day and Latchmer imagined even stranger things happening. Maybe it referred to Sarah Hughes or some unknown event in his future. Who knew what adventures lay ahead? There seemed no reason why the message couldn't concern him and a kung fu movie as well. That's how magic works, he had thought.

The elevator stopped at the eighth floor. Latchmer straightened his tie, transferred the begonia to his left arm, and practiced a smile. A natural, comfortable smile was not one of his qualities. Normally, his face was blankish, as if he was waiting for something or trying to fathom the punch line of a joke. He turned left out of the elevator and knocked on the first door.

Sarah Hughes must have been standing just on the other side because she opened the door immediately. She wore a blue dress with long loose sleeves and her right arm terminated in a gray glove. Latchmer was trying to get a close look at the glove when Sarah stretched forward her cheek to be kissed.

"Is that for me?" she asked. "I love begonias." Her blond hair hung loose down her back. Around her neck were three thin gold chains. She was just Latchmer's height and even her face was somewhat like his: long and thin with a long straight nose and blue eyes. Again he was struck by the size of her teeth. It gave her a ferocious smile. The teeth were not only large but looked sharp. If it weren't for the teeth, Latchmer thought, she'd look enough like me to be my twin. He couldn't decide how he felt about this.

Latchmer gave her the begonia and had just begun to

describe how he'd seen it and been unable to pass it up when a large red dog bounded into the foyer and began licking his hand.

"That's Jasper," said Sarah. "He's perfectly friendly. He's been with us forever."

"I like dogs," said Latchmer, who had never liked dogs. They smelled and licked their genitals. Latchmer thought of that as the dog continued to lick his hand, but he felt it would be rude to withdraw it too soon. He was a tall dog, taller than a Labrador, with short red fur and one floppy ear and one erect. The redness was particularly striking and Latchmer thought he'd never seen a dog quite that color. The fur was the same dark red that the sky sometimes gets at sunset. He was also an old dog with a lot of gray about the muzzle and droopy eyes. His ropelike tail kept slapping against Latchmer's leg. Then he turned and began poking his nose into Latchmer's crotch. Latchmer gently tried to shove him away but the dog pushed all the harder. He had a long blunt muzzle and once again he rammed his nose up into Latchmer's groin and snuffled.

Latchmer looked to see Sarah staring at the dog. Her lips were parted and her teeth seemed to be pressing out from between them. Then she glanced up at Latchmer and smiled. "You have to be rough with poor Jasper," she said. "He's very old and stubborn. If he wants something, he'll just take it."

Latchmer pushed the dog to one side. Jasper assumed he was trying to play and nipped at his hand.

"Lie down!" ordered Sarah. Jasper collapsed in a heap, looked gloomily at Sarah, then began licking himself. Sarah took Latchmer's arm above the elbow and gave it a little squeeze. "Come and meet mother," she said.

Still holding Latchmer's arm, she directed him into a long living room with a cream-colored rug and wallpaper that appeared to be blue silk with hand-painted flowers.

Against one wall was a white marble fireplace and at the far end of the room was a dining room table covered with a white tablecloth and set for dinner. Above the table was a crystal chandelier.

In the middle of the room were several soft-looking armchairs, a coffee table, and a sofa. Mrs. Hughes sat in the middle of the sofa. She was a trim, white-haired woman, probably in her late sixties. In her lap was a recent *New Yorker*, while balanced on the tip of her nose was a pair of tortoise-shell reading glasses. When she saw Latchmer, she removed the glasses, slipped them into a green silk case, and stood up.

"Mother, this is Michael Latchmer," said Sarah. "He's from Rochester."

Mrs. Hughes stretched out her hand and Latchmer took it. The hand felt hot and soft. "My husband was from Rochester," she said. "Before he died, he told me he wanted to be buried there, and when we went for the funeral I was surprised at how much it had grown. That was eight years ago and I'm sure it's even bigger now."

"Huge," said Latchmer. "Rochester is always growing." Mrs. Hughes was still holding his hand and Latchmer wondered if she had forgotten. He gave it another squeeze, then tried to pull free. After a slight resistance, she let go.

Mrs. Hughes wore a green silk kimono, and, glancing around the room, Latchmer saw that the Oriental style formed a motif. Near the door to the kitchen stood a black lacquer cabinet with a painting of pink clouds and a dragon. By the window was a tall folding screen showing a valley spotted with villages, rice paddies, and a great river with tiny boats. The drapes and the fabric covering the couch resembled the blue wallpaper with yellow finches and green leaves. The only object that seemed out of place was an old brown armchair next to the coffee table.

"Would you like a drink?" asked Sarah.

"Sure, anything."

"I've made some strawberry daiquiris in the blender."

"Sounds great," said Latchmer. He watched Sarah walk past the black lacquer cabinet to the kitchen and wondered if the dragon on the cabinet was the one he had to watch out for. Maybe the message had meant he shouldn't drink too much.

"That armchair is the most comfortable," said Mrs. Hughes. "It was my husband's favorite chair." She nodded toward the brown armchair, which was large and low to the floor.

Latchmer looked at the chair respectfully. When he sat down in it, however, he discovered the springs were broken. It was like sitting down in an inner tube. Even as Latchmer struggled to get comfortable, the dog trotted over and began licking his face. Latchmer tried to push Jasper away, but he was so low to the floor that the dog was actually above him. He rapped Jasper on the tip of the nose with one knuckle. The dog sneezed, then lay down. From the kitchen came the whir of the blender.

"Your dog is an interesting color," said Latchmer. "I've never seen a red dog before."

Mrs. Hughes had resumed her seat on the couch and glanced at the dog fondly. "He's part chow, part Rhodesian Ridgeback. My husband gave him to me twelve years ago, but Jasper was really my husband's dog. Jasper would follow him everyplace. Even long after Dale's death, Jasper would sit by the door waiting for him to come home. He still remembers him, even after eight years." Mrs. Hughes turned to the dog, which lay with his head resting on Latchmer's penny loafers. "Jasper," she said, "where's Daddy, go find Daddy."

The dog scrambled to his feet, looked around the room, and trotted over to the fireplace. In a silver frame on the mantel was a photograph of a rather fat, gray-haired man smoking a pipe. Jasper stared up at it and barked twice, a sort of woofing bark. Then he looked back at Mrs. Hughes and wagged his tail.

"Good dog," said Mrs. Hughes. "Come have your treat."

"That's amazing," said Latchmer.

Jasper trotted back to Mrs. Hughes. On the coffee table in front of the couch was a wooden tray with olives stuffed with anchovies, chunks of cheese, salami, and Triscuits. Mrs. Hughes took an olive and tossed it to Jasper, who caught it with a snap of his jaws.

"Jasper loves anchovies," she said. "The vet says they're bad for his heart, but now and then they can't do him any harm. Jasper's getting old just like the rest of us."

"He's a remarkable dog," said Latchmer. He took an olive for himself, then sat smiling at Mrs. Hughes. Jasper stood with his head in her lap. She stroked it and called him a good dog. Mrs. Hughes had a high, shiny forehead and large blue eyes. Her mouth and lips were surrounded by thin lines like the creases made by the drawstring fastening of a cloth bag. It was a narrow, restful face and slightly sad, as if her burden of memories was almost too great. As he stared at Mrs. Hughes, it occurred to Latchmer that he had seen her before. He didn't think it had been in New York City. On a table next to the couch was a photograph of Sarah sitting on a horse. Latchmer saw that in the picture she had two hands. She seemed about ten years younger, maybe just out of high school.

Sarah came back into the living room carrying a silver tray with three fat glasses and a glass pitcher filled with a red daiquiri mixture. "How are you two getting along?" she asked.

"Your mother's been telling me about the dog," said Latchmer.

Sarah set the tray on the coffee table and filled the

three glasses. "I don't know what we'd do without Jasper," she said.

The glove on her right hand was gray leather. Latchmer noticed that although she seemed to use the hand, she didn't lift anything with it. He wondered how it was connected. The fingers of the glove were slightly curled. As she leaned over to give him his glass, he saw that she wasn't wearing a bra. He started to look away, then didn't. A strand of her long blond hair fell forward and brushed against his wrist. Once again he was struck by how her face resembled his own. She resembled him; the mother resembled someone he couldn't remember, and the dog resembled nothing he had ever seen.

"Be careful of these daiquiris," said Sarah. "They're deceptive."

Latchmer sipped his drink, then took another olive when Sarah offered him the tray. Seeing the olives, Jasper left Mrs. Hughes and ambled over to Latchmer. Because of the lowness of the chair, Latchmer and the dog were on eye level. Jasper's eyes were red and gummy and he kept blinking them.

"Sarah tells me you work for Xerox," said Mrs. Hughes.

"Yes, I got a job with them right out of college."

"What do you do?"

"I help design software. My main skill is systems analysis, but I'm hoping to break into video games."

Jasper had again begun to nuzzle Latchmer's crotch. Latchmer gave the dog another olive and tried to push him away. The dog thrust his head forward into Latchmer's lap while making a wet snuffling noise. Glancing up, he saw Sarah watching the dog with a raised eyebrow. Latchmer shoved Jasper away and again struck the dog's nose with one knuckle so that he sneezed.

"What do you do at IBM?" Latchmer asked Sarah. His voice struck him as a trifle high.

She looked at him through two thick strands of blond hair, then flicked her head so the hair fell back over her shoulders. "I'm on the repair end of things," she said.

"Sarah's known as the best mechanic in New York City," said Mrs. Hughes. "She used to do all the work herself before her accident. Now she has a Japanese staff."

"What kind of accident?" asked Latchmer. Now it seemed his voice was pitched too low.

Mrs. Hughes patted Jasper's head. "A large Wall Street computer tried to suck her into it," she said. "It tried to absorb her."

"Oh, Mother, you know that's not true."

"Then what was it?" asked Mrs. Hughes sharply. "Didn't I talk to the technicians?"

Sarah leaned toward Latchmer. "It was rollers," she said. "You know, like the ones on a wringer washer, only bigger."

"In any case," said Mrs. Hughes, "we're lucky she's alive today. As it is, they were never able to find the hand. It's still in there someplace."

"How awful," said Latchmer, looking at Sarah's gray glove. "Do they know what went wrong?"

"According to one of the programmers," said Mrs. Hughes, "the machine had fallen in love with her. Or perhaps it was only desire—that dry sexual desire which only intelligent machines are capable of."

"It was nothing of the sort," said Sarah, "it was a brain malfunction."

"What's the difference?" asked Mrs. Hughes.

Jasper removed his head from Mrs. Hughes's lap and ambled over toward Latchmer. Hoping to avoid the dog's attentions, Latchmer tossed an olive, which bounced off Jasper's snout and rolled down his back. The dog spun around, wagging his tail. Latchmer's glass was on the edge of the coffee table. Too late, he tried to reach for it. The dog's tail hit it, knocking the glass toward Latchmer, spilling strawberry daiquiri over his shoes and the rug. The dog, oblivious to the accident, retrieved the olive from under the coffee table and gobbled it up.

Latchmer jumped to his feet. "I'm terribly sorry. That was my fault. Let me get a towel."

Mrs. Hughes tugged at one of Jasper's ears. "Jasper's always doing something," she said.

Latchmer hurried to the kitchen. "Let me help too," said Sarah, following him.

The kitchen was a long narrow room lined with white cabinets and white shelves. Latchmer took a sponge from the sink. "I feel like a fool," he said.

"I should have warned you about Jasper's tail," said Sarah. She brushed past him to get a roll of paper towels. "Don't worry about Mother, she goes to bed early." She brushed past him again, pressing her breasts against his shoulder.

When Latchmer returned with the sponge, he found the dog licking up the spilled daiquiri. Mrs. Hughes sat on the couch repeating, "Bad Jasper, bad dog," in a kindly voice.

Latchmer and Sarah knelt down by the spot on the rug and rubbed at it. Their heads bumped together and Latchmer sat back on the brown chair. Some of the daiquiri had spilled between the edge of his left penny loafer and sock. He slipped off the shoe and Sarah knelt in front of him, rubbing the inside of the shoe with paper towels. Latchmer could see right down her dress and, as she rubbed, her breasts swung back and forth. Uncertainly, Latchmer glanced up at Mrs. Hughes, who smiled and nodded at him.

When Latchmer had cleaned up as much of the daiquiri as he could, he returned to the kitchen to rinse out the sponge. As he stood at the sink, Sarah pressed past him to get to the waste basket. He felt her pelvis press against his buttocks, pushing him into the white counter top.

"Excuse me," he said.

He turned off the water and dried his hands on a white dish towel with pictures of butter churns. Sarah stood just behind him. "I like the way you handle Jasper," she said.

Latchmer turned so that his face was less than a foot from hers. Her mouth was slightly open and her teeth seemed huge. "Don't go home too early," she said. "I want to be your suck-oven."

Before Latchmer could reply, she pushed past him and returned to the living room. He paused to catch his breath, then followed her. Sarah sat down by her mother and gave Jasper a little poke with her shoe. The dog thumped its tail on the carpet. In the middle of the coffee table stood Latchmer's glass refilled to the brim with fresh daiquiri. He sipped it, then sat back down. As he looked at Mrs. Hughes, he saw that she was wearing gold earrings in the shape of tiny grand pianos. Again he thought she reminded him of someone, someone he had known a long time ago. Most likely it was someone in Rochester. Jasper stood up and stretched, then wandered over to Latchmer and tried to lick his face. When Latchmer pushed him away, the dog collapsed at his feet and began to fart—soft sloppy noises.

The silence made Latchmer uncomfortable. Both Sarah and her mother were looking affectionately at the dog. "I heard a story at work about a dog," Latchmer said, "about a college student who visited an aunt and uncle who had a dog."

"Is it a funny story?" asked Mrs. Hughes.

"Kind of," said Latchmer, "although it's more peculiar than funny." Why did he say that? He never told stories, was never any good at it. Mrs. Hughes was looking at him with polite interest. Much later Latchmer decided he had been crazy to tell the story, that the dog had upset him and he was getting even. But that didn't explain why he, a nonstoryteller, should suddenly tell a story. It was as if something else had forced him to tell it. Maybe it was the dog's influence, maybe the dog was responsible.

"This young man had never been away from home before," said Latchmer, "but in the same town as the college lived his father's brother, so his father told him to visit his uncle and even called up his brother to ask him to keep an eye on the boy. Well, the Sunday after the young man moved into the dormitory, he went to his uncle's for dinner. His aunt and uncle were nice people who had never had any children. They lived in a little bungalow with lots of little figurines on the tables, and they had a little dog: a red dachshund named Randy which they fed special dog chocolates.

"The next Sunday the young man came back again for dinner and he came back the Sunday after that. His aunt would cook a roast, which was much better than any cafeteria food. He even got used to Randy trying to climb into his lap and begging for scraps at the table. Well, on the fifth Sunday, the young man decided to play a little joke. During the week he had wandered into a novelty store and had seen a little dog mess made out of rubber. You know, four or five turds and very realistic. The young man bought the dog mess and took it to his aunt and uncle's that Sunday. Then, when he and Randy were alone in the living room, he took out the rubber dog mess and put it in the middle of the carpet, which was a thick, white carpet. Then the young man went back to reading the newspaper. The dog whimpered a little bit. He was about ten years old.

"After a moment, the uncle came out of the kitchen, saw the little group of dog turds and stared at them as if he was going crazy. Then he called to his wife. 'Agnes,' he said, 'come quick.' She came running out and the moment she saw the dog mess she burst into tears. The young man stood up. He began to realize he had made a mistake, but before he could speak, his uncle rushed across the room and kicked the dachshund so that it actually flew through the air yelping. Then he ran to the dog and began beating it. And his aunt too, she ran to the dog and was almost pushing her husband out of the way so she could hit it. And they weren't just slapping the dog, they were hitting it with their fists.

"The young man was shocked. 'Don't worry about the mess,' he said. 'I'll take care of it.' And he ran over to the rubber dog turds, scooped them up, and stuck them in his pocket. His aunt and uncle were so busy beating the dog they didn't even notice. The young man felt terrible, but he didn't see how he could say anything. Then his uncle picked up the dog by the scruff of the neck, ran to the door of the basement, and flung Randy down the stairs. He slammed the door and burst into tears. Both his aunt and uncle kept saying how Randy had never, never done such a thing, how he'd always been a good dog, and how embarrassing it was that this should happen in front of a guest, especially a relation. The young man said it didn't matter in the least. He was used to dogs and maybe Randy had a cold or something. His uncle said there was no excuse, that nothing, nothing, could ever forgive it. Then the young man said maybe he should go, that it didn't look like such a good Sunday to stay for dinner. His aunt and uncle nodded and his aunt made him a sandwich. The young man went back to the dormitory.

"The next Sunday he decided not to visit his aunt and uncle. Nor did he the Sunday after that. In fact, he stayed away for two months. When he finally visited again, there was no sign of Randy. He looked all over the house and not only was the dog missing but all his toys were gone as well. It was as if they'd never had a dog. The young man wanted to ask what had happened but couldn't bring himself to say the words. And even though he visited his aunt and uncle about once a month for the next four years, he never built up the courage to ask or learned what had happened to Randy."

Latchmer put his glass back on the coffee table and glanced up at Sarah and her mother. Sarah was squeezing the little finger of her gray glove, while Mrs. Hughes was staring at Latchmer as if doubting the evidence of her senses.

"What a horrible story," said Mrs. Hughes. "He should have told them."

"He was too embarrassed."

"But he turned against them."

"What do you mean?" asked Latchmer.

"They were his aunt and uncle and he betrayed them. They invited him into their home and he did them a bad turn. I call that betrayal."

"I'm not sure about that," said Latchmer. It seemed to him that Mrs. Hughes was taking the story too seriously.

"They probably had the poor dog put to sleep. How awful."

"Yes, that's what I thought myself," said Latchmer.

Sarah got to her feet and smoothed her blue dress down over her thighs. "I think dinner's just about ready," she said. "I hope you like roast beef."

"Love it," said Latchmer. He stood up as well. As he took a step, his foot brushed against Jasper, who jumped up and began moaning and turning in circles.

"See," said Mrs. Hughes, "you've upset Jasper."

"Don't be silly, Mother, Jasper couldn't have understood."

"Dogs know these things," said Mrs. Hughes. "That was a terrible story, Michael."

"I'm sorry if it offended you. Many people like it."

"They must be nasty people," said Mrs. Hughes.

Sarah stood in the doorway of the kitchen. "Could

you give me some help, Michael?"

The dog was still moaning and Mrs. Hughes was stroking his head. She fed him another olive. Latchmer looked at her but could think of nothing to say so he followed Sarah into the kitchen. He had lied about other people liking the story. He had never told it before. The whole thing had sprung ready-made into his brain. He had no idea where it had come from or even why he had told it. He thought again about the skywriter that had warned him about the coming of the dragon. Perhaps it wasn't the daiquiris which were like the dragon, but the story.

From the oven came the bubble and hiss of cooking food. Sarah stood near it with her gloved hand at her side. Latchmer wondered if the fingers could actually move. He knew there were ways to connect things. Sarah opened the oven door and a small cloud of steam rose to the ceiling. Using potholders designed to resemble chickens, Sarah lifted a pan out of the oven. The roast was the size of a child's head. Surrounding it were a dozen small potatoes.

"You shouldn't have told that story," said Sarah. "Mother is very sensitive."

"It was a mistake," said Latchmer. "I don't know why I did it."

Sarah put the pan holding the meat on the counter. She looked at him with a seriousness that made him think she was angry. Then she took a step toward him. Slowly she reached out her gloved hand. It was as if he knew what she was going to do before it really happened. He looked down at the gray leather glove and when it touched his genitals, he felt no surprise, just a tingling at the base of his brain. Sarah leaned forward and put her mouth to his ear.

"I loved the story," she whispered, "but I couldn't laugh. You understand that, don't you?" She touched her tongue to the inside of his ear. "Let me be your hot vacuum," she said.

"My what?" asked Latchmer.

Sarah shook her head. "Take in the roast. I'll get the wine."

Latchmer transferred the roast and potatoes to a blue ceramic platter, then carried the platter into the dining area. The table with its white cloth stood by a window looking out over Eighty-ninth Street. Three places had been set. By each place was a yellow napkin in a silver ring. Latchmer felt a little dizzy and hoped he wouldn't trip or drop anything.

"I think we're about ready," he said to Mrs. Hughes.

She stood up and walked toward him across the room. The hem of her green kimono just brushed the rug. "Sarah is a wonderful cook," she said.

Like her daughter, she was tall and slender, and as she walked toward Latchmer, he began to realize who she reminded him of. Not that he could remember a name or even the circumstances of where he had known her, but he knew that the person she resembled was someone he hadn't seen since he was a child. He began to think it was someone who had lived in the small town where he had spent a month each summer visiting his grandparents. For some reason the memory made Latchmer feel guilty. Latchmer felt a poking at his leg and he looked down to see Jasper. Thoughtfully, he scratched the dog's floppy ear.

Sarah came out of the kitchen with a bottle of red wine and a bowl of string beans with some sort of cheese and bread crumb crust. She put the wine on the table. "I'm afraid this hasn't had much chance to breathe," she said. "Will you carve, Michael? I love to watch a man carve."

"I'm not very good at it," he said. Now that he had started to remember the woman whom Mrs. Hughes resembled, he began to feel somewhat removed from the room. The feeling of guilt interested him. Latchmer never felt guilt; he thought it a waste of time. Therefore, he began to experience a little pleasure, even piquancy, in the feeling. As yet, he couldn't remember any specific events. It was like trying to remember a dream. He felt that if he could summon up one string of images, the rest would follow. As a matter of fact, he had almost no memory of his childhood, just a vague sense of being small and more confused. For that matter, he had little memory about anything. Memories held no interest for him. Consequently, it often seemed that his past was as much a mystery as his future.

Latchmer began carving the meat, driving the serving fork into the center, then slicing off thin portions. He stood at the head of the table, while Sarah and her mother sat on either side, looking at him expectantly.

"They give courses in carving at the New School," said Latchmer. "Maybe I should sign up for one."

"You're doing great," said Sarah. She had poured the wine into three long-stemmed glasses. Latchmer saw she was holding her glass with her gloved hand: two fingers curved slightly around the stem. If she had lost the hand while working, then presumably IBM had had to replace it. Latchmer thought that IBM could probably afford a really good hand, one that could do everything a real hand did and more.

"I have a few rare slices if anyone wants some," said Latchmer.

Sarah leaned forward so her hair fell across the white tablecloth. "Mother likes hers well done, but I love rare meat."

Latchmer put several slices of somewhat charred meat on a plate for Mrs. Hughes. The dog stood behind him with his head on Latchmer's chair, waiting for a little treat. He still moaned occasionally. It seemed to Latchmer that Mrs. Hughes kept looking at him with a certain coldness. He wondered how long he would have to wait before she went to bed. The more he thought of it, the more he was sure that the woman she reminded him of had lived in the same town as his grandparents. Latchmer's grandfather had been the local doctor: a tall, dark-haired man who had died unexpectedly when Latchmer was eleven. It was a small town in upstate New York, hardly more than a village. Latchmer hadn't been back in over twenty years.

Latchmer scooped some beans onto the plate with the overdone pieces of meat and handed it to Mrs. Hughes. "Did you ever spend much time in Rochester?" he asked. "You remind me of someone and I thought it might have been from there."

Mrs. Hughes put down her wine glass and pressed her napkin to the corners of her mouth. "My husband and I were married in Rochester. That was the only time I was there except for his funeral. We lived in White Plains for thirty years. Some years after my husband's death, I sold the house and Sarah and I decided to move to the city."

It seemed obvious to Latchmer that he'd never seen her before tonight unless it was on the street or in a store. But that wouldn't explain the guilt. Presumably she reminded him of an entirely different person. "It must be difficult to keep a big dog like that in an apartment," he said.

"He's a faithful friend," said Mrs. Hughes, "but I'm afraid something's bothering him tonight."

"I hope it wasn't my story," said Latchmer.

"Maybe it was the anchovies," said Sarah. She gave Latchmer a small conspiratorial smile.

Mrs. Hughes cupped Jasper's muzzle in her hand and stroked his head. Jasper's tail thumped against a table leg. "They never bothered him before," she said. "Do you remember that night he ate a whole can? If Jasper had his way, he wouldn't eat the olives, but he knows it's a trade-off. That's how smart he is. No olives, no anchovies. The olives are good for his coat. That's what makes his fur so red and shiny. I used to give him butter, but the vet said it was bad for his heart."

"He certainly has a handsome coat," said Latchmer. "I've never seen fur that red." He was slicing some rare meat for Sarah.

"Make it as rare as possible," she said.

"I'm trying to."

Latchmer's grandparents had had separate bedrooms in opposite parts of the house. His father had been their only surviving son and years later he told Latchmer they could barely tolerate one another. But because the town was small and his grandfather was the only doctor, and because his grandmother had her social position to protect, they had made a truce and to all appearances were a loving couple. His grandmother was president of the garden society as well as the Lady's Guild of the Episcopal Church. The only wrinkle was that his grandfather had a mistress: a woman he had been involved with for more than twenty years. Latchmer glanced at Mrs. Hughes and for a moment it seemed that his grandfather's mistress was sitting with him at the table.

"Just a small amount of beans for me, please," said Sarah. "Who is it my mother reminds you of?"

Latchmer experienced another flush of guilt. He put a few beans on Sarah's plate and passed it to her. What had been the woman's name? By now, if she weren't dead, she'd be in her eighties. All he could think of was that his grandmother had always referred to the woman as "your grandfather's whore."

"I'm not certain," said Latchmer. "It must have been someone when I was a kid." He began serving himself the reddest meat he could find. He was starving.

"You like rare meat too," said Sarah.

"I sure do," said Latchmer. "When I order steak in a restaurant, I like to tell the waiter, 'Just drive the cow through a warm room.'"

"I'm not sure that's very nice," said Mrs. Hughes. She had been cutting off small bits of meat and offering them to Jasper, who licked them off her palm with a swipe of his tongue.

"The waiters like it," said Latchmer. "Their job gets very boring, so they like customers who're a little different. It makes them serve you better if you can amuse them. They also like it if you ask them for their suggestions, I mean like, what's good today or what do they recommend. It makes them feel more like people."

"It still seems impolite," said Mrs. Hughes, looking down at her plate.

Latchmer didn't see why she should be put out by his remark. After all, that was what waiters were like. If she got angry at anyone, then it should be at the waiters. He looked at her again. Maybe she doesn't like her meat, he thought.

The woman who had been his grandfather's whore had been a grade school teacher. She had retired early, but maybe his grandmother had had her fired. She lived in a small white Victorian house on a street lined with large oaks and maples. The house had a screened-in porch and in the summer Latchmer would often see her sitting on the porch reading when he rode by on his bike. Some nights he and his cousin would sneak down just to see what his grandfather did there, maybe see them kiss or get undressed. They would sneak up to the house, peer over the sill of the parlor window, and there would be the woman and their grandfather sitting on the couch reading—she with a book, he with a newspaper. Sometimes they would be talking, but Latchmer could never hear what they said. Her name had been Miss Mitchell; "Miss Mitchell, the whore," that's what his grandmother had called her.

"You know a lot about restaurants," said Mrs. Hughes.

"Rochester's a big restaurant town," said Latchmer. He finished serving himself and took his seat. It was the shape of Mrs. Hughes's head that reminded him of Miss Mitchell, that and her high cheek bones and the way her white hair was parted in the middle and then pinned up in back. Also her eyes, her blue eyes. Latchmer wanted to stop thinking about it. He was certain he had not thought of this woman in twenty years. He disliked thinking about the past. It was always such a jumble.

"What do you like best about New York?" asked Sarah.

"I like it that people leave you alone. They respect your privacy. Why, in some penthouse apartment you can have a man who owns millions. He's completely anonymous, goes anywhere he likes. In Rochester, everyone would recognize him and nod and point. He'd never have any peace. In New York, people are all separate. I like that."

"Sometimes they meet," said Sarah. She stared at him over the rim of her wine glass.

"Yes, sometimes," said Latchmer, "but in New York people can have all kinds of interests that would get them in trouble anyplace else. I have a roommate who gets catalogs for rubber clothing, you know, rubber underwear and stuff. He's a pharmacist. He and a couple of friends sit around his room wearing rubber underwear and rubber bras and panties. Mostly they just sit and watch TV. If this was Rochester, I'd probably look for another apartment, but here I think, what the heck, it's just New York. As long as they don't make a lot of noise, I don't care."

Latchmer looked to see if he had offended Mrs. Hughes, but she was staring past him into the living room. "What's wrong with Jasper?" she asked.

Turning in his chair, Latchmer was surprised to see that the dog was running. It was a very slow run, more of a lope, and as Latchmer watched, he saw that Jasper was running in circles. The dog's tail was between his legs and he was snapping and biting the air. At first Latchmer thought it was some kind of trick. Jasper's head kept turning from left to right as if he were searching for something. His eyes were nearly all white and he kept bumping into things. Then Jasper began to moan and, as he ran faster, he began to moan louder. It was a guttural noise, something like a gargle. Jasper stumbled, fell against a chair, got to his feet, shook himself, and began running again.

Latchmer put down his fork. "Does he do this often?" he asked.

"No, never," said Mrs. Hughes. She got to her feet. "Jasper, stop that!"

The dog ran around the outside of the circle made by the couch and two armchairs. He began to make a yipping noise and bit the air as if biting at invisible creatures which flew above his head. He collided with a small table. A blue pottery lamp fell to the floor and smashed. The lamp shade rolled off toward the fireplace. As the dog began to run faster, Latchmer was reminded of the tigers running around the trees in *Little Black Sambo*. The dog's red coat made a similar blur, although it wasn't like butter but rather like red paint or catsup. Every so often Jasper would make a little hop and rise up behind the couch or one of the chairs. He was now yipping constantly. Suddenly he leaped high into the air, arching his back and twisting his head to make an almost pretzel shape. He snapped his jaws together so hard that Latchmer heard the click. Jasper sailed over the end of the couch and crashed against the side of the coffee table, upsetting it and spilling the tray of olives, cheese, and crackers to the floor. Latchmer waited to see what Jasper would do next, but he did nothing. He just lay with his eyes open among the wreckage while olives rolled off in all directions.

"My God," said Mrs. Hughes, dropping her napkin and hurrying to the dog.

Latchmer had just taken a large mouthful of roast beef and was trying to swallow. Both he and Sarah stood at the head of the table staring at Jasper. After a moment, Latchmer realized that Sarah was rubbing her gloved hand against his backside. It was like being rubbed with a piece of wood.

"Sarah, call an ambulance," cried Mrs. Hughes. "He's stopped breathing!" Her voice was high and frightened. She had knelt down and was holding Jasper's head in her lap.

Sarah picked up the phone. "Maybe there's some kind of pet ambulance," she said. "I'll try information."

Latchmer swallowed and was tempted to take another bite. He glanced down at the food getting cold on his plate. "It's sad," he said.

Sarah had dialed a number and stood listening. "The pet ambulance doesn't run on weekends. I got a record-ing. It said I should try the Humane Society."

Mrs. Hughes was still on her knees on the floor. There were tears on her cheeks. "Mr. Latchmer, you must do something."

Latchmer had continued to hold his fork. It was heavy and appeared to be solid silver. He carefully set it down next to his plate. No telling when he'd pick it up again. "I've had some CPR training," he said. "They made us take it at Xerox." As he crossed the room toward Mrs. Hughes, Jasper's blank eyes seemed to follow him.

Sarah had been dialing another number. She put her hand over the mouthpiece and looked at Latchmer. "The kiss of life," she said.

Mrs. Hughes stood up and touched Latchmer's arm.

Her face had a sad, pleading quality that made him uneasy. He tried to smile reassuringly, but felt too hungry to smile. He knelt down by the dog and pulled him away from some of the broken dishes. With a bright purple cocktail napkin, he wiped the crumbs from Jasper's face.

Latchmer could feel no pulse or heart beat. With the heel of his hand, he struck the dog in the chest where he thought the heart must be. He had taken the CPR class about five years before and never expected to use it. The class had practiced on a large rubber doll and the instructor kept wiping its mouth with alcohol. As Latchmer turned the dog over on his back, he realized that the big difference between a dog mouth and a human mouth was that a dog had five times as much lip. He didn't see how he could cover the sides of the muzzle efficiently enough to blow air into the lungs. How could he get a good seal?

"The Humane Society is closed," said Sarah. "I got another recording. It said I should call the Pound."

Latchmer wrapped both hands around the dog's muzzle and pressed his thumbs against the nostrils. It reminded him of one spring vacation in Key West when he had tried to make Polynesian warrior noises on a conch shell. It hadn't worked. Looking up, he saw Mrs. Hughes staring at him intently. He again felt a wave of guilt and realized he was still seeing her as Miss Mitchell, his grandfather's whore. But why should he feel guilt? There seemed no reason. He had liked Miss Mitchell and she had always been nice to him. He remembered one time when she stopped him on the street when he had his bicycle. It had been a warm summer day. She looked at him with great seriousness and he thought she was angry. Then she gave him ten cents and told him to buy an ice cream cone. "You look hot," she had said.

"The emergency number at the Pound doesn't answer," said Sarah. "I'll try the police."

Latchmer had crouched down and was sitting astride the dog's chest. Leaning forward, he pressed his lips against Jasper's mouth and blew. Jasper's lips were cold and bristly. Latchmer leaned back, let go of the dog's head, and pushed the heels of his palms against Jasper's chest at the top of his rib cage. He did this twice. The fur on Jasper's belly was getting gray and was almost pink in places. Latchmer again leaned forward, cupped his hands around Jasper's snout, and blew into his mouth. Then he leaned back and pressed his palms against Jasper's chest, pushing hard against the bone. The only sound was the wheezing noise of his own breath being exhaled from Jasper's lungs. Latchmer leaned forward again. The feel of the dog's cold mouth against his own was unpleasant. Opening the mouth, he moved the tongue to one side so that it wouldn't slide down Jasper's throat. Then he leaned back and again pushed down on his chest. Jasper made no response. Latchmer remembered his CPR instructor telling the class: "When you blow down the victim's throat, the first thing that happens is that he throws up on you. Then you throw up on him and continue like nobody's business."

Latchmer thought of all that Jasper had eaten in the last hour. The dog's breath smelled of anchovies and olives. Mrs. Hughes sat on the edge of the coffee table several feet away. When Latchmer leaned foward he kept brushing his arm against the folds of her green kimono. "Is there anything I can do?" she repeated.

"The police gave me a special pet emergency number," said Sarah. She spoke rapidly and her voice was strident. "They don't think anyone's there on Saturday nights, but I'll try anyway."

Mrs. Hughes bent forward so her head was only a few inches from Latchmer's. "If you knew how that dog loved my husband," she said, "you wouldn't let him die."

Latchmer kept thinking of the chance that the dog

might throw up. "Maybe you can get me a towel," he said.

Mrs. Hughes hurried toward the bathroom. Sarah was listening to something on the telephone. Leaning forward, Latchmer again blew into Jasper's mouth. He was certain he could taste anchovies. He glanced at his watch and saw that it was nine-fifteen. He'd been working on the dog a little more than ten minutes. He was tired and his back was sore.

"I got another tape recording," said Sarah. "It told me to call the canine section of the police department."

Mrs. Hughes returned from the bathroom with a large yellow towel. "Let me call," she said, "I can't stand doing nothing." She put the towel down beside Latchmer, then went to the telephone. Sarah and her mother embraced. Sarah was three or four inches taller and her chin pressed against her mother's forehead. She had her eyes shut. Latchmer blew into Jasper's mouth, then leaned back to push down on his chest. The dog was completely limp and every time Latchmer let go of the head, it bumped on the beige carpet.

As her mother began to dial, Sarah walked over to where Latchmer was straddling the dog. "Let me massage your shoulders," she said.

"Never mind, that's okay," said Latchmer.

Ignoring him, Sarah stood so that her dress rose behind him like a soft blue wall. She began to rub his shoulders, leaning forward when Latchmer leaned forward to blow into the dog's mouth, leaning back when Latchmer pressed against the dog's chest. Sarah's artificial hand felt hard and pinched Latchmer's skin. It made it difficult to concentrate. Latchmer had discovered that if he put the little finger of his right hand into Jasper's mouth, then he could press down upon the dog's tongue to keep it from sliding down the throat. It was hard to do this with Sarah pressing down on him from behind.

"Does that feel good?" asked Sarah.

"Feels great," said Latchmer.

Sarah kept pushing him down on top of the dog, then pulling him back against her thighs, which were thin and bony. When she pushed down on top of him, she pressed her groin against the back of his head.

"I want to be your sweat box," she told him.

Mrs. Hughes began shouting into the telephone. "Never," she said, "never, never, never!"

Sarah let go of Latchmer. "What's wrong?" she asked.

"The man told me to wait until Monday or put Jasper into a dumpster. Can you imagine? My dog in a dumpster, my dear dog? He's not going to die, is he? Mr. Latchmer, tell me that Jasper will get better."

Latchmer wiped his mouth, then pressed down on Jasper's chest. "Don't get your hopes up. I haven't had much experience with death, but this looks like the real thing." He leaned forward to blow into Jasper's mouth. By now, twenty minutes had gone by. Thirty was his limit, vital signs or no vital signs.

As he leaned back again, he glanced at Mrs. Hughes who stood staring at the rug, hugging herself with folded arms. After Miss Mitchell, his grandfather's whore, had given him the money for the ice cream cone, Latchmer had made a point of riding by her house on his bike every day: not in hopes that she would give him more money but just to inspect her. She had two long flowerbeds with dwarf marigolds and some small blue flowers and sometimes she would be out pulling weeds or watering the flowers with a red watering can. Latchmer had been too shy to stop, but he would wave or shout hello. She had been taller than Mrs. Hughes and her hair had been more old-fashioned—curled in a bun on top of her head. She drove a two-tone blue 1950 Chevie and for years Latchmer had been unable to see a 1950 Chevie without remembering her.

Latchmer continued to lean forward, blow into Jasper's mouth, then lean back and press down on his chest. The dog made no response. Every few seconds Latchmer looked up at the old Seth Thomas clock on the mantel. Two minutes went by, then five, then eight. When ten full minutes had passed, Latchmer got to his feet. "This dog is dead," he said. Mrs. Hughes began to sob. Latchmer's joints were stiff and his knees hurt. He looked down at Jasper and shook his head. The dog had peed slightly and a puddle had formed on the rug. Latchmer opened the yellow towel and spread it over the dog. It completely covered Jasper except for his long red tail.

"What can we do now?" asked Mrs. Hughes, still sobbing.

"You'll have to wait till Monday, then see about getting him buried," said Latchmer. "There are special pet cemeteries."

Mrs. Hughes knelt down beside Jasper and drew the towel back from his head. The dog's mouth was open and his long pink tongue lay on the rug. Gently, she closed the mouth, then kissed his forehead. "We can't leave him dead on the rug for the next day and a half," she said.

"Don't you have a storage room?" asked Latchmer. "Just spread him out naturally so you can still move him when he gets stiff." He glanced over at the food on the table. Although starving, he didn't want to put anything in his mouth. He wished he could brush his teeth.

"He needs to be buried now," said Mrs. Hughes.

"He can't be, Mother," said Sarah.

"He has to be." She knelt with her hand on Jasper's head and looked from Latchmer to her daughter.

"Just wrap him in a sheet and put him in the back of a closet," said Latchmer. "You won't even know he's there."

Mrs. Hughes stood up and took a few steps toward

Latchmer. "It must be tonight," she insisted. "There's Riverside Park. Jasper loved Riverside Park."

"It's not safe to go there now and we don't have a shovel," said Sarah. "Anyway, the police would stop us. It's no place to bury a dog, especially a big dog." She stood beside Latchmer and again began rubbing his buttocks with her artificial hand. This is a peculiar place, thought Latchmer to himself.

"I won't be able to sleep until he's buried," said Mrs. Hughes. "He was your father's favorite dog, he should be buried in Rochester."

"You mean, drive to Rochester?" asked Latchmer. "That's pretty far."

"If not Rochester, then someplace with trees and green grass. Please, Mr. Latchmer, you could bury him tonight, I know you could."

"Do you have a car?" asked Latchmer.

Sarah shook her head. "We didn't think we needed one. Do you?"

"One of my roommates has one."

"Could you borrow it?" asked Mrs. Hughes.

"Probably." Even as he said it, Latchmer knew he had admitted too much, but the hard artificial hand stroking his buttocks distracted him.

Mrs. Hughes took a white handkerchief from the sleeve of her kimono and blew her nose. "We would be very grateful. Jasper doesn't want a pet cemetery. He wants his own piece of earth with maples rising above him."

"You think you could find a place tonight?" asked Sarah.

"Maybe someplace over in New Jersey, you know, toward the Delaware Water Gap. I've never buried a dog before."

"How long would it take?"

"Two or three hours. One of my roommates has a lot of camping gear, including a shovel." Latchmer wondered what he was getting himself into. "But it would be a lot easier if you could wait till tomorrow or even Monday."

Mrs. Hughes made a sobbing noise. Sarah again touched Latchmer's buttocks. "It would be best if you could do it tonight. Mother's health isn't good. But even if it takes six hours I want you to come back."

Mrs. Hughes again blew her nose. "And bring a small handful of dirt from Jasper's grave."

"Do you have something I can carry the dog in?"

"Jasper's too big for a suitcase," said Sarah. "We have some heavy-duty garbage bags. Perhaps I could put several inside each other."

"He must have his blanket," said Mrs. Hughes. "And his dishes, he can't be buried without his food and water dishes. And his leash and his red rubber ball." She hurried toward the bedroom.

"I'll call my roommmate and have him bring over the car," said Latchmer. He picked up the phone and dialed. After it rang six times, he hung up and dialed again. This time he let it ring ten times. Sarah had gone into the kitchen to get the garbage bags. From both the kitchen and bedroom, Latchmer heard drawers opening and closing, cupboard doors slamming.

Latchmer hung up the phone. This particular roommate had a girlfriend who lived nearby. He was probably seeing her, but Latchmer couldn't remember her name. However, he knew where his roommate parked his car and where he kept an extra set of keys. He would get the car, drive back, and pick up the dog. It would be an adventure: driving into New Jersey in the dead of night with a dog's corpse. Latchmer wondered if he would have done this if Mrs. Hughes hadn't reminded him of Miss Mitchell. Why did he feel guilty? As he tried to think he again remembered those summer evenings when he and his cousin would prowl around Miss Mitchell's house trying to catch a glimpse of her and his grandfather, to see them naked or doing something illicit. But they saw nothing. Often Miss Mitchell would sit on the front porch swing until quite late. She would rock and the swing would creak, while from inside would come the sound of the radio—sometimes music, sometimes a dramatic program like Ozzie and Harriet or the Fat Man.

Mrs. Hughes returned to the living room with a ragged blue blanket, a red ball, and a rubber squeaky toy in the form of a pink-eared mouse. She smoothed the blanket out on the floor, then began pulling and tugging Jasper until he lay in the center. She put the leash, ball, and squeaky toy next to his chest, then folded over the sides, covering the dog so he was no more than a blue mound on the living room rug.

"I'll get his dishes," she said, walking quickly to the kitchen.

At the kitchen door, she bumped into Sarah, who was hurrying back to the living room with the garbage bags.

"I put six inside each other," said Sarah. "They seem quite strong."

"Let's see if Jasper fits," said Latchmer.

They spread the opening of the bag behind the dog, then began to push him into it. His blue blanket bunched up on the rug. Sarah held the bag open, while Latchmer lifted first the back half of Jasper, then the front. Latchmer could still taste the dog when he touched his tongue to his lips: the salty taste of anchovies. Once Jasper was partly in the bag, he slid easily on the black plastic.

"Let me see if I can pick him up," said Latchmer.

"You forgot his dishes," said Mrs. Hughes.

"They'll have to go in another bag," said Latchmer. By bunching the bag at the neck, he could just manage to hold it. He guessed it weighed about seventy-five pounds. He set it down again. There was a squeaking noise as the body of the dog collapsed onto the toy mouse.

"But they must go into that bag," said Mrs. Hughes. "Jasper will miss them."

"There's no room, Mother. Michael will carry them in another bag and then put them with Jasper when he buries him. Won't you, Michael?"

"Of course."

"Do you want another squeaky toy?" asked Mrs. Hughes.

"One's probably enough," said Latchmer.

"Did you reach your friend?" asked Sarah.

"He's out, but I know where he keeps his car. I'll go get it, then drive back. It should only take about thirty minutes."

"But you can't," said Mrs. Hughes, raising her voice. She was kneeling on the floor with her hand inside the garbage bag, giving Jasper his last pats. "You have to take Jasper with you. You can't leave him here."

"It will only be for a short time," said Latchmer.

"I don't want him here, I don't want him here any longer!" She stood up and touched the lapel of Latchmer's brown corduroy suit coat.

"I guess I could take him in a cab," said Latchmer.

"Could you, are you sure?" asked Mrs. Hughes. "You'll never know how grateful I am. Just let me finish saying goodbye." Kneeling, she folded back the bag to expose Jasper's head. Then she lifted it, leaned forward, and whispered something that Latchmer couldn't hear. Afterward, she kissed the tip of Jasper's nose. Standing up, she covered her face with her hands and hurried toward the bedroom.

Latchmer watched her go. "It's a shame," he said, taking hold of the mouth of the bag.

"Can you carry him all right?" asked Sarah.

"Oh sure, I'm as strong as a horse." He lifted the bag so he cradled it in both arms. The plastic was slippery.

He walked to the door and Sarah followed him.

"Don't forget to come back," she said. "No matter how late." She stood in front of him by the door, leaning against the bag. She stared at him and Latchmer could see her pupils getting bigger. Her teeth seemed huge, great fat teeth suitable for tearing and rending. She reached toward him, took hold of his testicles, and began to squeeze them. Latchmer realized she was squeezing him with her artificial hand.

"Do you know how to do the pressure cooker?" she asked.

"Pardon me?" She was hurting him and Latchmer was afraid he would drop the dog.

"When you come back, I'll show you how to do the pressure cooker."

Latchmer shut his eyes. "I'm going to drop the dog," he said.

Sarah let him go, then opened the door. "I won't kiss you now," she said.

The dog kept slipping and Latchmer jostled him into a better position. "I'll be back as soon as I can."

He took the elevator down to the lobby. The Indian or Pakistani was still on duty and opened the door for him. Pressing the plastic bag to his chest, Latchmer stumbled out onto the sidewalk. The air was cool and he took a deep breath. He had never had a dog before, not even a dead one. He walked to the curb and began looking for a cab. With every step, the toy mouse made a slight squeak. Latchmer thought once again of the dragon that the skywriter had warned him against. Perhaps Jasper was the dragon, not alcohol or his inability to keep his mouth shut. Maybe the big danger was Jasper himself.

CHAPTER TWO

Michael Latchmer stood on the corner of West End and Eighty-ninth looking for a taxi. It was ten-fifteen Saturday night. Theaters were just getting out and taxis were in short supply. In fact, those he saw were all filled with people having a good time: ladies in fur coats, gentlemen with cigars. The weather had turned chilly and what had earlier been a spring day was now a winter night. The puddles along the curb were covered with a sheen of ice. Bits of paper chased each other down West End Avenue in confused spirals.

Latchmer lifted the black plastic bag, holding it with both arms. It was heavy. There was no way he could carry Jasper the twenty blocks to 109th Street. Down by Eighty-eighth, he saw a taxi stop to let someone off. Latchmer hurried into the street. As he did so, he saw a man waving to the taxi from the other side of West End Avenue. Latchmer waved more frantically and ran into the middle of the street still clutching the dog. The other man saw him and began to sprint toward the cab. Being unencumbered except for an umbrella, he could move more quickly.

"Hey, that's my cab," shouted Latchmer.

The taxi stopped and the other man gave Latchmer an exaggerated salute as he climbed into the back seat. The taxi made a U-turn and headed downtown. Latchmer gave the dog a slight heave to get a better grip and the squeaky toy squeaked. He turned and walked back toward Eighty-ninth. It was cold and dark and he saw no stars. Every few moments he put down Jasper so he could wave at a taxi, but they were always full. A police cruiser slowed beside him and a patrolman eyed him suspiciously. Latchmer wondered what would happen if they knew he was carrying a dead dog. They would call it "transporting" a dead dog. Latchmer hated explanations.

"Laundry," he said to the police car. "It's just my laundry." But the patrolman was too far away to hear.

Far up West End Avenue, Latchmer saw a taxi with its light on, indicating it was empty. As it drove toward him, he saw other men and women dart out into the street to wave at it. The taxi passed them without slowing. Latchmer put down the dog and combed his fingers through his hair. He lifted his arm and stepped out into the street, straightening his back in order to give him more authority. Was the taxi slowing a little? He thought it was. Just a young black cab driver by himself. Latchmer caught his eye and began to wave. Staring at Latchmer, the driver slowed, swerved toward him, then shook his head and accelerated, missing Latchmer by about three inches. He came so close that Latchmer had seen the glitter of a gold tooth. Jumping backward, Latchmer stumbled over the dog, then caught himself on a car parked at the curb.

"Damn," said Latchmer as he watched the taxi disappear.

At that moment another car honked its horn from about two feet away. Latchmer scrambled around and again tripped over the dog. In front of him was a beat-up green Plymouth station wagon. The driver was black and had a very round, moon-shaped face. He stared at Latchmer for several seconds, then winked. Reaching to his right, he lowered the visor on the passenger's side. Attached to the visor with rubber bands was a printed card that read, "Delivery Service." The driver flipped the visor up again and nodded at Latchmer encouragingly. Latchmer picked up the dog and lugged him to the window.

"Where you going?" asked the driver.

"Broadway and 109th," said Latchmer. "Are you a taxi?" He kept wondering where the station wagon had come from.

"A special taxi. You see the sign? I'm Delivery Service. How much you pay most times to go that far?"

"I don't know, maybe two fifty."

"I do it for two bucks."

"Two fifty is okay," said Latchmer, opening the back door.

"I say two bucks and two bucks it will be." The driver spoke very precisely, giving each syllable the same intonation. The way he spoke reminded Latchmer of the talking computers they were developing at work. The driver wore some kind of African looking shirt with streaks of orange and brown. He had glasses with square brown frames that resembled the ones once worn by Buddy Holly. Latchmer thought he was about twenty-five.

"Are you insured?" asked Latchmer.

"Sure, I'm insured. I'm no gypsy cab. Delivery service, we carry $1,800 insurance. If I crash, we fix you up as far as $1,800. Past that and you are already dead."

Latchmer pushed the body of the dog into the backseat. Then he got in with the bag of dishes and slammed the door. The taxi was very hot and smelled of rancid mayonnaise. "I'm in your hands," said Latchmer.

"You can trust me fine," said the driver.

"Where're you from?"

"Haiti," said the driver. "I come all the way from Haiti

to drive you tonight." He pushed down on the accelerator and the station wagon leaped forward in the direction of downtown.

"I'm going uptown," said Latchmer.

Without slowing, the driver spun the wheel. The car had power steering and the driver spun the wheel using only his index finger. With a screech, the station wagon hurtled itself into a U-turn. Latchmer was positive the street was not wide enough, that they would hit the cars parked along the opposite curb. He squinched his eyes and gripped the back of the front seat. The right front fender of the Plymouth lightly kissed the door of a parked Mercedes, then fish-tailed up West End Avenue. Two normal, safe-looking yellow taxis slammed on their brakes in order not to hit them. The Haitian kept accelerating through a red light. A half-tuned radio in the dashboard was playing reggae. Through his many levels of anxiety, Latchmer listened as Bob Marley sang, "So Much Trouble in the World."

The Plymouth hit a pothole and bounced. The toy mouse squeaked in Jasper's bag. They hit another bump and the mouse squeaked again.

"What is in the bag?" asked the driver. From the backseat he was no more than a silhouette. He had stiff black hair that stood straight up on his head in lengths varying between half an inch and three inches. His hair didn't look cut so much as grazed by a thoughtful ruminant. Latchmer saw the Haitian was watching him in the rearview mirror.

"My laundry," he said. "Have you been in the States long?" He saw no point in discussing Jasper.

The Haitian swung the Plymouth into the lane of oncoming traffic in order to pass several slower taxis. The station wagon moved like a canoe in fast water. There was hardly any sense of movement, just a gentle rocking motion. Only the buildings and other cars rushing by made Latchmer feel he might be in danger.

"No, not long," said the Haitian, "but I have wanted to come ever since I was a little boy. I hoped to go to Montana. I would be a hunter and grow famous hunting the wombats. Some wombats have wings five feet long. They fly down at sunset so they are almost invisible. Big fat birds but tricky to catch. The poor people of Montana, if they catch a healthy wombat they can eat well for two or three weeks. They can make soup from the bones and the feathers they wear in their hats. But these wombats have big claws and sharp teeth. Sometimes the poor people eat the wombats. Sometimes the wombats eat the poor people. It evens out. So I would become famous hunting the wombats. The best way is with a boomerang, because if you miss, you don't lose the boomerang. So in my village in Haiti, I would make boomerangs and practice. But I never became any good, nor did my boomerangs come back to me, although one time I killed a cat. It was sleeping. I just walked up and whacked it over the head."

"Wombats don't fly," said Latchmer, who was wondering if there was any easy way to get out of the car.

"I've heard that was true," said the Haitian. "I have also heard they no longer live in Montana." He ran another red light, then bounced over another pothole. The toy mouse squeaked. "Tell me," said the Haitian, "what is really in that bag?"

"My laundry," said Latchmer. "Do you have to drive so fast?"

"Speed is good for the circulation," said the Haitian. "You know, one time I picked up a man with a plastic bag and I didn't say anything. Then, maybe an hour later, I picked him up again with a second plastic bag and I still didn't say anything, and an hour after that I picked him up with a third plastic bag and you know what he was carrying? It was his wife. The police, they were angry with me for not being more curious. He had his wife in lots of plastic bags. So tell me, what is really in that bag? It is too heavy to be laundry and laundry does not squeak."

"It's none of your business," said Latchmer. "If the bag bothers you, why don't you let me out right here." It had gotten even hotter in the station wagon, and Latchmer loosened his tie. In the rearview mirror, he saw the Haitian still looking at him. He never seemed to look at the road.

The Haitian swerved around another taxi, coming so close that Latchmer could have snatched the cigar from the driver's mouth. On the next block a patrol car was pulled up behind a pickup truck. Its blue lights were flashing.

"Why make it so difficult?" asked the Haitian. He ran another light, then drew up behind the patrol car, pumping his brakes and stopping about two inches from the bumper. "Shall I tell these policemen you have something funny in a plastic bag?"

Latchmer didn't answer. One of the patrolmen stood by his car looking back at the Haitian. He wore a black leather jacket and didn't appear friendly. Latchmer imagined the patrolman getting angry at him. He could see him pointing down at Jasper in his plastic bag and shouting rude remarks. But it wasn't Latchmer's fault that Jasper had died. If the patrolman got angry at anyone, it should be at the dog. Then Latchmer considered getting out of the car and just walking away. After all, it was only ten more blocks to his own apartment. He was strong, he could walk. But on the other hand, why bother? What would the Haitian or the police or anyone care that he was transporting a dead dog between point A and point B?

"It's a dog," said Latchmer.

"Why does it squeak?" asked the Haitian.

"It's the dog's toy, a little rubber mouse."

"Is this dog dead?" asked the Haitian.

"Of course."

"Then why does the dog need a toy?"

"It had sentimental value for the dog."

The Haitian turned around and leaned over the seat. He had large lips and tiny ears pressed flat against his head, almost a cat's ears. His nose was a little stub right in the center of his black moon-shaped face. To Latchmer he looked peculiar—the round face, ragged hair, the Buddy Holly glasses. But Latchmer knew that such a thought might be racist. Perhaps other blacks would find him handsome. Then again, perhaps *that* was racist. All Latchmer knew for certain was that he, personally, found the Haitian odd-looking.

"Let me see the dog," said the Haitian.

Latchmer folded back the top of the bag to expose Jasper's head. The Haitian flicked on the interior light and carefully inspected the dog, even looking at his teeth and lifting out one of his front paws.

"He's a nice dog," he said. "What's in the other bag, a cat?"

"No, the dog's dishes."

"Sentimental value?"

"That's right."

"When did the dog die?" asked the Haitian. He had begun to scratch Jasper behind the ears.

"About an hour ago."

"Did you shoot him?"

"No, it was a perfectly natural death. He was pretty old. I think he had a heart attack."

"What's the dog's name?"

"Jasper."

"That's a nice friendly name. What are you going to do with Jasper?"

"I was going to bury him," said Latchmer. The patrol

car turned off its flashing lights and drove away. The Haitian was still leaning over the backseat. His face was only a foot from Jasper's. Latchmer kept staring at the man's ears. They looked so rudimentary. As if they had just begun to develop and then stopped because of a lack of iodine or Vitamin E or iron or whatever it is that makes ears grow. But then again, perhaps in Haiti small ears were considered beautiful.

"Why do you wish to bury the dog?" asked the Haitian. "Is that too sentimental value?"

"In this country," said Latchmer, "that's what people normally do with dead dogs."

"Why not sell him?" asked the Haitian.

"Sell him?"

"Sure, a big red dog like that, he's worth a lot of money. You say he died only an hour ago? It would be a shame to bury him."

"But I promised his owner," said Latchmer.

"The owner, he is not here, right?" asked the Haitian. "We sell the dog, split the money fifty-fifty, then you go back and tell the owner the dog is buried. We sell the dog, we sell the dog's dishes, we sell the rubber mouse. This is New York. People will buy anything."

"I don't know," said Latchmer, "it seems like cheating."

"That's because you see it through the owner's eyes," said the Haitian. "From the dog's eyes, he would think you were doing him a kindness. He is tired of this easy life. He wants to be of use."

"I can't do it," said Latchmer, "I made a promise." But he began to think how far it was to the Delaware Water Gap, how he would have to borrow his roommate's car, drive for two hours, dig a hole, then drive two hours back. It could be five o'clock in the morning before he returned. What chance would he have then to learn about the pressure cooker?

"What was he?" asked the Haitian, "what was this

Jasper? Just somebody's pet? For his whole life he did nothing but lie around and eat or go out for a walk or maybe chase a squirrel. What a foolish life! Now maybe he can do something. Maybe he will be of use to his fellow creatures. If you bury him, he will be useful only to worms. But if we sell him, who knows, maybe the important part of his life is just beginning."

"But who'd want to buy him?" asked Latchmer. If he could get rid of the dog by midnight, then he could be back at Sarah's maybe no later than one o'clock. He could dig up a little dirt from the park and say it came from Jasper's grave.

"I know a laboratory," said the Haitian. "They do experiments on animals which maybe the authorities they frown upon. All the time they need dogs—dead dogs, living dogs. Many times they have bought dogs from me. It is a big business."

"Where is this place?" Latchmer swore if it was very far, he would refuse to go.

"It is over by Columbia, you know, the university. They work at night so nobody will notice. They are very professional."

"And you're positive they're open?"

"Absolutely. During the day, they must do regular work. You sit back and relax. From now on we are business partners." The Haitian stuck out his hand. "What is your name?"

"Latchmer, Michael Latchmer." The Haitian's hand felt as hard as the artificial hand that Sarah kept concealed with her leather glove. Perhaps this guy's the dragon, thought Latchmer, he's the guy that the skywriter was warning me about.

"My name is Jean-Claude," said the Haitian. He pronounced it something like Shawn-clue and for a long time Latchmer thought it was an African name like Sambo or Bantu.

"So," said Jean-Claude, "now we will make our fortune." He hit the gas and Latchmer was thrown back in his seat. The Plymouth turned right on 105th. As they passed under the street lights, the interior of the car brightened and darkened.

Latchmer looked down at Jasper's head poking out of the plastic bag. Idly, he tugged at one of Jasper's ears. It had bothered him that he'd never been allowed to have a dog while growing up. His mother said they were too dirty. But his grandmother had had a fat black cocker spaniel and Miss Mitchell had a collie. The first time Latchmer had seen the collie, he'd been riding by Miss Mitchell's house on his bike. The dog came galloping out, frightening Latchmer and nearly making him crash into a parked car. But the dog didn't bark, had only run along beside him in an affable sort of way. When Latchmer got off his bike to push it up over the wooden railway bridge, the dog trotted along beside him and let Latchmer scratch his ears. Then it accompanied him the three more blocks to the state highway, where it turned around and trotted home. After that the dog often went with him for those six blocks past Miss Mitchell's house. Latchmer rode an old blue Schwinn that belonged to one of his cousins. Usually he had playing cards attached to the fender supports and they riffled through the spokes making a noise vaguely like a motorcycle. Latchmer had imagined it was that riffling noise which attracted the collie, whose name, he later learned, was Copperfield. It was almost like having a dog, a part-time dog that remained with him for six blocks and no longer, since it refused to cross the highway. Latchmer began to bring it bones and bits of meat from his grandmother's house, even a cookie and once a slice of chocolate cake, and for those six blocks he and Copperfield were pretty good friends.

Jean-Claude drew up to the light on Amsterdam Avenue where two other cars were waiting. Glancing casually over his shoulder, he accelerated through the light, then turned left in front of the two cars. A taxi heading uptown on Amsterdam slammed on its brakes and skidded sideways with a screech of tires. Jean-Claude didn't seem concerned or attempt to hurry in any way. The skidding taxi missed them by about two feet.

"Sometimes," said Jean-Claude, "I think of what they bury in this country and I tell myself it is a great waste. Think of those great cemeteries across the river in Queens. Think of those bodies lying side by side—fresh bodies, rotting bodies, little heaps of bones. Think of all the clothes and rings and gold teeth. Think of people buried with their watches and dentures, their pacemakers and artificial legs, their wigs and glass eyes and contact lenses. In Haiti when a poor man dies they often sell his body to the United States. The government sells the bodies to medical schools because Haitian bodies are so cheap. That is the easiest way for a Haitian to come to the United States—to die poor. Then he can go to Harvard or Princeton or Yale just like a rich man's son. When I came to this country, I came on a boat that I helped make myself. Two men fell off and fish ate them, maybe it was sharks. But even to be eaten by fish is better than being put in the ground. The fish get fat, they make other fish fat. Then we catch them and we get fat. But a man in the ground just poisons the ground. His body is full of chemicals and maybe he is in a metal box. What about you? When you die, what will you do?"

"I hadn't thought about it," said Latchmer. He hoped he wasn't going to get embroiled in a philosophical conversation. Latchmer hated philosophy and the way it always seemed to turn against you.

"Maybe we will still be friends then," said Jean-Claude, "and maybe you will give me your body and I will do something useful with it. In Haiti, I know a man whose body was put in a field to keep the birds away from the crops. He hung up on two big sticks. Bit by bit the crows ate the body until all that was left was a skeleton, and when the wind blew, the skeleton rattled and so frightened the crows that they never came back. The man who owned that field had the best crops in the whole village."

"I'd like to be buried in Rochester," said Latchmer. "That's where my parents are buried." It seemed he was always getting chatty cab drivers.

Even though there was little traffic, Jean-Claude swerved from lane to lane as if just for the pleasure of it. Many of the storefronts on Amsterdam were boarded up and all the people on the street were black. When Latchmer first came to New York, he had been warned away from neighborhoods like this one.

"You think only of yourself," said Jean-Claude. "Your body is like a great shopping basket full of rich things to be sold. When you go to the market, you come out with a bag full of steaks and lobsters and fine things to eat. Do you just throw them away? Of course not, you have a party for your friends and we all come and we eat your steaks and lobsters and maybe we sing songs and maybe we dance. It should be the same when you die. We will sell everything and have a big party. We will sell your eyes and kidneys and heart. We will have a joyful time and you will be proud."

"I'll be dead," said Latchmer.

"Just a small problem. Your spirit will be there and it will be happy. Right now the spirit of Jasper is running alongside the car. He is running like a young dog because this is the first time in his life he is free. And every time I stop for a light, he stops and wags his tail."

"You don't stop very often," said Latchmer.

"That is the nature of lights."

Latchmer looked down at Jasper's head. The dog's large brown eyes were open again. Latchmer brushed his hand over the eyelids so they closed.

Latchmer's grandfather had had a carpentry shop behind the house where he would relax on the weekends by making little tables, chairs, cabinets which he gave away at Christmas. For the entire summer before the summer of his death, Latchmer's grandfather had built a coffin using cherry-wood boards. There had been no screws or nails of any kind. His grandfather had said he found it soothing to consider his death in the particular rather than in the abstract. Latchmer hadn't known what that meant. He had been ten at the time and watched his grandfather from the vantage point of a high metal stool. On the lid of the coffin, a picture of an owl had been burned into the wood. In honor of Athena, his grandfather had said.

Looking out at Amsterdam Avenue, Latchmer tried to remember what else they had talked about. Mostly Latchmer sat on the tall stool and watched. But his grandfather had had a second son who had been killed in the Battle of the Bulge. He would talk about what this son had been like as a child, how he looked like Latchmer, how he was a terrific third baseman, how he'd meant to become a doctor. His grandfather would talk about the war and politics, Governor Dewey and Wendell Willkie. The Korean War had recently ended and Latchmer was constantly mixed up as to what war was being discussed. Back in Rochester, Latchmer had seen a man on the street with only one leg. He'd asked the man if he had lost his leg in the war but the man said, No, a load of lumber had fallen on it. A cable had snapped on a crane and he had looked up to see this mass of wood falling out of the sky. He had leaped but hadn't leaped far enough. Latchmer remembered the conversation with the one-legged man much more clearly than his conversations with his grandfather.

But he remembered one day he had asked his grandfather about Miss Mitchell. His grandfather had been reluctant to talk about her. He had large red hands with freckles on the back and even now, sitting in the Plymouth, Latchmer could see him fitting the cherry-wood boards to each other, running his fingers back and forth over each board to judge its smoothness. His grandfather had told him that Miss Mitchell was his friend and was Latchmer's friend as well. He had been very insistent about that. He added that Latchmer should treat her with respect and help her whenever possible. Still, Latchmer had wanted to ask why he went there and what he did since he had a perfectly good house of his own. He had heard his grandmother call Miss Mitchell "your grandfather's whore," and even at ten Latchmer had a rudimentary idea of what a whore was.

He had tried looking it up in the dictionary but thought it began with an *H* and all he could find was a word for frost. But then, asking his cousin, Latchmer had been amazed to learn there were women whom one could hire. He himself was very shy with girls and it was a relief to think he could circumvent his shyness by simply renting someone. Every other Friday afternoon at school his fifth grade teacher would take his class down to the gym, put on records, and teach them to foxtrot. The girls stood on one side of the gym and the boys on the other. Latchmer had hated to ask the girls to dance, had hated to hurry across the floor with all the other boys. He hadn't even liked dancing. And sometimes a girl would say, No, she wanted to dance with someone else. How embarrassing it was. How much simpler just to rent someone, to take one's allowance and say, Let's dance. How wise of his grandfather to have solved this problem.

Jean-Claude began pumping the brakes and made a right turn onto 126th Street. Then he pulled up to a fire hydrant and stopped. "Does Jasper look presentable?" he asked.

"What do you mean?" asked Latchmer.

"Is there much blood?"

"Oh no, maybe some cracker crumbs and anchovies."

"Anchovies?"

"He was eating them before he died."

Jean-Claude turned on the interior light and looked at Latchmer as if trying to read his thoughts. "But do you think we should brush him?"

"I don't think so. He looks pretty good."

"Maybe you should take out the rubber mouse."

Latchmer dug down into the bag and found the mouse, then he squeaked it several times for Jean-Claude's benefit and put it on the seat. "There's also a red rubber ball and a leash," he said.

"Why does a dead dog need a leash?" asked Jean-Claude. "Ah, I forget, sentimental value. In Haiti, dogs care only for bones. Even when they are tied with a rope, they do not like that rope. We will leave the leash and the ball in the car. Maybe we can sell them later. Anything else?"

"There's his collar and he's wrapped up in an old blue blanket. It was his favorite blanket."

"I understand that," said Jean-Claude, "I too have a favorite blanket. But these scientists, they will not understand such a friendship. For them, it is all cut and slice. We will leave the blanket in the car."

Latchmer removed the leash and red rubber ball, then began to pull the blanket out from around the dog. It required getting on his knees and turning Jasper over. He kept bumping his head on the ceiling.

"Do you need help?" asked Jean-Claude.

"No, I got it all right." Latchmer tugged the blanket free.

Jean-Claude felt the material between his thumb and forefinger. "Good cloth, but it is old. Too bad to waste it on a dog, even a good dog like Jasper. Maybe someone will want to buy it. That is the wonderful thing about New York City. No matter how bad a thing you have, there is always someone who will buy it." Jean-Claude turned out the light and got out of the car. "You bring the dog and I'll carry the dishes. Good dishes are always useful."

Latchmer pushed Jasper back into the bag, grabbed hold of the top, and dragged him out of the station wagon. Jean-Claude waited by the front door of a narrow, four-story, brick apartment building. Latchmer was surprised to see that Jean-Claude was quite short, only five feet five or six. His head came up to Latchmer's chin.

There was a buzzer to the right of the door. Jean-Claude pushed three short, one long, three short, one long. "That is the beginning of a Beethoven Symphony," he said. "These guys might cut up dogs, but they are still classy guys."

A peephole slid back. "Who is it?" said a voice.

"Jean-Claude."

The door opened. Jean-Claude entered briskly while Latchmer followed carrying Jasper. The door was shut by a young man in a white laboratory coat who then shone a flashlight on Latchmer's face. "Who's this?" he asked.

"He's my friend," said Jean-Claude. "We've brought a first-class dog."

The young man turned and led the way up the stairs. The hall was lit by a tiny bulb. Plaster had fallen from the walls, and the stairs were littered with it. At the top was another door. The young man knocked three times, paused, knocked again, paused, knocked three more times, then paused again, knocked again. The door opened and bright light poured down the stairs.

"Come on," said Jean-Claude.

Latchmer got a better grip on Jasper, then passed through the doorway into an extremely bright room. The door shut and locked behind him. There were big lights on the ceiling and the walls were covered with insulation backed with tinfoil. The whole room glittered. Covering the floor were thick sheets of compressed Styrofoam. It made the floor seem bouncy. Attached to the door was an old mattress that was torn and spotted with blood.

A young woman in a white laboratory coat had opened the door. Latchmer blinked at her. When she saw the plastic bag, she said, "Let me get a table."

Moments later she returned wheeling a small aluminum table. Latchmer put the bag on top, then rolled the black plastic away from Jasper's head. One of his eyes had come open and seemed to be lazily inspecting the room. Latchmer shut it again. Jean-Claude stood by the table looking proprietorial. The huge frames of his glasses kept slipping down his nose and he shoved them back in place with one knuckle of a fist.

"Nice dog," said the woman. "What a beautiful red coat."

"He's had a lot of love and attention," said Latchmer, brushing some crumbs from Jasper's snout.

"Was he poisoned?"

"No, he died naturally. He had a heart attack after eating a whole mess of anchovies."

The woman nodded sympathetically. "Let's wheel him in to the doctor," she said.

Latchmer followed the woman through another door. She was very thin and two black braids hung down the back of her laboratory coat. The walls of the second room were also lined with insulation. From far, far away, Latchmer heard a faint barking. Jean-Claude brought up the rear, carrying the bag with Jasper's red and blue weighted bowls.

The woman opened another door and immediately the faint barking became loud and frantic. It was punctuated by shouts such as "Get back, Watch out, Hit him!" The woman turned and smiled at Latchmer apologetically.

As he passed through the doorway, Latchmer looked

for the source of the commotion. Before he could even begin to focus, a Great Dane came galloping toward him, bounced against him, knocking him into the door frame, then ran into the next room. Latchmer was just recovering his balance when two men in white coats raced through the doorway after the dog. Latchmer was again knocked aside. The younger man actually put his hand in the middle of Latchmer's chest and shoved. "Excuse me," he said. "Get that dog!" shouted the other. He was waving a revolver. Latchmer raised his arms to defend himself but the two men were already in the farther room, chasing the dog, shouting and clapping their hands.

The Great Dane had a dark brindle coat and ran with its tail between its legs. Its silver choke chain and identity tags made a constant jingling noise. The dog galloped in a circle and the two men ran after it. They shouted like wild Indians and aimed kicks at the dog whenever they got close. Latchmer and Jean-Claude watched from the doorway. The older of the two men continued to wave the revolver above his head. The dog's long tongue was lolling out of its mouth and its eyes seemed all white. It had a kind of galumphing run, like a giant rabbit in slow motion. It careened against the tinfoil covering the insulation. The younger man aimed a kick at it, missed, fell down on his back, cursed, jumped to his feet, and kept running.

"Okay, that's enough," shouted the man with the revolver.

The younger man flung himself down on the floor. The other man shakily aimed the revolver at the Great Dane which was making hoarse, panting noises as it continued to circle the room. It jumped over the man lying on the floor and he swung a fist at it. The man continued to aim the revolver and when the dog reached a far corner of the room, he fired twice—great booming noises—and the dog crashed against the insulation, then fell to the floor.

"Perfect!" shouted the man. "Good job. Cut off his head."

The younger man got to his feet and wiped his brow with the back of his hand. The Great Dane lay motionless by the farther door. The man grabbed its hind legs, dragged it across the room and into the next room toward an area of sinks and metal tables where half a dozen people were working. A thin stream of blood trailed after the dog. Another woman in a white coat began to mop it up.

"Don't butcher it," called the older man. "I want a clean head." Tucking the revolver into his belt, he turned to Jean-Claude and Latchmer. "John Cloud, good to see you again. You bring me another dog?"

"A nice red one," said Jean-Claude.

"I'm Dr. George," said the man, holding out his hand to Latchmer.

"Michael Latchmer," said Latchmer. The hand felt damp and cold.

"I like to see a nice-looking dog," said Dr. George. "How did he die?"

"Heart attack," said Latchmer.

"City life," said Dr. George, patting Jasper's rump. "You take a good healthy dog, bring it to the city, and it starts to worry. They're not mentally equipped for it. In no time, they get ulcers. They develop hardening of the arteries and aphasia. I once came across an aphasic dog— all it could do was grunt. Dogs are meant to live on farms, to bully the sheep and chase the chickens. It breaks my heart to see a dog in a bad environment."

Dr. George was a kindly looking, bald-headed man with gold-rimmed glasses. His white laboratory coat had the name "Dr. George" embroidered in red thread over his heart. He was a trifle portly and the white fabric of his coat was stretched across his round belly.

"Watch out!" cried someone from the other room, "Here he comes! He bit me, the little bastard. Kick him!"

There was the crash and rattle of metal falling against metal, then the high yelp of a dog. Latchmer stood back against the wall. A small beagle came dashing across the room chased by two men. One man ran to the door next to Latchmer and tried to block it. He bent over and waved his arms back and forth like an umpire signaling a runner safe. The other man ran after the beagle with what looked like a broom handle. He kept swinging it at the dog and missing.

"Is he ready?" shouted Dr. George drawing the revolver from his belt. "Is he ready?"

"Almost," shouted the man with the broom handle. He swung again and hit the metal leg of the table that held Jasper. The dog ran around and around the room.

"It's hard to hit the little ones," said Dr. George to Latchmer. "Watch out, here he comes."

The man guarding the door knelt down to block the dog which skidded past him, banged against the metal table, and came to a stop cowering between Latchmer's legs. Immediately, the man with the broom handle rushed over and began poking at the beagle. He kept hitting Latchmer's knees. Dr. George cocked his revolver and tried to push his way around the man with the broom in order to get a good shot. The dog snarled and barked. Latchmer was sure he would get a bullet in his leg, but whenever he tried to grab the dog it snapped at his hand. At last the beagle jumped into the air, landed on the metal table, jumped through the doorway past Jean-Claude, and ran into the next room to the farther door where it began scratching frantically at the mattress.

Dr. George ran after it. "Stand back!" he shouted. He shot once and missed. The beagle was tearing great gobs of white batting out of the mattress. Dr. George shot a second time and the beagle tumbled upside-down onto its back and lay still. "Good job," shouted Dr. George. "Cut off its head!"

The man with the broom handle scooped up the beagle and ran with it into the laboratory. The woman with the mop began to clean up the blood. Dr. George shoved the revolver back into his belt and looked at Latchmer with an expression of melancholy. Latchmer's ears were ringing from the gunshots.

"You've caught us at a bad time, Mr. Latchmer," said Dr. George. "Let's wheel this dog into my private lab."

He led the way with Jean-Claude while Latchmer pushed the metal table. They passed through a large laboratory where about fifteen people were working. The Great Dane lay headless on a high counter with a black top. Along the left-hand wall were stacked about twenty cages, each containing a dog. A few were sleeping but most were whining or yelping or barking, so the laboratory was full of noise. The white-coated men and women joked and talked cheerfully to one another. As Dr. George walked past them, they all turned and nodded or smiled. Time and again Dr. George paused at one, then another, asking if this one had gotten over his cold or how his sore arm was doing or if his brother had at last found a job. Some of the men and women were dissecting dogs, others were fussing with microscopes or test tubes. One was putting something into a centrifuge.

Dr. George passed through a set of double glass doors into a smaller laboratory. When he closed the doors after Latchmer, the room was completely silent. The smell of chemicals burned Latchmer's nose. Several Gauguin prints of colorful Tahitian women were tacked to the wall. In the far corner was a large desk, several soft-looking leather chairs, and a tall bookcase with glass doors. On top of the bookcase was a bottle of expensive brandy and four snifters.

"Now, let's see what manner of dog this is," said Dr. George. He had a strong, hearty voice that Latchmer found reassuring. "Or would either of you like a cognac. Mr. Latchmer? Mr. Cloud?"

"Just a taste," said Jean-Claude.

Latchmer also took a glass. The three men stood grouped around Jasper's body sipping their cognac.

"I love to see a dog like this," said Dr. George. "He's obviously received a lot of good treatment and has lived in a proper home surrounded by people who gave him the kindness and affection he deserved. How old did you say he was?"

"Twelve," said Latchmer. There were tears in his eyes from the chemicals.

Dr. George wrinkled his brow and looked disappointed. "That may be a little old for us, I'm afraid. Kidneys, heart, liver, they're just about gone on an old fellow like this." He set down his snifter and began to inspect Jasper more closely, looking at his teeth, feeling his joints. He kept sighing and shaking his head.

"But I just sold you an old dog last week," said Jean-Claude.

"That is entirely true, Mr. Cloud, but those old dogs belonged to our group of controls. Now we have all the old dogs that we need and to add more would throw off the age proportions. At this point what we require are young dogs that have died of natural causes. Hard to come by, I'm afraid."

"So you don't want Jasper?" asked Latchmer. Along with his disappointment, Latchmer felt relief. Although why he should feel relieved, he couldn't say.

"It's not that I don't want him," said Dr. George kindly, "it's that I don't need him. If it were up to me, I'd take him in a second, but our grant money is tight and, as I say, we have all the controls we require. Live dogs is what we want now, a whole truckload of live dogs. It's a pity we couldn't have gotten poor Jasper before his heart gave out."

"If it wouldn't be rude to ask," said Latchmer, "just what do you do with these dogs?"

Dr. George finished his cognac and set down the glass by Jasper's nose. "We're studying the tritiated imipramine binding sites in their frontal cortexes."

"Oh?" said Latchmer, "and what's that?" He held out his glass to Jean-Claude, who filled it with more cognac. He knew that the plan to sell Jasper had been too good to be true.

"Nothing to it really," said Dr. George. "Let's say you take two groups of people—half of them die naturally and half commit suicide. It has been discovered that among the suicides there are approximately forty-four percent fewer tritiated imipramine binding sites than among the controls. Well, this is very important. What causes such a strange phenomenon? Some scientists say fear, some say depression, some say a diminished life wish. Personally, I'm on the side of fear and that's what these experiments are all about. We have two sets of dogs. One set has died naturally, like old Jasper. The other has died in a moment of terror. Are the binding sites the same or different?"

"And what have you found?"

"The results aren't in yet."

"How do you learn about binding sites?" asked Latchmer, who imagined they must be like a dock or a cage or even a straitjacket.

Dr. George took off his glasses, folded them, and tapped them against his open palm. "You must understand, Mr. Latchmer, we're using techniques being used all over the world. In a thousand laboratories like this one, the search continues. Bit by bit we add our pieces to the gigantic puzzle of what it is to be a human being." He poured himself more cognac. "The procedure itself is relatively simple. First we cut off the head, then we take samples from the frontal cortex. These are mixed with a little hydrochloric acid and homogenized in a Brinkmann Polytron. Then we take the homogenate, send it through the centrifuge, and we get a little pellet. Then we do this and that, it's a tedious process. But if there is reduced binding in the frontal cortexes of dogs that have died in a state of terror, then this will indicate a functional decrease in serotonergic neuronal activity which could possibly be related to a diagnosis of a major affective disorder. It's much too soon to talk about cures, Mr. Latchmer, but something as common as fear might be curable. Think of the difference this could make to our civilization. The terrified flight from the cities, the fear of nuclear holocaust, the booming business in dead-bolt locks, mace, pacifiers, night lights, even guns—all this could become treatable with a little pill. Tell me, Mr. Latchmer, are you afraid of World War Three?"

"A little bit," said Latchmer.

"If the theories which we are attempting to test in this laboratory tonight turn out to be true, then that little fear of yours will be curable. You'll crawl into bed each night without a care in the world."

"But won't there still be bombs?" asked Latchmer.

Dr. George waggled a finger in Latchmer's face. "That's entirely another issue," he said. "What we are talking about is fear. Whether they blow up the world or don't blow up the world is a different subject altogether."

"So you don't want this nice dead dog?" asked Jean-Claude.

"I'm afraid not."

"What about dishes," said Jean-Claude, "I have two nice dog dishes." He took the red and blue plastic bowls out of the bag and put them on the table next to Jasper.

Dr. George lifted one, then the other. "They're weighted," he said. "I like that."

"Five bucks apiece, ten bucks together," said Jean-Claude.

"I'll give you five for the two," said Dr. George.

"Let's see your money. Cash on the line."

Dr. George took a five dollar bill from his wallet and gave it to Jean-Claude, who tucked it under his African shirt. Then the two men shook hands.

"Have another cognac," offered Dr. George.

"I'll have a touch," said Latchmer. He liked the doctor and felt kindly toward him and his work. Although he was disappointed about Jasper, it wasn't a big disappointment. "You know," he continued, as he rested one hand on Jasper's head, "I heard a story the other day from a man I work with about a dog."

"Is it a funny story?" asked Dr. George, pouring himself more cognac.

"Pretty funny. But strange, too. I guess I'd call it out of the ordinary."

"I love funny stories," said Dr. George. "It's not off color, is it?"

"No, nothing like that," said Latchmer, who had never heard the story from anyone. It had just popped into his head as he watched the five dollar bill disappear under Jean-Claude's shirt.

"So let's hear the story," asked Dr. George.

"It's about this college student," said Latchmer. "He was a shy kind of fellow and although he's handsome, he doesn't meet women easily. One of his friends set him up with this blind date and, when the night came along, the young man went over to the woman's apartment in order to take her out to dinner. She was tall, thin, and right away he thought she was just beautiful. She invited him in, then took him into the living room and asked him to wait while she finished putting some spray stuff on her hair.

"Well, her old mother was also in the living room.

She'd suffered a stroke a few months before and was propped up in a wheel chair, completely unable to move or speak. The young woman talked to her mother like she was just fine and introduced the young man and then said she'd be back in a few minutes. The only movements the old woman could make was that she could blink and squinch up her eyes. One blink for yes, two for no— something like that.

"The young man stood in front of the old woman for a few moments while she blinked her eyes in what was meant to be a friendly manner. Sort of like small talk. But it made the young man nervous and after a bit he went and plopped himself down in a big armchair to wait. When he next looked at the old woman she appeared to be having a fit. She was blinking furiously and scrunching up her face. The young man stared at her, not knowing what to do, but feeling uneasy. The daughter had said that the mother's nurse would be arriving soon and so the young man decided he should just wait and maybe the blinking would stop. But it didn't stop. The old woman blinked and squinched and looked like she was going crazy.

"After a couple of minutes, the young man couldn't take it any more and he stood up. The armchair was uncomfortable and there was an afghan or rug or something on the seat. He started to smooth it out when he saw that the rug was covering a little dog, a little bald Chihuahua. And he'd killed the dog. I mean, he'd just sat on it and killed it without even knowing. Maybe he'd crushed it, maybe he'd suffocated it. Anyway, that's what the old woman had been blinking about. She'd been trying to tell him that he was sitting on her Chihuahua but hadn't been able to. And now she was furious and she was still blinking like crazy and there were tears in her eyes.

"Well, the man couldn't decide what to do with the

dog. He couldn't just leave it on the chair because his date might see it. Against the wall was a big chest of drawers and the young man opened the middle drawer. It was full of lace tablecloths. He scooped up the Chihuahua, which hung limp in his hands. It was really ancient and hardly had any teeth. Then he put it on top of the tablecloths and shut the drawer. What else could he do? He looked at the old woman and shrugged. Then his date came out and said, 'Have you two been having a nice time?' 'Great,' said the young man. The old woman was still blinking like crazy. His date kissed her mother and they left. They had a wonderful evening—went to a French restaurant, the theater, then went back to his apartment and made love. But the young man never saw her again, you know? Every time he thought of calling her, he would see that dead Chihuahua lying on the lace tablecloth and the girl's mother blinking like crazy, and it paralyzed him."

Latchmer finished his cognac and put his glass on the metal table. Jean-Claude was reading the titles of the books in the bookcase. Dr. George was staring at the floor with his hands folded behind his back.

"That's a horrible story," said Dr. George at last.

"I thought it might interest you."

"Why in the world would you think a story like that might interest me?"

"We better put Jasper back in his bag," said Jean-Claude.

"Lots of people find it an interesting story," said Latchmer, "even a funny story."

"What can they possibly find funny in an awful story like that?"

"Well, the blinking is sort of funny," said Latchmer.

"Help me with the dog," said Jean-Claude. Latchmer held open the bag and Jean-Claude pushed Jasper down inside it. As Latchmer pulled together the mouth of the bag, he bumped against his brandy snifter, which fell to the floor and broke. Latchmer bent down to pick up the pieces.

"Leave it," said Dr. George. "I just want you out of here as soon as possible." He spoke in a tight, impatient voice that reminded Latchmer of Sarah's mother.

"My friend is sorry," said Jean-Claude. "It was very rude. I won't bring him again."

"I should hope not," said Dr. George. He stood on the other side of the metal table as if purposefully keeping it between him and Latchmer.

"I really thought you'd find it funny," said Latchmer. "All of my roommates found it funny." But to himself he kept asking, Why'd I tell such a crazy story?

Dr. George put the bottle of brandy back on the bookcase. "The trouble with people like you is that you like to upset people. You prey on their sensitive feelings. You're a vampire, a vampire of the heart."

"I have sensitive feelings too," said Latchmer, "lots of them." He picked up the bag and Jean-Claude opened the door. Again they were half-deafened by the yelping of the caged dogs.

Dr. George led them quickly through the laboratory and the two following rooms to the front door. Then he unlocked the door and pulled it open. "You can make this up to me, Mr. Cloud, by bringing me some nice live dogs. Medium size would be best."

"I'm not a vampire," said Latchmer, "I'm sorry I upset you." But Dr. George was already walking back across the room.

"We better go," said Jean-Claude. He led the way down the stairs to the street. Latchmer followed, pausing every few steps to get a better grip on Jasper. The air outside was cool and refreshing. Looking at his watch, Latchmer saw that it was nearly 11:30. There was still time to borrow his roommate's car, bury the dog, and get back to Sarah in time to learn about the pressure cooker. Perhaps he wouldn't have to drive as far as the Delaware Water Gap. Perhaps he could bury Jasper somewhere along the Garden State Parkway.

Jean-Claude opened the back door of the station wagon. Latchmer heaved the dog onto the seat and got in. Climbing in the front, Jean-Claude turned the key and began revving the motor to louder and louder degrees of mechanical passion.

"I liked your story," said Jean-Claude, "but I could not say so in front of the doctor because he is a business associate. I found your story both affecting and touching. It is sad when a small dog dies suddenly."

"I guess I should've kept my mouth shut," said Latchmer. "Why don't you drive me over to my apartment and I'll go bury Jasper. It's getting late."

"Bury him?" asked Jean-Claude. "Waste a handsome dog like that on the worms? No, sir, already we have made five dollars from the dishes. That is just the beginning."

CHAPTER THREE

Latchmer's grandmother had always contended that her husband died under suspicious circumstances. In fact, he had died in the house of Miss Mitchell. His grandmother suggested that he had died while engaged in some herculean yet distasteful labor. For her, any mention of sex or the more private affairs of the body was so veiled in euphemism and innuendo that for years Latchmer believed his grandfather had died while carrying out the trash.

When Latchmer had learned more about whores, he was surprised to think of the word as applying to Miss Mitchell, who dressed sedately and went to church. Latchmer would search his memory for the smallest symptom which would link her to the scarlet women of whoredom. In summer she wore dark dresses and in winter she wore dark suits, often with a white blouse. Latchmer couldn't even remember any jewelry.

His grandfather had died in July, just a few days after the Fourth. A few fireworks were still being set off around town and the eleven-year-old Latchmer had thought that appropriate. He was only sorry he had none left himself. All he possessed were a handful of sparklers, and to express his grief he had burned these in the dark of his room until the smell caught the attention of his aunt, who came running with a pail of water.

His grandfather was a notorious early riser and got up each morning at 4:30. Latchmer too would get up early and sometimes it seemed that the basis of their friendship were those five a.m. breakfasts where his grandfather would feed him a cereal still known as Shredded Ralston. He would pour the cereal into a blue bowl, then slice peaches to put on top. Latchmer remembered how his grandfather would stand at the sink with a sharp knife, skinning the peach in a long spiral which he tried not to break. If he was successful, he would hold the spiral up for Latchmer's inspection. Sometimes Latchmer would peel a peach, but his spirals invariably broke. His grandfather would turn up the kerosene heater in the kitchen stove so the kitchen was always warm. The sun would be just poking its yellow head through the pine trees behind the house. Latchmer, chewing his Shredded Ralston, could almost feel the other people asleep upstairs, grunting or snoring with the warm smell of sleep thick upon them. On the counter by the sink would lie three or four peach skins like the discarded skins of snakes.

Often during these breakfasts his grandfather would open his black leather doctor's bag for Latchmer's inspection. Latchmer would take out the stethoscope and sometimes listen to his own heart and sometimes to his grandfather's heart and sometimes to the heart of the gray kitchen cat. The cat's heart made a high rapid sound. His own heart also seemed rapid. When it came to be his grandfather's turn, his grandfather would unbutton his white shirt and set the end of the stethoscope against his chest, which was speckled with white hair. After a moment, Latchmer would hear DaDum, DaDum, slow and steady, the strongest sound in the world.

His grandfather had died late in the evening and then was brought back to his own house so no one would know he had died under suspicious circumstances. He had been laid out in the downstairs bedroom and covered with a sheet. The next morning Latchmer had gone downstairs early, expecting to find him at breakfast. The kitchen was empty except for the gray cat.

Latchmer went into the downstairs bedroom and found his grandfather in the brass bed covered with a sheet. He knew right away he was dead, not just because of the sheet but because of the way he was lying—lying as still as a piece of wood. He pulled back the sheet and touched his grandfather's bare shoulder. It wasn't the coldness that surprised him but how hard it was. He searched around for the doctor's bag, wanting to find the stethoscope, but couldn't find it anywhere. His grandfather's face didn't look like a real face. His mouth was slightly open and seemed caved in because he wasn't wearing his false teeth. Latchmer noticed them on a small table to the left of the bed. He took them and held them in his hands as if trying to warm them, running his fingers over the teeth and pink plastic gums. The gray cat kept rubbing against Latchmer's legs, winding in and out between his ankles.

He thought of the cherry-wood coffin resting on sawhorses in his grandfather's carpentry shop behind the house. Watching his grandfather build the coffin the previous summer had robbed the death of much of its surprise. Latchmer had never thought about it, but once it happened he was able to tell himself that he had known it would happen.

He put the teeth back on the table, then went into the kitchen to feed the cat. When his aunt found him two hours later, he was peeling peaches. He had peeled nearly two dozen and at last had been able to peel the skin in a single long spiral which he held up for his aunt's inspection. She thought he was crazy.

* * *

Jean-Claude double-parked the Plymouth station wagon in front of Paco's Bar and Grill and ran inside. Latchmer sat in the back seat with Jasper's head in his lap. The dog seemed to be getting stiff, but perhaps Latchmer was just tired. He found it soothing to stroke Jasper's head. It allowed him to be affectionate yet have no responsibilities. On the car radio, Bob Marley was cheerfully singing that total destruction was the only solution.

Latchmer thought of his grandfather, realizing that he hadn't thought of him for many years and feeling somewhat startled by the amount of detail flooding into his mind. He also thought about the child he had been and how different he seemed to be now. The differences were not differences he understood and he supposed that was one of the reasons he rarely bothered about the past. He glanced out of the window in time to see Jean-Claude emerge from the bar. He ran to the Plymouth and jumped into the front seat. They were on Columbus just above 110th.

"Here," said Jean-Claude, handing a small paper bag over the back of the seat. It was a pint of rum. "They were your dog dishes, so you get the first drink."

Latchmer shifted the dog off his lap and broke the seal on the bottle. He didn't much like rum but took a drink anyway. It was hot on his tongue and reminded him that he had missed dinner. "Is there someplace we can get a sandwich?" he asked.

"Sure," said Jean-Claude. He hit the gas and Latchmer was again thrown back in his seat. A little rum slopped onto his tie. "You like hot dogs? I know a place on the next block."

Just as Latchmer was regaining his balance, Jean-Claude hit the brakes, throwing Latchmer forward and sending Jasper onto the floor.

Jean-Claude turned and leaned over the seat. His Buddy

Holly glasses were perched on the very tip of his nose. "You like chili on yours?" he asked. "I get you the works. This is my treat. You just give me a couple of bucks and I'll pay you back when we sell the dog."

Latchmer gave him the money and Jean-Claude hurried into the little restaurant. Latchmer took another pull from the bottle of rum, then began dragging Jasper back onto the seat. Jean-Claude had double-parked next to an old blue Buick. Two fat women sat on the hood. They were white and Latchmer guessed they were whores. One of them slid off and walked the two or three steps to the window of the station wagon, rolling from side to side just like an elephant. She wore a long gray coat which was unbuttoned to reveal a loose white blouse and gold hot pants. She motioned to Latchmer to roll down the window. He thought she must weigh over three hundred pounds. After a moment, he unrolled the window.

The whore stuck her head through the opening. She had short blond hair with black roots. Her face was the shape, texture, and color of a boiled potato. It was a pleasant face, but its nose and eyes seemed about to be swallowed up in the way that wet mud can swallow a rock. As she leaned through the window, her mammoth breasts seemed on the verge of tumbling into the back seat.

"Like some butter?" she asked.

"I'm just waiting for my friend to get a couple of hot dogs," said Latchmer.

"I give good butter," said the whore. "You never had better."

"I guess I just don't feel like it tonight." Latchmer said this as politely as possible so the whore wouldn't think he was being rude.

The whore shrugged and her breasts rolled forward half out of her white blouse. "What's in the bag?" she asked.

"A dog."

"I had a dog once," said the whore, "a little yellow dog. He was hit by a car."

"This dog died naturally," said Latchmer. He offered the whore some rum and she took a sip. After she drank, she wiped the mouth of the bottle on the lapel of her coat and handed it back.

"You know what I could do to your body for only twenty dollars?" she asked.

"I've had a pretty busy evening already," said Latchmer apologetically.

"You gay?"

"No."

"Then you're missing a bet," said the whore. "What're you going to do with the dog?"

"We're trying to sell him." Every time he glanced at the woman, he was aware of her breasts poised above him like soft boulders.

"Let me see the dog," said the whore. She opened the back door and got in. The whole right side of the station wagon sagged several inches. Latchmer flicked on the top light, then rolled back the mouth of the bag to reveal Jasper's head.

The whore reached out and patted Jasper's nose. "Nice dog," she said. "What's his name?"

"Jasper."

"Nice name," said the whore.

"You want to buy him?" asked Latchmer.

"I don't really need a dog. What kind of collar does he have?"

Latchmer turned Jasper's head so she could see the collar. It was dark orange leather with about twenty brass studs.

"I like the collar," she said.

Latchmer unfastened the collar and held it up. The license and identity tags jingled. One of the tags read,

"My name is Jasper," then gave an address in White Plains.

"It's yours for five bucks," said Latchmer.

"What about three?"

"Can't do it. This is a quality collar. Just the tags are worth a buck."

"Okay, four."

"Done."

The whore took the collar and fastened it around her neck. It was loose and the tags hung down between her breasts. "How does it look?" she asked.

"Nice," said Latchmer. "What about my four bucks?"

"You want to take it out in trade?" asked the whore. "I can give you a hand job."

"I'd rather have the money," said Latchmer. "What's your name?"

"They call me Big Pink," said the whore. She took four one dollar bills from the side pocket of her coat and gave them to Latchmer. Whenever she moved, the identity tags made a little jingling noise. "Are you sure it looks nice?" she asked.

"Makes you look like a million dollars."

"You're sweet," said Big Pink.

"You know," said Latchmer, "my grandfather was in love with a woman who was supposed to have been a whore. It's always made me think well of them."

"Was she East Side or West Side?" asked Big Pink. "It makes a difference. I mean, emotionally I'm pure East Side, but people say I've got a West Side appetite."

"No, she lived in a little town upstate. I don't think she charged anything, but 'whore' was what my grandmother called her."

"Amateurs," said Big Pink, "they're always trying to crowd us out. They should pass a law saying every woman has to wear something like a parking meter strapped to her waist. That's the only fair way to do it."

"What do you think about betrayal?" asked Latchmer. Big Pink was leaning against him and his shoulder was going to sleep.

"I don't much like those passive pleasures," said Big Pink, "but I'm ready for anything tonight."

Latchmer considered telling Big Pink about Miss Mitchell and Mrs. Hughes and how he had promised to bury Jasper but was planning to sell him instead. It felt related somehow but the threads were all mixed up, like a Gordian knot of colored ribbon. Latchmer hated confusion. It made him doubt himself, and once one admitted the possibility of doubt then all definitions, opinions, and even one's sense of well-being began to unravel.

Jean-Claude came out of the restaurant trying to balance six chili dogs covered with onions and sauerkraut. He got into the front seat and looked at Big Pink. "Who's that?" he asked.

"She bought Jasper's collar for four bucks," said Latchmer, "doesn't it look nice?"

"Looks great," said Jean-Claude. "Where's my half?"

"I'm keeping it," said Latchmer. "It'll pay me back for the money I lent you for the hot dogs."

Jean-Claude raised his eyebrows so his glasses slid down his nose. Then he handed Latchmer three hot dogs. "You want to buy the leash?" he asked Big Pink.

"What do you think I am?" she asked.

"Just a girl looking for a good time."

"That's about right," said Big Pink. "What about you, you want some butter? I like chocolate."

Jean-Claude turned out the top light. "Get out of the car," he said.

Big Pink shrugged and threw herself back in the seat. "Poof," she said. "Let me have a bite of your hot dog?" she asked Latchmer.

"Here." Latchmer held up one of the hot dogs and Big Pink maneuvered her mouth so as to enfold her lips around the bun. Most of the hot dog disappeared with a loud sucking noise.

After a minute of chewing and swallowing, she said, "I love hot dogs." Latchmer looked down at the little stub of hot dog left in his hand. Jean-Claude sat with his back to them, pretending to ignore them. Big Pink took out a small mirror and some lipstick. Her lips puckered outward like the mouth of a milk bottle. She caked on the dark red lipstick, then pouted at herself in the mirror. Latchmer finished the stump of hot dog. He could taste her perfume on the roll.

Big Pink reached under Latchmer's suit coat and began unbuttoning several buttons of his shirt. Reaching under to his bare stomach, she felt around until she found some loose skin. This she squeezed sharply, making Latchmer almost drop the remaining hot dogs.

"Love handles," she said. "I got plenty." She started to get out of the car. "You change your mind about the butter, you know where to find me."

"Okay," said Latchmer.

"You sure the collar looks nice?"

"Fan-tastic."

Jean-Claude started the engine and before Big Pink had a chance to shut the door, the car shot forward with a squeal of its tires and the door slammed shut by itself.

"You shouldn't sell Jasper's stuff to just anybody," he said.

"It seemed like a good price." Latchmer tried to balance the hot dogs and bottle of rum on his knees without getting any chili on his suit. He took another drink of rum and handed the bottle to Jean-Claude, who was steering with his elbows as he ate.

"The price is not important," said Jean-Claude. "You should only sell to people you respect. Girls like that are trouble. If you loved poor Jasper, you would be more careful who you sold to. Think of that girl on the street wearing Jasper's collar. What if a friend of Jasper's came along and saw it and found out what happened? How could you hold up your head?"

"I didn't know Jasper very well," said Latchmer. He was sorry that Jean-Claude was angry he had sold the collar to Big Pink. But it wasn't his fault she had found the collar attractive and wanted to buy it. If he got angry at anyone, then it should be at Big Pink. Glancing down, Latchmer saw he had spilled chili in his lap. At least it was more or less the same color as his suit. "You get any napkins?" he asked.

"I forgot," said Jean-Claude. "It is true I did not know Jasper as a living dog, but I feel that in his death I have become his friend. What is more, I respect him. That is why I am taking him to an A-1 place. We will make a bundle which we will split fifty-fifty."

Not knowing how else to get the chili off his fingers, Latchmer carefully wiped his hands on Jasper's belly. "Where're we going?" he asked.

Jean-Claude chose not to answer. After a moment, he said, "You know, when I was small, I thought the United States was the most generous place in the whole world. If a man had two cows, he would give his neighbor one. Once I saw a movie about cowboys and cattle drives and I thought each of the cowboys owned maybe twenty of the cows and the reason they were going to the city was to share them with those who had no cows until every man in the United States had his own cow. Yes, it was strange, but no stranger than having snow-capped mountains or having ice on the ground for month after month. My village was small and there was only one radio. Every day the same things would happen. The same people would get drunk and fight. They would say the same things day after day. I would think of the United States and know that here different things happened every day. That's what it meant to be rich—every day there could be something different."

"You have any more of that rum?" asked Latchmer. "These hot dogs are pretty hot." He thought of philosophy and how much he disliked it. A philosophical discussion was like hearing a description of cancer symptoms. Immediately, Latchmer would think he had caught the disease. What was the point of talking about stuff that made everyone uncomfortable?

Jean-Claude passed him the bottle. "When you were small, what did you want to do most?"

"I wanted to fly airplanes like crazy."

"And what do you do now?"

"I work with computers."

"Do you like it?"

"It's great." Latchmer passed him back the bottle.

"I like to drive this car more than anything," said Jean-Claude. He pressed down on the accelerator and did a series of S-shaped curves down the middle of Columbus. "It moves down the road like a snake moves through the grass."

"You get many tickets?" asked Latchmer. It was difficult to eat while Jean-Claude kept whipping the wheel back and forth.

"Not me," said Jean-Claude, "I don't have a license. They can't give you a ticket unless you have a license. That's the law. I think that's what's wonderful about this country. Whenever I break the law, the law still protects me. And the more wrong I do, the more I am protected. It is crazy. In Haiti, if a man does wrong, they just shoot him. I mean, maybe they say he was escaping or cutting up or something, but no, he was just sitting in a chair and they shoot him. They say a man who does wrong once will do wrong again so why fool around? There are many, many people in Haiti and if a man is shot, then right away there is someone else to take his place. Say the man next door has a wife, ten kids, and a goat. Say the police shoot him. Right away there's another man living in the house with the same wife, ten kids, and same goat. What has been lost? The men look about the same. They're the same age and they are both poor. You don't even realize someone is missing. But in the United States many times there is not enough people. When a man disappears, it makes a hole and the wind whistles through that hole and it gets louder and soon people ask questions and they find out why the man is missing and sometimes there are problems. But in Haiti, all the holes are filled up lickety-split."

"We're out of rum," said Latchmer, draining the last of the bottle. "Here's the four bucks from the dog collar. Maybe you can get some more." Another problem with philosophical discussions, thought Latchmer, is that they make the choices of one's life suddenly suspect, as if one could have done better or acted better or lived better. Why stir up the pot, why muddy the water? Better to draw a veil of silence across such problems.

Jean-Claude pulled up in front of a bar. "You gave too much rum to that whore," he said.

"She was a nice girl. She liked me."

"You sink into a girl like that," said Jean-Claude. "It is like dropping a penny into a bowl of thick potato soup. All your friends, they will gather around her naked body and they will call out, Latchmer, Latchmer, but there will be nothing, just a kind of bubbling noise and maybe a week or so later one of your shoes will float to the surface." Jean-Claude got out and went into the bar.

Latchmer leaned back with his arms outstretched on the top of the seat. He felt tired but not really sleepy. His stomach ached a little, but whether from rum or hot dogs, he couldn't decide. A police car with its blue lights flashing roared downtown. Maybe some kid had gotten into the rat poison or an oldster had had his heart give out. On the corner someone in a dark overcoat was pawing through a trash container. Latchmer couldn't tell if it was a man or a woman. The bar was a rundown storefront with the name "Rico's Fun Spot" painted across the top in red glitter letters.

Miss Mitchell, his grandfather's whore, wasn't at all like Big Pink—not in size, shape, age, or dress. During the few days after his grandfather's death, Latchmer had ridden his bike past her house several times every morning and afternoon. Each time Miss Mitchell was standing on her front porch, standing just above the top step as straight as a post. Latchmer couldn't figure out what she was doing. Then, sitting on his bike at the corner, he had seen his grandmother's green Dodge drive slowly down the street. Part of the tailpipe had come loose and dragged on the pavement. He had watched how his grandmother sat stiffly behind the wheel without turning her head or making any sign that she was aware of Miss Mitchell, who in turn stared at the car but made no motion or gesture. A little later Latchmer had seen his grandmother drive by a second time. And not long after that she had driven by again—very slowly and staring straight ahead. The broken tailpipe made an ugly scraping noise on the pavement. Miss Mitchell had stood on the porch watching her. But she too had no expression. The only sign that anything was different was that Miss Mitchell had been wearing a black dress.

That night his grandmother had gone to bed early. His parents and sister were visiting his aunt and Latchmer had been downstairs looking at cartoons in several back issues of *Collier's*. When he went upstairs, he heard a noise from his grandmother's room. At first he thought she was crying and he went to her door to listen. It took a few moments to realize his grandmother was laughing—a high, delicate laugh. It was a sound like glass breaking, as if she had taken a hundred wine glasses and was smashing them one after another. There was no light coming from under the door or through the keyhole. Latchmer had imagined his grandmother sitting at her dressing table in the dark and just laughing, laughing at the dark mirror, at the dozens of bottles of creams and lotions and perfumes, at the little pinwheel snippets of white hair that she pinned up into her real hair each morning.

One time the previous summer he had gone with his grandmother way up on the hill behind town where she had shown him her family's farm, which was now an antique store with a treasure barn full of junk spelt junque. Across the road had been the family graveyard. His grandmother had walked him through it, showing him the graves of her parents, grandparents, great-grandparents, plus an assortment of cousins, aunts, and uncles. They had spent much of the afternoon pulling weeds and planting flowers. Latchmer had found the grave of a great-great-aunt who had died just at his age: ten. A stream ran along the side of the graveyard and Latchmer gathered small white stones and used them to make a decorative border around the grave of his great-great-aunt who had died eighty years before. His grandmother had talked about the dead as if they were her living family. They worked until it was too dark to see and got home long after dinner was over. His parents were worried and angry. But his grandmother had ignored them and, taking him by the arm, brought him into the kitchen where she made melted cheese sandwiches. They had eaten the sandwiches, drunk ginger beer, and whispered together like conspirators.

The morning after he had heard his grandmother laughing, Latchmer went out to his grandfather's workshop to look for the coffin. He felt there was a connection but wouldn't have been able to explain what it was. In any case, the coffin was gone. He assumed it had been sent to the funeral home and would reappear at the wake.

But just to make sure, he asked his aunt. She said, No, his grandmother had picked out another casket at the funeral home the day before. She had no idea what had happened to the cherry-wood coffin. Maybe it didn't fit. But Latchmer knew that wasn't true because there had been a day at the end of the previous summer when the coffin was finished and his grandfather set it down on the cement floor and got inside and wriggled his shoulders to get comfortable, then folded his hands on his chest and winked at Latchmer and said it fit just right. And after that they got canoe paddles and both sat in the coffin paddling like wild, pretending they were shooting the rapids on the Black River which was fast and dangerous and where each summer there were children who did not listen to their parents and drowned.

After talking to his aunt, Latchmer had asked his parents, cousins, and uncles. No one knew about the coffin. He also kept asking his grandmother. She said she knew nothing as well, but he knew she was lying. She had been a short, heavy-set woman with a huge bosom, and when she shook her head her whole body swung back and forth.

Latchmer had explained he would like the coffin for himself. He wasn't sure what he would do with it but had a vague notion of using it for bookshelves or a boat.

His grandmother had been going through his grandfather's closet, separating the clothes between those to sell and those to give away. She explained she couldn't give him the coffin. It no longer existed. She had decided it would be humiliating for her husband to appear at his wake in a homemade coffin with a picture of an owl burned onto the lid. Whoever heard of Athena anyway? Consequently, she had gotten the man who did their yard work and they had taken the coffin into the field behind the house and burned it. She was sorry, but she hadn't wanted it around. Latchmer asked if there was any little piece left and she said, No, she had stayed until the entire coffin was turned to ash.

That afternoon Latchmer had again ridden his bike past Miss Mitchell's house. She was standing on the porch in her black dress. They had looked at each other for what seemed a long time. It felt to Latchmer as if he was falling into her eyes. Even his bike had swerved toward her, but then he had grown frightened and stopped himself. With his grandfather dead, where did his loyalties belong? That night there had been no noise from his grandmother's bedroom.

Glancing from the car window, Latchmer saw Jean-Claude emerge from Rico's Fun Spot with a small paper bag. The person with the brown overcoat who had been pawing through the trash container stood nearby holding up a pair of torn work pants flecked with white paint. Presumably the person was deciding whether they would fit. Without pausing, Jean-Claude snatched away the pants, got into the station wagon, and accelerated down Columbus. Latchmer glanced back at the person, who was still standing with his or her hands up in the air as he or she had stood while holding the pants. The person had long gray hair but appeared clean-shaven. He or she was staring after the station wagon but didn't appear visibly upset. A white van cut across Columbus blocking the person from view.

"Everything has a purpose," said Jean-Claude. "Each day in New York millions of dollars worth of useful things are thrown away. You could build a city under this city and fill it with poor Haitians and when you think you have something to throw away, you just throw it out the window and it falls down to the city of poor Haitians and they will do some useful thing with it."

"Was that a man or woman back there?" asked Latchmer.

"I didn't notice."

"You buy the rum?"

"Sure," said Jean-Claude. He removed the bottle from the bag, opened it, drank a little, then passed it back to Latchmer.

"So where are we taking Jasper now?" asked Latchmer. He drank a little rum and it seemed to soothe his stomach.

"I know a place in the twenties where they buy him for sure."

"What kind of place?"

Jean-Claude ran a light at Seventy-second Street. A yellow cab slammed on its brakes and slid toward them sideways. Jean-Claude sped up a little in order to avoid it, then reached into the back seat for the bottle. Peering through the rear window, Latchmer saw the cab had come to a stop facing the opposite direction.

"It will be a surprise," said Jean-Claude. "But it is an A-1 place and you will not be disappointed."

Latchmer took back the bottle, drank a little, then looked out at the street. It was past midnight but there were as many people walking around as during the day. Jean-Claude was swerving from one lane to another through the traffic. He drove with his left hand on top of the steering wheel and his right stretched out along the top of the seat. On the car radio Bob Marley was complaining that he couldn't roam where he wanted any time he wanted. Jean-Claude turned up the volume.

Latchmer kept thinking about his grandmother watching his grandfather's coffin burn. The field behind his grandparents' house was on a hill and surrounded on three sides by pine trees. From the top of the hill one could see all of the village. The man who had helped her was a tall ex-lumberjack by the name of Cecil Poorhouse. He was thin with long white hair and wore blue denim coveralls both winter and summer. Latchmer imagined them standing on either side of the fire. Perhaps Cecil had held a rake or stick with which to poke the flames. Most likely they had soaked the coffin in gasoline. It would have taken some moments for the wood to catch and so the coffin must have been outlined in flame up there near the top of the hill while Cecil kept prodding it with his stick or whatever. They had burned it after dark. A bright coffin-shape outlined by flame with his short round grandmother on one side and tall thin Cecil on the other. Latchmer imagined the smoke and sparks rising above the fire, swirling together until they formed the figure of a man.

Jean-Claude drew up to a light at the corner of Broadway and Fiftieth Street. Near a trash barrel two black men were fighting. Each held a jacket wrapped around his left hand and a knife in the other. They circled each other around the trash barrel, waiting for an opening. Both were well dressed in dark suits. The light changed and Jean-Claude pulled away.

Latchmer thought again of his grandfather's coffin. He wondered how much he was remembering and how much he was making up. It had been years since he thought of that time and at least twenty since he had thought of Miss Mitchell. He wished he could stop but he knew he still hadn't reached the center of the memory, the part lodged in his gut. In any case, he couldn't control it. The memory pulled him forward. He imagined Miss Mitchell standing in the dark on her front porch, then noticing a light and looking up the hill toward his grandparents' house where something was burning in a field.

Jean-Claude abruptly began pumping the brakes and swerved. There was a loud thump from the right front fender. Jasper slid off Latchmer's lap to the floor as the Plymouth came to a stop. A figure was lying by the curb a little behind and to the right of the car. Jean-Claude

backed up so the person was in front of them. It seemed
to be an elderly white man and he was lying on his back.
Gathered on the sidewalk and dressed in ragged coats,
six other elderly men stood in a semicircle with bent necks
and shoulders so they looked like so many ragged arcs
as they watched the man lying by the curb.

"Did you hit him?" asked Latchmer.

"It's the old trick," said Jean-Claude. "He slapped the
car with his fist and then fell down. Now he hopes we
will make him rich." He honked the horn. After a moment, the old man got to his feet and stood swaying a
little. Jean-Claude honked again and the man stumbled
onto the sidewalk, rejoined the other men, and they all
wandered off down Broadway, some limping, some
weaving back and forth.

"It's a pity," Jean-Claude continued, "because if I had
hit him, then I could have sold him no trouble. In fact,
I owe somebody a body already."

"Owe somebody?"

"Yes, I sold a cadaver but the man turned out not to
be dead. I had him right here in the back of the car and
he woke up. These drunks, sometimes you can't tell.
Anyway, I have already spent the money so I have to
find another body or give the money back. All day I
drive around looking for a body but it's no go. That is
why my heart gave a little leap when I thought I might
have hit that old fellow. Just my luck to have missed him.
The best time is when it is cold. You drive down to the
Bowery around four or five in the morning and you find
some old fellow who did not use enough newspapers to
keep warm. So you toss him in the back of the station
wagon and sell him. But now that the weather is changing, the bodies come from gang fights or the river. Both
are difficult to get. You know, they drag 150 bodies from
the river each year and those are only the ones found by
the police because I always get some too. But the bodies

from the river are wet and ugly. And the gang fights, they are generally unfriendly. It is like a disease. You stick one man with a knife and immediately you want to stick another man with a knife. So I come along hoping to pick up a body and do these gang-fighters see me as a human being trying to earn his living? No, I am just another person to stick with a knife and I am forced to hurry away."

"You should work with computers," said Latchmer, hoping to steer Jean-Claude away from another philosophical conversation.

"When I was a little boy," said Jean-Claude, "there was a pinball machine in my village. I would make coins out of little round pieces of metal which I cut from tin cans. For years I played this machine and I won hundreds of games. For this reason I am very tired of pinball machines. These computers, I think they are like that. They are like very serious pinball machines with no flashing lights and no pretty girls with big tits going bomba-bomba. They have taken away the lights and girls and steel balls and all the wacka-wacka noises and now it is called a computer. No, I think I know enough about them already."

Jean-Claude turned onto a street in the upper Twenties, drove half a block, and parked in a tow-away zone. "Here we are," he announced.

Latchmer looked out the window. There were a few clothing stores and furriers, as well as a couple of buildings that looked like warehouses. He saw no lights or people. "Is it open?" he asked.

"Sure it's open," said Jean-Claude. "These guys, they never sleep. Twenty-four hours a day, every day except Saturday. You bring the dog and I'll bring the leash, the ball, and the rubber mouse. You never know what they might want."

Latchmer got out of the car. It was cold. He bunched

together the top of the garbage bag and pulled Jasper onto the sidewalk. A gray rat scurried along the side of a building. Latchmer picked up the bag and held it in his arms.

"We are going to see a man named Marty," said Jean-Claude. "Don't be a wise guy or anything. Marty is very serious. What is more, he has a bad temper." Jean-Claude rang a buzzer next to a gray metal door.

"Who is it?" asked a voice that came over a tiny speaker.

"This is Jean-Claude. I have a dog for Marty."

There was the sound of several locks being unfastened. "Don't try any funny stuff," said the voice. "I have a gun."

Jean-Claude winked at Latchmer. "They are always joking," he said. Jean-Claude's hair stood up in a way that reminded Latchmer of the silhouette of a famous mountain range, maybe the Alps, maybe the Andes.

The door creaked open. Latchmer didn't see anyone. Jean-Claude gave him a push and he stumbled into a narrow hall which was lit by a small bulb hanging from a wire. He still didn't see anyone. Then the door slammed shut. Standing behind it was a very young man in a gray suit, white shirt, gray fedora, and two little black curls, one by each ear. He also wore gold-rimmed glasses and had an extremely large revolver which he pointed first at Jean-Claude, then at Latchmer. He was short, not much taller than Jean-Claude, and when he pointed the gun at Latchmer, he appeared to be pointing it at his nose. He held the gun with both hands and seemed nervous. Latchmer shifted Jasper up a few inches so the dog covered his heart and chest area. The revolver looked like a .45 and Latchmer guessed the bullet would go through Jasper like a finger through a piece of wet Kleenex. Latchmer moved a few inches to his right so he was standing behind Jean-Claude. He thought the young man with the fedora was about sixteen.

Jean-Claude raised his hands over his head. "What's the grand idea?" he asked.

"I don't recognize you," said the young man.

"That is because you have not been here before. I am Jean-Claude and I have brought Marty many dogs. See, I have a dog right here in this bag. Show him the dog, Latchmer."

"Wait," said the young man. "No tricks. There could be a kid in that bag with a weapon. We've seen everything here. Maybe an eight-year-old with a small automatic. Let me shoot the bag a couple of times."

"Impossible," said Jean-Claude, shielding the bag with his body, "it would ruin the dog. Let us just show you the head. We will do it very slowly. Show him the head, Latchmer."

Carefully, Latchmer pulled back the plastic. Jasper's head lolled to one side and looked sleepy.

"Maybe it's just the head of a dog," said the young man. "And the little kid inside the bag is holding it up on a stick. He's just waiting for me to put down my gun, then he'll blast me."

Someone was coming down the stairs behind Latchmer. It was an older man dressed almost exactly like the man at the door, except he didn't wear glasses and his curls were longer and lusher. "What's the problem?" he said.

The young man waved the revolver at Latchmer. "They got a little kid inside that bag with a gun."

The man pushed past Latchmer, reached into the bag, and grabbed Jasper by the scruff of his neck. Then he heaved backward, lifting the dog out of the bag. He held Jasper up to the light. "Nice dog," he said.

He shoved the dog toward the young man's face so the tip of Jasper's black nose bumped against the young man's glasses. "What do you call this?" he shouted. Then he gave the dog back to Latchmer and they wrestled him back into the plastic bag. Latchmer thought the man smelled of strong tea. The older man turned back to the man by the door. "Put down the gun," he said. The young man shoved the gun under his coat and stared down at his shoes. The older man reached out and slapped him twice across the face. "Stupid," he said.

He turned back to Latchmer and Jean-Claude. "Come with me," he said, then led the way up the stairs. "New help, there's always trouble with new help. I tell Marty, but will he listen? We get these boys right out of the *schule* and tell them how the niggers, no offense my friend, how the niggers try to break in with their machine guns, then we stick them downstairs in a dark hall all night long and they go crazy. The one last week shot himself in the foot."

At the top of the stairs, they went down a dimly lit hall with a wooden floor. The plaster on the walls was chipped and cracked. At the end was a steel door. Next to it was a large easy chair, a small table with a stack of paperback romances, a high-intensity lamp, and a double-barreled shotgun. The man unlocked the steel door, then collapsed into the easy chair with a sigh. "Go on up to the top," he told them. "Hershel will be there. And give my best to Marty. I never see him anymore."

As they climbed the next flight of stairs, Latchmer asked, "Isn't this sort of complicated?"

"They've had trouble," said Jean-Claude, "and they get upset easily. I don't know, perhaps it's the Palestinians." There was a door at the top of the stairs. Jean-Claude knocked.

The man who opened the door also wore a dark suit, white shirt, and a fedora. He was older than the others and his curls were gray. "Johann Klug," he said, "this is a pleasure. Please follow me." He led them down another hall and up a third flight of stairs. He had a bad limp and his right leg dragged on the floor with a loud scraping noise. Jasper seemed to be getting heavier and Latchmer kept pausing to shift his weight. He kept telling himself that if he had gone right home, he would now be approaching the Delaware Water Gap.

At the top of the stairs, they passed through a metal door into a huge space like a church or large gymnasium. The only light was a dim glow that came from someplace far ahead. Looking up, Latchmer couldn't see the ceiling. Above him were a series of galleries or balconies disappearing into the dark. The air was thick with the smell of tannic acid.

Strung out across the open space and going up level after level were cables that connected two sides of the warehouse like clotheslines. Hanging from the cables were furs, skins, feathers, pelts—all the epidermal possibilities available to living creatures. Near him on the floor, Latchmer saw the shells of several gigantic tortoises. The room was cool and there was a breeze blowing from somewhere.

The skins mostly hung from their hind feet with the noses pointing down. To Latchmer's right was a row of raccoon skins. Just above them was a row of red fox skins. Then Latchmer saw some cat skins, perhaps a dozen and all from marmalade cats. Beyond them were some skunk and beyond the skunk was a long line of rat skins. As his eyes grew accustomed to the light, Latchmer began to see dog skins hanging to his left: the skins of twenty Irish setters, a dozen chows, maybe fifteen or so golden retrievers. There were even the skins of fish: medium-sized sharks, salmon, flounder. High above him, he began to pick out the skins of birds: pigeons, orioles, cardinals, jays, even some crows. They were swaying slightly and it created the illusion of arrested flight.

"I will take you to Marty," said Hershel, "but I warn

you, don't dawdle, and stay right behind me. If you see anything peculiar, don't look at it. If we meet anyone, don't speak."

Then Hershel set off through the forest of skins, often making detours to avoid particularly large skins that hung down to the floor: zebras, three white horses, and something that might have been a camel. Latchmer hugged Jasper to his chest and walked between Hershel and Jean-Claude. The warehouse had a wood floor but the skins absorbed the noise of their footsteps, making them sound dull and truncated. Latchmer kept peering around him. He saw the skins of black panthers, dalmatians, Manx cats, black rabbits. He almost expected to see the skin of the dragon he had been warned against, but there was no sign of it.

Abruptly, Hershel signaled to Latchmer and Jean-Claude to stop. Cutting across in front of them were six young black men carrying bags over their shoulders. Whatever was inside the bags was alive and squirming. Latchmer heard a whimpering noise. The six men wore black berets, black fur vests, and black leather pants. Each wore a thick silver chain around his waist. They slowed when they saw Latchmer and Jean-Claude and glanced at them with what Latchmer thought of as mild hunger, the way one might look at a cracker and a piece of cheese late in the afternoon. Only the last one stopped. He halted in front of Latchmer and stared into his face. Slowly he reached out and touched Latchmer's cheek, stroking it. Latchmer didn't move. The black man hissed softly and Latchmer saw that his teeth were pointed. Latchmer pulled back and the man hissed louder.

"Leave him alone," said Hershel. "He's protected."

The black man glanced indifferently at Hershel, then slipped away into the dark after his companions.

"They are very proud," said Hershel. "They say that

before you can join them, you must take a test where you skin a human being. I do not think I could do that."

"Would you want to?" asked Latchmer.

Hershel tugged at one of his gray locks. "Sometimes it is useful to know a trade," he said.

They followed Hershel until they came to a large open area lit by four spot lights. Three men sat at a long table: one in the middle and the others at either end. All three wore dark suits with vests, dark ties, white shirts, and fedoras. The two on either end had beards. The one in the center wore a black overcoat with a black fur collar. All were in their fifties and had long gray curls dangling by their ears. The two men at either end of the table were leafing through stacks of papers. Occasionally, they would stop to write something on yellow pads or add up figures on their calculators. The man in the center was looking over a number of small white furs that resembled little handkerchiefs. His left elbow rested on the table and he supported his chin in his hand. Near him was a white bowl filled with rectangular green mints.

About ten feet beyond the table stood a row of fifteen boys. They were dressed like the others and looked hopelessly bored. They were thin and all of different heights, ranging from five to almost seven feet. To Latchmer they resembled a bar of music, a series of thirty-second notes or demisemiquavers, and he tried to hum it to himself. When they saw Hershel with Latchmer and Jean-Claude, they began to whisper to one another.

"Marty," said Hershel, "I have brought you a friend."

The man at the center of the table looked up. "Johann Klug," he cried, "it has been too long. Irving, Joseph, see who is here. Have I not been saying where is Johann Klug?"

The other two men looked up, nodded, then went back to their papers.

Jean-Claude walked to the table. "I am happy to see you, Marty. I have brought a friend and a nice skin for you."

Jean-Claude reached out his hand and Marty stood up and took it in both of his. The row of young men continued to whisper, holding their hands to each other's ears and whispering behind them. Then, from somewhere in the darkness, came a high scream like the scream of a rabbit. This was followed by the scampering of feet on the wood floor, then the louder thumping of human feet. Latchmer looked but couldn't see anything. It seemed that the human feet were bare human feet. All the others were listening as well: the line of boys, the two men at either end of the table. They appeared to be waiting for something. Suddenly, there was another scream, then everything became silent.

"Introduce me to your friend," said Marty, as if nothing had happened.

Latchmer approached the table, set the bag down on the floor, and stretched out his hand. Marty clasped it in both of his own. Latchmer thought that Marty's hands were very soft and hot, as if he had been soaking them for a long time in hot water. Marty smiled at him. It was a kindly, paternal smile.

"Welcome to my humble place of work," said Marty. "If you are a friend of Johann Klug, you will always be welcome here."

"I appreciate that," Latchmer.

"I better get back," said Hershel. "You got any messages for the boys downstairs, Marty?"

"Tell them to keep up the good work."

Hershel touched a finger to the side of his nose and disappeared behind some large skins that might have been walrus.

"What small things do you have there?" asked Jean-Claude, pointing to the white pieces of fur on the table.

"Aren't they wonderful," said Marty, handing one to Latchmer. "Touch it to your face. See how soft it is. This is the skin of a gerbil, a nice friendly animal. The trouble is, they are so small. You know how many top-quality gerbils it takes to make a full-length fur coat? Over a thousand, and the women who sew them do not last long. It is a sad story. And the coats, they are very expensive. But now there may be a solution, although even the solution is difficult. It was this that I was brooding about when you found me. Perhaps you can give me your advice."

"What is the problem?" asked Jean-Claude.

"My research laboratory has been working several years breeding bigger gerbils. We had some success, but a big gerbil, it was still very small. Then last year my scientists found they could transplant growth hormone genes from bigger animals into the gerbils. At first, they had little success. You see it is a matter of finding the right bigger animal. They had to be compatible. So now they have found the right bigger animal and this is where the problem lies."

"Why?" asked Jean-Claude.

"The bigger animal, it is a puma," said Marty. "You see, by themselves the gerbils are very friendly and very dumb and breed very fast. These new animals, these puma-gerbils, they also breed fast but they are no longer very friendly and dumb. In fact, they are very unfriendly and very smart. The bigger we make these puma-gerbils, the smarter and less friendly they become. And it continues like that. Today we have one gerbil the size of a German shepherd. Not only is it smart, it is angry. Smart like a pig. And vicious. It half killed the boy taking care of it. One escaped into the warehouse and screamed at us from the rafters. They had to kill it with a special bomb. If we decide to raise them for their fur, some will escape. As I say, they breed very quickly. Soon there would be many puma-gerbils hiding in the dark corners of the city. You see, it is a moral problem. I tell Joseph and Irving, how can we unleash this terror on our neighbors just for the sake of a fur coat? What do you think, Johann Klug?"

Jean-Claude sat down on the edge of the table and took a mint from the white bowl. "This is a changing world, Marty. Every day there are new dangers. Can we be responsible for each person? If man is to continue on this planet, he must adapt. Think of it this way, if you do not breed a giant gerbil, someone else will. Human beings have become soft. The herd has grown too big. Perhaps it needs to be made smaller."

Marty nodded slowly, then tugged at the brim of his fedora. "I will consider what you say. There is a chance we can breed these gerbils without teeth and if that is the case, then that is the way we will go. But they are very smart. They will learn to carry knives."

"You are a good man," said Jean-Claude, "not everyone is such a humanitarian."

Marty looked pained and wrinkled up his face. "It is a great sacrifice. You know how many giant gerbils are needed for a coat? Maybe four. And the fur is better than sable. And cheap. Such a coat would be cheaper than wool. And you can feed the living gerbils on the meat of their dead brothers and sisters. Everybody could afford such a coat. The most disgusting beggar on the street could be wearing a coat now beyond the dreams of kings. Such a coat could mean the Nobel Prize. On the other hand, I think of packs of puma-gerbils roaming the streets, preying on the blind, the slow, the elderly. I think of my own parents being hunted down by such an animal, and I balk."

"Are they really as big as a German shepherd?" asked Latchmer.

Marty held out his hands to Latchmer, palms upward.

"What do I know? Maybe they are a little smaller than a German shepherd. But you know these angora rabbits? Big, husky rabbits with big, husky bodies? They are really hamsters. A man in Peru developed them so they would breed big. And rats. You can breed rats until they are bigger than cats. It's all a matter of fooling with the growth-hormone genes. My gerbils may be a little smaller then German shepherds, but they're mean and they're fast."

There was another scream from somewhere in the warehouse. A little chill ran up Latchmer's spine. Then came a scampering of feet, then silence, then the sound of many bare feet running on the wood floor. They all waited. At last there was a second scream.

"Was that a gerbil?" asked Latchmer.

"No, no," said Marty. "I'm not sure what it was, but I know it wasn't a gerbil. The puma-gerbils only scream when victorious."

"Who's running around out there?" asked Latchmer.

Marty took off his hat and wiped his forehead with a gray handkerchief. He was almost bald. "Sometimes it is difficult to get good help," he said. "But enough of my troubles. Let me see what you brought. Put it right up here on the table."

Latchmer lifted the bag onto the table, then rolled it back away from the dog. He arranged Jasper's legs to look as if he was trotting through a field and moved back an ear from where it had flopped over his closed eye. The jaw had fallen open and Latchmer shut it.

"But he is beautiful," said Marty.

"I thought you should see him first," said Jean-Claude.

"The red fur is perfect, rarely do I see such nice red fur."

Isaac and Joseph at either end of the table put down their papers to look at the dog and even the row of young men stopped their whispering and craned their necks.

"Can you get me a dozen?" asked Marty.

"I am afraid it is impossible," said Jean-Claude. "This dog is one in a billion. I thought maybe a muff or something to wear around the neck. Something nice for someone special."

Marty took out a magnifying glass and began to study Jasper more carefully. Irving and Joseph returned to their papers and the young men to their whispering and giggling. Latchmer tried to look into the dark of the warehouse but could see nothing but thousands of pelts around and above him. He felt uneasy and thought he was being watched.

Marty put away the glass and straightened up. "A pity," he said, "a great pity."

"What is wrong?" asked Jean-Claude.

"This dog is too old. The fur wouldn't stand up under the tanning process. I'm terribly disappointed. If you had brought him to me five years ago, then maybe I could have done something, but now it is too late. He might as well be dead."

"He is dead," said Jean-Claude.

"It was just a figure of speech," said Marty.

"He looks okay to me," said Jean-Claude. "Couldn't you fake it?"

"Impossible. When they get this old, the hair follicle becomes big and sloppy. Look at this." Marty took a pinch of Jasper's fur and yanked it out. He threw it into the air and bits of red dog fur floated down over his shoulders.

"Hey," said Jean-Claude.

"See how easy it is?" said Marty. He yanked out another tuft of hair.

"Stop that," said Jean-Claude, "you are ruining a good pelt." He tried to smooth down the places where Marty had yanked out the fur but little bald spots remained: one on Jasper's shoulder, another on his hip.

"Believe me," said Marty, "no one will want that pelt, not even for a rug. We have done much business, Johann Klug, and I agree that this dog is a wonderful color and I fully appreciate the chance to see him. Get me a dozen puppies like this and I'll give you five hundred dollars per skin. But this old fellow, he has had a full life." Marty took one more pinch of fur from the belly and sprinkled it over Jasper's head.

"Cut it out," said Jean-Claude. "It is not respectful."

Marty briefly covered his eyes with one hand and bowed his head. "You are right and I am sorry. Perhaps you have something else I can buy."

Jean-Claude picked up the other bag and removed Jasper's leash, blue blanket, rubber squeaky mouse, and red rubber ball. These he put on the table. Marty looked at each in turn, then shook his head. Joseph and Irving walked over to the small collection and studied them with interest.

"No collar?" asked Irving.

"He already sold it," said Jean-Claude.

Irving sucked his teeth and went back to his papers. Then the young men came over in single file and each, in turn, picked up and studied the leash, ball, blanket, and rubber mouse. The last young man was very short and looked about twelve. His face was heavily freckled and his two curls were bright red.

"How much for the ball?" he asked.

"Three bucks," said Jean-Claude.

"I'll give you two. No more."

"Done," said Jean-Claude.

The young man removed two crumpled dollars from the inside pocket of his suitcoat and gave them to Jean-Claude. Then he took the ball and tossed it to one of the other young men, who tossed it to a second, who tossed it to a third, until all fifteen were hopping and jumping and waving their arms, trying to catch the red rubber ball, even though none of them said anything or smiled or made any noise.

Marty looked disgusted. "These boys, they all have good fathers. They come on bended knee and beg me to teach their sons a trade. How can I refuse them? And so in twos and threes their sons come and watch what we do. If a boy is smart and pays attention, then someday he will learn the business. But look at them. Give them half a chance and they again become boys. He shouldn't have paid more than fifty cents for that ball."

Jean-Claude gathered up the leash, mouse, and blanket, then he and Latchmer began pushing Jasper into the bag. Again there was an animal scream and the sound of running—both animal and human. This time the running came so close that Latchmer could hear the sound of heavy breathing. Marty got to his feet and stared into the dark warehouse with a nervous intensity that made Latchmer move behind Jean-Claude. Then there was another scream and silence. Latchmer gathered together the top of the bag and pulled it off the table. He thought it was time to go.

"What about your friend," said Marty to Jean-Claude. "He has had little to say for himself. Maybe we have been impolite. After all, he has been carrying the dog."

Jean-Claude tugged reflectively at his earlobe. "He can tell stories," he said after a moment.

"We like stories here," said Marty. "The boys get bored."

"He tells stories about dogs," said Jean-Claude.

"Even better," said Marty.

"Nobody likes my stories," said Latchmer.

"Too modest," said Marty. "We are all amicable."

"People get cross," said Latchmer. "Besides, I was warned about the coming of the dragon and I think these stories may be the dragon. They only get me in trouble."

Marty made a clicking noise with his tongue. "Kung

fu movies," he said, "we all saw the same skywriter. You can't take that kind of warning seriously."

"Tell the story," said Jean-Claude.

Latchmer put the bag down on the floor and stretched. Looking at his watch, he saw it was one o'clock. No wonder he was tired. He would tell the story and if they got angry, it would be their own fault. After all, Marty had insisted. Then he would get rid of Jasper in the nearest bit of earth he could find and return to Sarah's. He glanced down at Jasper's head and tried to think of what sort of story he would tell, then, as he wondered, the story began to fill his mind.

"There was a young man who left home and went away to college," he said. "His family was poor and although the young man had a scholarship, he also had to get a part-time job. At last he found a job in a bakery, a huge factory that sold bread in four different states. The young man's job was to carry messages and soon he knew the factory like the back of his hand. Because it was so big, the bakery was completely automated. The bread dough was mixed in huge vats and stirred by machines. When the dough was ready, it was spat into baking pans on a conveyor belt, allowed to rise, and then delivered to the oven. Afterward the bread would be sliced and bagged. During the whole process it wasn't once touched by anyone.

"The owner of the factory was a generous and likable man, but unfortunately he was always accompanied by his wife, who was a terrible busybody. This wife had a little dog, an ancient Chihuahua that was the one thing she loved. She said it was almost twenty. It was deaf and nearly blind. All it had left was its bark and it barked all the time—a high, squeaky, coughing kind of bark.

"In the front office was a secretary whose job it was to take care of the Chihuahua, whose name was Dip-dip. The secretary's name was Betty and she hated Dip-dip.

The young man thought Betty very beautiful, and although he was shy and had never spoken to her, he would smile and she would smile back. But one day the young man went into the front office with a message and found Betty and Dip-dip all alone. The young man sat down to wait for the owner. As Dip-dip sniffed at his ankles, the young man told himself he had to overcome his shyness and speak. So he asked Betty what was her favorite ice cream. Then he asked what kind of music she liked and if she liked to dance. They talked and after a few more minutes the young man built up the courage to ask her out for Friday night and she accepted. Then she looked around the office. 'Where's Dip-dip?' she asked. Suddenly they saw the door was open. Dip-dip had escaped into the factory. 'My lord,' said Betty, 'if anything happens to that dog, I'll be fired.' 'I'll catch him,' said the young man. 'Everything will be all right.'

"The young man ran out of the office. He searched everywhere. There was no sign of Dip-dip. At last he went into the great room where bread was being made. The huge silver vats that held the bread dough towered above his head and the only sound was the steady slushing of the automatic stirrers. The young man glanced up and to his horror saw Dip-dip tottering along one of the catwalks above the silver vats. In a flash, the young man climbed one of the ladders to the catwalk. Then Dip-dip saw him and began to bark. The young man approached the dog slowly, not wanting to upset it. But the dog barked and snapped and backed away from him. In fact, it backed right over the side of the catwalk. Even as it fell, it barked. It barked when it landed in the bread dough. It even barked as it sank beneath the surface.

"The young man flung himself down on his stomach and tried to reach into the vat but it was too far. He considered leaping in after Dip-dip, but the vat was twelve feet deep and he knew he'd never get out. The young man climbed down from the catwalk and hurried down to the next floor where the bread dough was spat into the baking pans. But all that took time. Doors were locked, keys had to be found. An assistant baker told him they were making the whole wheat extra-size family loaf. The young man shuddered.

"By the time he got downstairs, great gobs of dough were being shot into the pans. The young man stood by the spout waiting for Dip-dip. Nothing happened. The whole vat was emptied and still no Dip-dip. Perhaps he had gotten stuck. He ran back upstairs and looked into the vat. No Dip-dip. With horror, he realized that Dip-dip was probably in one of the first pans. He rushed downstairs in time to see the conveyor belt carrying the pans into the oven. He poked into some others but it was no good. Dip-dip was being baked.

"All he could do was to wait for Dip-dip to come out the other side and find him when the bread was cooling. But again there were delays, more locked doors and missing keys. By the time the young man got to the cooling room, the first loaves were already cool and moving forward on the conveyor belt toward the cutter. In fact, some had already been sliced and were being bagged and stacked. In a panic, the young man rushed to the storeroom and arrived to see the first loaves coming out of the bagger. But how could he find Dip-dip? Then he realized that even though Dip-dip was tiny, he still weighed twice as much as the bakery's whole wheat extra-size family loaf. Rushing to the neat pile of freshly baked bread, it took the young man only minutes to locate the loaf that was suspiciously heavy. Here was Dip-dip, baked and sliced in a loaf of bread. The young man ran out of the storeroom. He would put Dip-dip in the back seat of his old VW. Later he would bury him.

"But just as he was passing the office, the owner stopped him. He grabbed the young man's arm and dragged him inside. There was the owner's wife and Betty all nervous and upset. 'Where's Dip-dip?' they asked. The young man was forced to lie. 'He's down in the cupcake section with the frosters.' The owner's wife was under the illusion that everyone in the factory loved Dip-dip. 'Just as long as they don't give him too much frosting, I guess it's all right,' she said.

"As the young man started to leave, the owner snatched the loaf of bread from under his arm. 'Is this fresh bread?' he asked. 'I'm starving.' 'No, no,' said the young man, 'that's a test loaf from the laboratory.' 'Then I'll test it myself,' said the owner and he carried the loaf to an inner office where he kept his butter and jam. Horrified, the young man watched the owner open the bag and take out the end slice. It appeared to be perfect, but then he saw a suspicious speck in its center. Before the young man could look more closely, the owner slapped butter and jam on the slice and gave it to Betty. 'The first slice is for you, my dear,' he said. Then he took a second slice. This too appeared perfect, but it also had a speck and this time the speck was bigger. The owner spread butter and jam on the slice and gave it to his wife. The owner took a third slice. The speck was now the size of a dime. He buttered the slice, put jam on it, and handed it to the young man, who nibbled a little of the crust. He felt paralyzed. The owner took a fourth slice. The speck was the size of a quarter. 'Good bread,' said Betty. 'It's crunchy,' said the owner's wife, 'may I have another slice?' 'Of course,' said the owner, and he took a fifth slice. The speck was the size of a fifty-cent piece. The owner covered it with jam. Then the young man realized that these specks were slices of Dip-dip's tail. They were moving up the tail and soon the owner would reach Dip-dip's rear end, which would look like a slice from a loaf of pâté. 'I'm still hungry,' said the wife, 'I want more.' 'Me too,' said the owner, 'I could eat this bread all day. How about you?' he asked the young man. But the young man waved his hands in front of his mouth and began backing out of the office. When he reached the door, he turned and ran. He ran all the way to his VW, then drove like a maniac back to the dorm. He never went back to the bakery again, never got his last paycheck, never saw Betty. For weeks, some one kept calling, but his roommate said he was gone, had died, or had flown to Europe. After about two months, the phone calls stopped."

As Latchmer had been telling the story, he had kept his eyes on the floor. When he finished, he looked up. Marty was staring at him in the same way he had stared into the dark warehouse moments after the strange animal had screamed. Joseph and Irving were also staring. The fifteen young men had stopped tossing the red rubber ball and were staring as well. Jean-Claude was looking down at the floor. Latchmer was pleased with the story. He had never thought of himself as inventive and now he was going great guns.

After half a minute of silence, Marty said, "I don't know why you did that."

"Pardon me?" asked Latchmer. Maybe they hadn't liked the story. What was the point in being inventive if it only got you in trouble? It occurred to him that these people might be touchy about food.

Marty took a white handkerchief from his breast pocket and blew into it. "I think you should leave."

"Now Marty," said Jean-Claude, "it was just a story."

"I realize that, but we all have our feelings and you should know that some of us might have found the story offensive. Maybe you should take your friend and get out of here."

"It was a true story," said Latchmer.

"Shut up," said Jean-Claude. "Marty, he didn't mean anything by it."

"Distasteful," said Marty. "I'm sure most of us found

that story distasteful. In fact, you wonder about a person who can tell such a story. Is he human, does he have feelings?"

"I thought you'd find it funny," said Latchmer.

Marty blew his nose again. "Can you find your way downstairs by yourselves?"

"Have someone show us," asked Jean-Claude.

"I don't want to."

"We need a guide," said Jean-Claude. "You know we can't get downstairs without one. Give us a guide, Marty."

"I don't feel like it."

"Please, Marty, think of the good things I have brought you. Don't let one mistake wipe out our friendship."

Marty looked down at his hands. His fingernails were shiny as if covered with transparent polish. "All right," he said, "but remember, I am a good man. And no more dogs. If you come back again, bring something special like a wolverine or a vicuña. And come by yourself." He snapped his fingers at the smallest of the young men, the one with red curls. "Show them downstairs and do it fast."

The young man trotted off and Jean-Claude and Latchmer followed him through the maze of hanging furs. Latchmer hugged Jasper to his chest so he wouldn't drop him. Once they got away from the open area, Latchmer was certain he heard footsteps all around them and even saw dark faces staring from behind the legs and buttocks of elands and gnus.

"If I had known you were going to tell that story," said the young man, "I would never have bought the red rubber ball."

"It's too late to get your money back," said Jean-Claude.

They followed the young man through the warehouse. He moved quickly and they had to run to keep up. Jasper's head kept bouncing and hitting Latchmer in the chin. At the steel door, the young man said, "You're lucky you weren't eaten." He opened the door. "You can go the rest of the way by yourself."

Latchmer and Jean-Claude hurried down the stairs, down the long hall, then down the second flight of stairs, past Hershel and the other man until they reached the front door where the youngster with the .45 was cleaning his teeth with a gold toothpick. He unlocked the door and Jean-Claude and Latchmer hurried out on the street. Latchmer took a deep breath. The air felt clean and fresh. They turned right and walked toward the Plymouth station wagon.

After they had gone a few steps, Jean-Claude said, "I thought you were going to tell the story about the Chihuahua that got squashed."

"You'd already heard it."

"I liked the other story better," said Jean-Claude. "You should have told it. They would have laughed about the man sitting on the dog."

"Maybe next time," said Latchmer. "Can I bury Jasper now?"

"Are you pulling my leg? Why do you give up so easily? This is a big town. If one man does not want a dead dog, another will."

They were back in the station wagon and barreling uptown on Franklin D. Roosevelt Drive. Latchmer sat in the front seat with Jean-Claude, and Jasper lay between them with his head on Latchmer's lap. Jean-Claude's attack style of driving still made Latchmer uneasy and he felt that sitting in the front seat was only a little safer than sitting on the hood ornament. He stared longingly at every patch of dirt they passed and wished he had a shovel. It was just one-thirty and Latchmer knew that if he had driven straight to the Delaware Water Gap, then right at that moment he could be tossing flowers on Jasper's grave.

Jean-Claude passed him the pint of rum. Latchmer took a sip and handed it back.

"When I was a little boy," said Jean-Claude, "I thought every inch of the United States was paved like a parking lot. I told myself that was what freedom meant. You could drive to every corner of the country, even on roller skates. You could take a roller skate trip all the way to Yellowstone Park."

"How could it be a park if it was covered with concrete?" asked Latchmer.

"I don't know. Maybe they would have pictures of geysers on billboards or painted the concrete different shades of green or maybe the bears and things just sat on the curb. But in Haiti we had only dirt roads and the jungles were not safe, so I thought the difference between my country and the United States was just a matter of pavement, and that when each little American is born, the government gives him a car and he drives off into the sunset, just like in the movies. Maybe you think that is foolish, but when I drive this car, I remember those ideas and I feel this is when I am most American, and the faster I drive, the more I think this country is mine."

He had kept accelerating as he spoke and was now doing about eighty. Latchmer squinted at the road through half-closed eyes. "Perhaps you should forget about being a patriot. We have to sell Jasper first."

Jean-Claude took his foot off the gas. "You are right, I think only of myself. Poor Jasper is our first task. You were not frightened?"

"It's okay if I keep my eyes shut." Whenever they hit a bump, which was often, Jasper's head took a little bounce on Latchmer's lap. "What do you think about selling this dog," he asked, "doesn't it seem the owner might be upset?"

"You mean the old lady?"

"Sure. Mrs. Hughes. She wants Jasper underground."

"She doesn't want part of the money?"

"No, she just thinks a dead dog should be buried. I keep thinking of that skywriter that said, 'Beware the coming of the dragon.' I didn't bother about it much at the time, but since then all sorts of strange things have been happening."

"Like what?" asked Jean-Claude, puzzled.

"Like this dog dying and then trying to sell it. I've also been thinking a lot about my grandfather and the woman who was his mistress. She looked like Mrs. Hughes, and seeing Mrs. Hughes reminded me of her."

"What does it have to do with the mistress?" asked

Jean-Claude. "It seems perplexing."

"I don't know, except that I probably did her a bad turn too and now I'm remembering about it. It's like a machine that's started up in my head and I can't make it stop."

"Where does the dragon come into it?" asked Jean-Claude.

"I'm not certain. At first I thought the dragon was alcohol, you know, too many daiquiris, then I thought it was Jasper, then I thought it was those dog stories I've been telling. The only thing I know for sure is it's out to get me."

"Your life is too mixed up," said Jean-Claude, swerving around a tow truck that was pulling a wrecked taxi. "You should be like me and do nothing more complicated than drive a cab. Why worry about betrayal or the expectations of the people around you? You must understand, there are forward-looking people and backward-looking people. If you are backward-looking, you will think of burial. But if you are forward-looking, you will see that the fact of Jasper's death is no hindrance to his possible usefulness. Certainly, there has been a change, but the way I see it is that Jasper has developed a kind of maturity. He no longer needs anything. He has achieved a self-sufficiency not available to the living. Is this not enviable? No longer is he prey to embarrassment or humiliation. Personal success or failure mean nothing to him. As for his sins, it is as if he had been finally and completely forgiven. So you see, it is wrong for you to think about betrayal. Probably that is a problem in your own mind. You should look at it, then discard it. Such problems can be a real nuisance."

"Maybe you have a point," said Latchmer.

"You try to sleep now," said Jean-Claude, "the most important part of the evening is yet to come."

"I'll just rest my eyes," said Latchmer. But when he

shut his eyes, he began to think of Mrs. Hughes. Of course she'd be angry. How could he think differently? He imagined her standing straight and tall in her green kimono, then raising a finger and shaking it like all the grade school teachers who had ever scolded him. He saw her impatiently tapping a ruler against the palm of her hand. He tried to turn his mind from her and found himself thinking of Miss Mitchell. If she weren't dead, she'd be in her mid-eighties. Latchmer hoped she was dead.

Again he began to recall the days between his grandfather's death and the funeral. Because his grandfather was the town doctor and knew hundreds of people, the wake had been held in the funeral home instead of in his own house. For three days the body was on display in a large cream-colored room with wicker cornucopias full of flowers. The coffin was open and stood on a platform in front of several red and blue curtains that reminded Latchmer of the curtains at Radio City Music Hall.

His grandfather had worn a dark blue suit and a vest. His hands were clasped on his belly and on his left wrist was a gold wrist watch. Latchmer had looked closely and saw it was running. He had spent some time inspecting his grandfather. His graying brown hair was combed to a degree of perfection never achieved in his lifetime. Even his eyebrows were combed. And although Latchmer knew that his grandfather's teeth were on the table in the bedroom, he still appeared to be wearing them. Presumably there was something else in his mouth that made it look like he had teeth. As he leaned over the body, Latchmer realized the skin was covered with a pinkish cream and that it had been slightly powdered. He touched his grandfather's cheek. It was still very hard. His shoes were shiny and black and brand-new. The soles had been polished and reflected the lights of the chandelier. Their black laces were tied in perfect bows and each of the four loops was exactly the same length. Latchmer wondered about the things his grandfather used to carry in his pockets: a lucky silver dollar, a small ivory-handled pocket knife, keys, comb, and a souvenir change purse from Niagara Falls. Asking his aunt, he learned they were back at the house and he had worried about his grandfather entering his death with stiff black shoes and no lucky silver dollar.

Near the front door had been a table with a book bound in blue leather where visitors signed their names and sometimes wrote a brief sentiment such as, "A branch broken off too soon," or "The old wagon has been un-hitched from the faithful horse." Afterward, his grandmother had kept this book on the mantel next to her husband's picture. She would read through it again and again, trying to determine who had not signed and who had written down sentiments which she thought hypocritical. On the last page was a plain signature and sentiment left by Harriet Mitchell that had nearly driven his grandmother wild.

Over and over she asked Latchmer if he had seen Miss Mitchell at the funeral home and he denied it. If the signature hadn't been on a page full of other signatures, his grandmother would have probably ripped it out. But she was a woman who hated flaws of any kind, and later Latchmer guessed that she hadn't destroyed it just because she didn't want to damage the book.

Of course he had seen Miss Mitchell. She had arrived early in the evening on the last day of the wake, shortly after suppertime. His grandmother had gone home half an hour before and Latchmer suspected Miss Mitchell of knowing that. There had been ten other people in the room but no relatives other than Latchmer himself. The other people were townspeople and all made little displays designed to show Miss Mitchell she was being ignored, such as abruptly turning away and heaving their shoulders.

Miss Mitchell seemed not to notice. She walked straight to the coffin, then, very slowly, she had reached out to touch his grandfather's cheek. Latchmer expected her to touch the cheek, then jerk her hand away, because that had been his own impulse. But she didn't. She kept her hand against the cheek, pressing it with the backs of her fingers. Tall and thin with her white hair gathered in a bun, she had worn a dark blue dress that was enough like mourning to make the other people feel scandalized. She had stood for about ten minutes, simply touching his cheek and staring into the coffin. It seemed to Latchmer that most people had hardly glanced at his grandfather or if they did it was only to say something like how well he looked or what a good job the funeral home had done.

At last Miss Mitchell stepped back from the coffin, although she continued to stare at the body as if memorizing each detail. Latchmer had come closer so he could watch. Just as he was getting a little bored, he saw her remove a silver ring from her finger and slip it under his grandfather's jacket and into his vest pocket. Then she turned and saw Latchmer. For a moment she just looked at him, then she walked over to where he stood.

"Walk me home, Michael," she had said.

"I've got my bike."

"You can wheel it beside me."

So they had left together, she pausing only long enough to put her name in the blue leather book. After her name, she wrote, "Soon to follow."

The funeral home was four blocks from her house. Latchmer pushed his bike along the edge of the sidewalk, hoping that his grandmother wouldn't drive by. For a block neither of them spoke. Miss Mitchell was about a foot taller than Latchmer and stood very straight. She looked neither to the left or right but stared up the street toward her own house. Her first words to Latchmer had been: "Did you know that your grandfather died while visiting me?"

Latchmer admitted that he did.

"Just now in the funeral home, did you see me put something in your grandfather's pocket?"

Latchmer started to say no, then changed his mind. "Yes," he nodded.

"That was a ring your grandfather gave me. If your grandmother knew it was in his pocket, she'd take it out and throw it away. She'd destroy it in the same way she destroyed the cherry-wood coffin. I want the ring buried with him and I want you to promise you won't say anything. Will you promise?"

Latchmer hadn't wanted to. He had walked beside her, wheeling his bike, trying not to step on cracks, and thought that to keep silent would be unfair to his grandmother. Until that moment, he had never thought of telling his grandmother. He was sure about that. He even knew his grandfather would want him to keep silent and he felt pulled and divided between his grandparents, uncertain what he should do. Part of him even felt proud to have such a confidence, to have an adult trust him in such a way. Part of him felt that such a trust was a burden, that he was eleven years old and too much was being asked of him.

"Your grandfather often told me about having breakfast with you," Miss Mitchell had said. "He told me that sometimes when he was depressed or didn't want to get up, he would think about how you would soon be coming downstairs and how much he enjoyed those times."

Sitting in the front seat of the Plymouth, Latchmer tried to reconstruct the conversation he had had nearly twenty-five years before. Certainly he didn't remember the exact words and again he wondered how much he was inventing just to feel guilty. But he clearly remembered walking with Miss Mitchell down the tree-lined street with its white Victorian houses and large lawns. He clearly remembered it had been sunset and the last light had reddened the white paint of the houses, flickered on the tips of the maples. And he remembered how Miss Mitchell rested one hand on the saddle of the bike and how he had walked slowly in order to keep pace with her.

And so he had sworn not to tell.

"I have something else to ask of you," she then said. "Not really a promise but a favor."

Latchmer began to agree automatically. After all, having given his promise about the ring, what else could matter? But she told him to wait, that he should know exactly what she wanted.

"I hadn't meant to go to the funeral," she said. "I thought it would be enough to say my goodbyes in private. But when I saw him just now, I knew I'd have to go all the way to the end, that despite your grandmother, I must go to the church.

"When I get there tomorrow, people will pretend I'm invisible. No one will speak or look directly at me. No matter how crowded it is, there will be a space around me. What I'm asking is that you don't do the same. If you see me, then speak to me. You don't have to say much, just hello or how are you or it's a nice day for a funeral. Just don't pretend I'm invisible. Will you do that?"

At eleven years old, the request seemed easy. By that time they had reached Miss Mitchell's house and stood in the driveway. Latchmer hadn't wanted to stop, was still afraid his grandmother might drive by and see him. But he couldn't imagine not being able to speak to Miss Mitchell. Nor did he believe that people would ignore her. In any case, he agreed.

After leaving her, he had gone up the hill to his grandparents' house. Dinner was long over. His grandmother was sitting by herself on the side porch looking at the last traces of red in the sky. She sat in a tall green rocker with her back to Latchmer. In front of her was the field where she had burned her husband's coffin.

Latchmer stood in the doorway and had a huge desire to speak about the ring. It was as if he was standing on a steep hill. He felt himself about to fall toward her. If she had seen him, he surely would have told. Instead, she stared out across the field until the last red glow of the sun was just a speck between two layers of darkness. Latchmer had hurried away. He had gone to the kitchen to get an apple and a handful of Oreos, then went up to bed.

That night a barn burned farther up the hill. Latchmer woke at three to hear the bawling of cattle. His room was full of flames, the very walls seemed to flicker and burn. He sat up in bed, thinking about his grandmother and the ring. Then he saw that the fire was really a reflection in the room's two mirrors. The flames that leaped around him, lighting the room, dancing over the bedsheets, had nothing to do with him.

"You have any more of that rum?" Latchmer asked Jean-Claude. As he had been thinking, he'd been running one finger across Jasper's lower teeth. They felt like small mountain peaks and reminded him of the morning after his grandfather's death when he had held his grandfather's false teeth in his hands.

Jean-Claude passed him the bottle. "Just a bit left. When we sell Jasper, we'll buy more."

Latchmer drank the rest of the rum. He still didn't like it. In fact, he rarely drank and was only drinking now, he told himself, because the hot dogs had upset his stomach and because the night was so strange. "You have any family still in Haiti?" he asked. They had just crossed into the Bronx and the landscape was beginning to look ragged.

"My mama is there. Aunts and uncles too. My brothers and sisters are scattered all over the world."

"What about your father?"

"One night he went out and never came back. They say Papa Doc got him, but they never even found his head."

"Was he involved in politics?"

"Who Papa Doc got or did not get, it was like something falling out of the sky. It didn't matter what you were doing."

"Did that make you angry?"

"I was a little boy. Does one get angry at the wind? It was like that. One day my papa was in the house, the next day he was gone. Soon my mama had another man and he was nice to me. Then one night he disappeared and soon my mama had another man after that. My mama was a big woman and could have lots of men."

Latchmer thought of his own mother, who had been small and always seemed to have a cold. Jean-Claude had turned off the expressway and was driving through an area that appeared to have been bombed: block after block of burned-out buildings, rubble, crumbling brick walls, destroyed automobiles. There were no people or stores. The gutters seemed full of garbage.

"Nice neighborhood," said Latchmer.

"Every place has its troubles," said Jean-Claude. "Some places have their troubles on the outside of their skin like a leper, some are on the inside like a crazy man. This place has both."

Jean-Claude turned down another street and as they approached the end of the block Latchmer saw that three wrecked cars had been pulled across the road. The street lights were not working and there were no lights in the buildings. Jean-Claude slowed down and flicked on his high beams. The cars were rusted and burned, without tires or seats or engines or doors. They resembled the husks of locusts. There was no way to get around them.

Jean-Claude put the station wagon into reverse. Broken bricks were scattered across the pavement and the Plymouth bumped over them. On one side was a burned-out apartment building with plywood over the lower windows. On the other was a large open area of rubble and mounds of debris. Jean-Claude backed up quickly, weaving from curb to curb. Before they had gone half the block, Latchmer saw that three more cars had been pulled across the street, penning them in.

"Those weren't there before," he said.

Jean-Claude slammed on the brakes, shoved the Plymouth into first gear, then bounced across the curb into the open field of rubble. Immediately, two small vehicles came rushing out from behind a brick wall and began to pursue them. At first Latchmer thought they were motorcycles because each had only one headlight. Then he saw they were like dune buggies—round tubular frames covered with heavy wire from a chain-link fence. Both had huge tires and bounced across the rubble making high screaming noises like mammoth mosquitoes.

Jean-Claude accelerated, bouncing over the bricks, scraping the bottom of the Plymouth on chunks of concrete. The dune buggies rushed up on either side. Jean-Claude yanked the wheel to the left, side-swiping one and sending it into a spin. Quickly, it regained its balance and roared after them again. As unnerving as the vehicles themselves was the fact they appeared to be driven by midgets wearing colorful ski masks.

"How much money do you have?" asked Jean-Claude, trying to side-swipe the second dune buggy.

"About a hundred bucks. Why?"

"Take all but a few dollars and put it in your shoe.

You have a watch? Put that in the other shoe."

Latchmer did as he was told, even though he was being bounced back and forth across the seat. Jasper had fallen to the floor. At least, thought Latchmer, the dead are uncomplaining. He saw Jean-Claude take some money from his back pocket and stick it down inside his sneakers.

"Remember," said Jean-Claude, "we are taking poor Jasper to bury him in the country."

He swerved again at the second dune buggy but it just dropped back a few feet, then rammed them from behind. A metal barrel suddenly appeared in front of them. Before Jean-Claude could turn, he smashed into it, knocking it back over the hood so that it bounced on the roof. The Plymouth kept banging its underside on the ground. Jean-Claude skidded past another brick wall onto a smooth asphalt surface. It was a large playground, only a little smaller than a football field. Around its perimeter, Latchmer saw a dozen bent and rusted basketball back-boards. The asphalt had been swept clean of any debris. On the far side was a wall of about thirty wrecked cars piled two or three deep.

Jean-Claude yanked up the emergency brake, accelerated, and spun the wheel. The Plymouth made a sliding U-turn and immediately slammed into one of the dune buggies, sending it crashing into the wall of a deserted apartment house. It bounced off, skidded into reverse, and roared back at them. Looking toward the entrance of the playground, Latchmer saw an old wrecker dragging a string of four demolished cars across the place where they had come in.

Jean-Claude made another sliding U-turn, accelerated, and hurtled around the perimeter of the playground, searching for a way out. The second dune buggy cut in front of him and he knocked it into a wall of cars. On the far side, between the corner of a building and the rusted shell of a UPS delivery truck was a narrow opening and Jean-Claude pointed the Plymouth at it. Before he had gone twenty yards, however, a single headlight flicked on from inside the opening and a third dune buggy roared into the playground. Then came a fourth and fifth until at last there were ten dune buggies swarming around the station wagon and carooming into its sides like giant bees after a bear. Spinning the wheel, Jean-Claude clipped a dune buggy that had cut in front of him, sending it skidding back into two others.

Their lights were all aimed high and kept blinding Latchmer as he tried to brace himself in the front seat. Jasper bounced around on the floor. Jean-Claude hit another dune buggy particularly hard and it rolled over several times and came to rest on its roof, whirring its motor and spinning its wheels. All the dune buggies were painted gun-metal gray. Because of their tubular frames and wire mesh, they banged off each other like Ping-Pong balls. Jean-Claude kept circling the playground, side-swiping and ramming the small cars. At last he pulled into the middle of the playground, honked twice, and stopped.

The nine remaining dune buggies formed a semicircle in front of the Plymouth and began flashing their lights. The tenth dune buggie still rested on its roof, roaring its motor.

"Get out of your car with your hands up," said a voice. Even though it was being amplified through a speaker, Latchmer felt there was something wrong with it.

"Get out very slowly," said Jean-Claude, "and take Jasper with you."

Latchmer opened the door, then pulled the bag containing Jasper up off the floor and hugged it to his chest. He walked around to the front of the Plymouth, which was a mass of scratches and dents. A little column of steam rose from under the hood.

"What is in the bag?" said the voice.

"My dog," Latchmer answered. He thought the voice seemed too high.

"Put it on the ground."

Latchmer set the bag down on the asphalt in the front of the Plymouth. It was difficult to see because of the glare of the headlights. He could dimly make out people standing behind the dune buggies but could tell nothing about them except that they seemed short. He tried to decide if the dune buggies looked like dragons, but they didn't.

"Stand back away from the bag," said the voice.

Latchmer backed up until he was standing next to Jean-Claude.

"No talking," said the voice. "Take everything out of your pockets and put it on the ground in front of you."

They did as they were told.

"Now take off your shoes and socks, put them with the other stuff, and sit up on the hood of the car."

Jean-Claude and Latchmer both hesitated. Slowly, they took off their shoes and socks. Latchmer was already cold and the touch of the asphalt against his bare feet made him shiver. As he sat back on the hood of the car, he saw a figure come out from behind the flashing lights. Certainly, he was under five feet tall. He wore jeans and a black ski mask with red and orange lightning flashes across the eyes. Hurrying to the plastic bag, he pulled back the top, exposing Jasper's head.

"It's a dog," he said in a squeaky voice. "It's a dog and he looks dead." Gently, he folded the bag back away from Jasper.

"What are you doing with the dog?" asked the voice.

"We were taking him into the country to bury him," said Latchmer.

The figure in the ski mask went over to the little pile of shoes, keys, wallets, loose change, and a pocket knife. After a moment or two, he cried out, "They were carrying their money in their shoes!"

Latchmer heard Jean-Claude groan. Very quietly Jean-Claude said, "Tell a sad story about Jasper."

"I saw you talking," said the voice. "We don't like people who hide money in their shoes."

Neither Latchmer nor Jean-Claude said anything. The hood of the Plymouth was cold and Latchmer's feet felt like ice. He turned up the collar of his jacket. As he tried to make out the figures standing behind the lights, they began to move forward until about twenty little figures stood between them and the dune buggies. All wore jeans, jean jackets, and ski masks. Several were carrying sawed-off shotguns. Latchmer found himself thinking about Rochester, about what a nice town it was and what a fool he had been to leave there.

"Tell me the truth about the dog," said a figure standing in the middle of the group. He was taller than the others, about five feet two, and his ski mask was embroidered with purple and orange and green spirals that went round and round his head. Attached to each shoulder of his jean jacket was a little rectangle of gold braid.

Latchmer cleared his throat. He was sitting on the hood with his legs crossed and trying to warm his toes with his hands. The prospect of invention pleased him. It was something new in his life, an ability he had not known he possessed.

"My dog died in the night," he began. "We had known it was coming but even when it came it was a shock. We had always considered him one of the family. Not a perfect dog by any means. A dog given to sloth and slovenliness and greed like any other, but still a dog which greeted us with love and affection when we came home after a long day, a dog that tried to make each of our minutes a happy one. Yes, he was taken from us tonight. At one moment he was there, frollicking, asking us to share in his exuberance and life. And the next moment, he lay motionless on the floor, the warmth and passion for the world oozing out of him. It was his heart. We had been to specialists, we had been all over the city, but the consensus was that his candle had almost reached its nub. Any day could be his last. There he was, eating a Triscuit from my open hand, and the next moment it was all over. I don't need to tell you how my children responded, how my wife wept. I'm sure all you young men have had dogs of your own. Suffice it to say, that among my children many little hearts were broken. And even I, who am no stranger to death, even I felt the sobs break from my chest.

"Although Jasper was a family dog, at home as long as he was with us, he had been born on a farm. And sometimes at night I would see him staring from the window and I knew he was thinking of those days when his life was bounded by the low of the cattle, the quack of the duck, when there was green grass to play upon and ancient trees to protect him from the heat of the sun. Yes, he was happy with us, but part of him yearned for the barnyard, part of him still lived in the open spaces of his youth, the rivers and fields, the smell of growing things, and sometimes I would hear a little catch in his bark, a hesitation in his growl, and I would know that the memory of those happy days was pressing hard upon his heart. He would not have left us. He would not have openly complained, but there were weekends when I would take him out to the country and let him run through the grasses, and when he was done and tired and all his wildness spent, he would return to where I was waiting and lay his red muzzle upon my knee and I would know he was saying, Thank you.

"Yes, my friends, Jasper died tonight. He died in the midst of the concrete, in the midst of glass and steel, in the midst of the great stone field that is Manhattan, but as he died the sound of wind through the tall grasses was a whisper in his ears, the smell of the barnyard and the clucking of hens—these spoke to him as the last spark went out and with his remaining strength he looked at me and, gentlemen, I recognized that look. I felt its yearning and heard its last request.

"Suffice it to say that Jasper will not be buried in the city. He will not be given to men in white laboratory coats to burn in some underground furnace. Tonight, with the help of my good friend Jean-Claude, I am taking Jasper back to the farm. We are taking him to the field just east of the house where the rising sun will warm his grave, where the little brook will tell him the stories of its travels and lull him with its song, where the tall sugar maples will protect him from the rain and cover him with a blanket of golden leaves when the snows threaten from the north, where the chickadee and jay, the robin and mourning dove will say, Welcome home, Jasper, it's good to have you back. Yes, my friends, it was to that farm in the rolling Connecticut hills that my companion Jean-Claude and I were making our way when you stopped us."

Latchmer lowered his head and looked down at the hood of the Plymouth. A cold wind blew across the playground. His toes seemed frost-bitten. Next to him, Jean-Claude was sitting with his head bowed. The wind ruffled the fur on Jasper's neck, rippled the edges of the black plastic bag.

The leader of the group stepped forward. He was holding a sawed-off shotgun loosely in the crook of his arm. He looked at Jasper, then bent down and laid the shotgun next to the dog's body. Straightening up, he took off his ski mask. Latchmer saw he was only about ten years old: a thin, black child, perhaps a little tall for his age. Then the others also took off their masks. They were all children ranging from between six and eleven, both boys and girls, mostly black but some white and even one Chinese. They stood spread out in a line behind their leader. Those with weapons put them down on the asphalt or back in their dune buggies. Four or five were dabbing their eyes with the sleeves of their jean jackets.

The leader went to the pile of keys and wallets and combs and shoes and socks, gathered them up, and carried them to where Latchmer and Jean-Claude were sitting.

"Take these back," he said. "We are sorry to have interrupted your journey."

"You must have had a dog yourself," said Latchmer.

"No," said the child, "but I've seen a lot of movies."

Latchmer gestured to the little pile of money on the hood of the Plymouth. "Please take something," he said. "I'm sure you could use it."

"I couldn't," said the child. He had a very black, narrow face with large eyes and perfect teeth.

As they talked, Latchmer saw the other children go up to Jasper one by one, kneel down, and pat him. Jean-Claude still sat with his head bowed. After a moment, he began putting on his socks and sneakers. Latchmer put on his shoes as well.

"Tell us more about your dog," said the child. He was standing before the grill of the Plymouth, looking up at them.

"There's not much to tell," said Latchmer as he tied his shoes. "He was a regular dog. He would let my children pull his ears and dress him up in their clothes. He would lie by my feet at night as I read the paper. He would fall asleep and his paws would twitch as if in his dreams he was chasing a rabbit across the fields. I would take him to Riverside Park and he would try to catch the gray squirrels. He would sit beneath a tree for half the afternoon looking up with a hopeful, yearning expression as the squirrels chattered at him. He would chase them from tree to tree, each time believing he would be successful. He never gave up thinking he would catch one of those squirrels, yet he never got any better or faster. He never gave up hope."

"You should have shot one of those squirrels," said the child.

"It was the chase he liked best," said Latchmer. "If he had actually caught a squirrel, he wouldn't know what to do with it. He liked to rush across the grass and skid to a halt at the foot of the tree, to bark and bark as the squirrel mocked him from its little branch."

"I would of shot the squirrel," said the child. "Just fuckin' blown his ass outta the tree."

"Then he'd have nothing to chase."

"Maybe you got a point," said the child.

During these minutes, the other children had brought out a long black skate board which they dusted off and cleaned so its silver wheels sparkled. Very gently, three of the children lifted Jasper and laid him on his belly on the skate board with his four feet dragging on the ground. They put a little pillow under his chin, then propped up his tail with a stick attached to the back of the board. The tail rose up in the air and seemed to wag back and forth. They attached a rope around Jasper's neck and, when they pulled it and the skate board rolled forward, it was as if they were taking Jasper for a walk as his tail wagged and his four feet dragged on the asphalt. One of the little girls hung a chain of flowers around Jasper's neck, red flowers that were limp and brown at the edges. Another child had found some ribbons and tied up bits of Jasper's fur with little bows.

The leader left Latchmer and Jean-Claude and disappeared into the dark. Moments later he returned with a box of candles that he passed out to the other children. They turned out the lights of the dune buggies, then one by one they lit the candles. The leader picked up his sawed-off shotgun and stood at attention with the shotgun resting on his shoulder. The two little girls pulling Jasper on the skate board took their position behind him. Then, two by two, the other children lined up behind the skate board. Slowly, the leader stepped forward and all the children followed. Jasper's tail wagged back and forth on its stick. The lights from the candles flickered on their faces and on the wall of burned-out cars and buildings.

Soon the children began to sing. They sang very slowly in high, tremulous voices. It sounded like a dirge or some church hymn and it was only after a few moments that Latchmer realized it was a rock and roll song he had known for nearly twenty years, but so changed and melancholy, so slowed down that it would have been unrecognizable if it hadn't been for the words.

> When I'm drivin' in my car—
> And that man comes on the radio;
> And he's tellin' me more and more about some
>   useless information
> Supposed to fire my imagination.
> I can't get no, no, no, no,
> I can't get no satisfaction.

The children marched around the perimeter of the playground, dragging Jasper on his skate board, taking him for his last walk. The candles threw their shadows on the surrounding buildings, wavering, ghostly shadows that seemed to shiver to the music. Jean-Claude and Latchmer remained on the hood of the Plymouth and kept their mouths shut.

> When I'm watchin' my TV—
> And that man comes on to tell me

How white my shirts can be,
Well, he can't be a man, 'cause he doesn't
    smoke the same cigarettes as me.
I can't get no, no, no, no,
I can't get no satisfaction.

The high voices of the children echoed off the walls
of the buildings. It was a clear, moonless night and Latchmer could see some stars. He began to search for a constellation, any constellation, but the stars seemed different,
as if he were looking up at the sky from the southern
hemisphere or even from a different planet. Yet he was
sure the stars were forming constellations, new unnamed
constellations which he didn't have wit or knowledge to
recognize. There, perhaps, was the Great Dog and there
the Dragon.

At last the procession wound its way back to the Plymouth. The children blew out their candles, then carefully
untied Jasper and put him back in the plastic bag. While
his head was still sticking from the opening, they all filed
by and patted it. Then they closed the bag and four of
the children put it in the back seat of the station wagon.

Latchmer went to the front, opened the door, and took
out Jasper's old blue blanket. Unfolding the blanket, he
walked to where the leader was standing and put it over
the boy's shoulders so that it hung down like a cape.

"I want you to have this," Latchmer said. "It was
Jasper's blanket as a puppy and the blanket he slept with
for his entire life. I meant to bury him with it, but I want
you to have it instead. It must get cold here at night.
Perhaps the blanket will bring you comfort. When you
wear it, think of Jasper and think of us as well."

The child stood with his head lowered, feeling the
blanket with his fingers, stroking it where it hung over
his breast. Then he looked up at Latchmer. "I will always
keep it with me," he said. "My men will guide you out

of the playground and back to the road."

Jean-Claude and Latchmer got into the front seat of the station wagon. Jean-Claude still hadn't spoken and Latchmer wondered what he was thinking. As they looked at the wall of wrecked cars, part of it was pulled aside. Jean-Claude started the Plymouth and drove slowly out of the playground. Latchmer rolled down his window and looked back. The children stood in a long line and were waving to them. As the Plymouth passed between two hills of rusted metal, Latchmer leaned across Jean-Claude and gave three short beeps of farewell on the horn. The Plymouth bumped across the field of bricks and rubble. A single dune buggy led the way. It stopped at the curb to let them pass. A little blond girl was driving it. She waved at them as they reached the street.

"I'd side-swipe it," said Jean-Claude, "but they'd probably catch us."

He drove to the end of the block. The chain of three wrecked cars had been pulled back to the curb. Jean-Claude pressed his foot down on the gas. The muffler of the Plymouth had been damaged and the car roared as it accelerated northward.

"I bet you could have made that kid give you a buck for the blanket," said Jean-Claude.

"Maybe."

"Seems like a waste."

Latchmer slouched down until his head rested on the back of the seat. He didn't feel like talking to Jean-Claude about the children. He closed his eyes. The roar of the muffler effectively shut out any sense of the city. He considered the children with their dune buggies and thought of his own life at that age. The leader was only a little younger than he had been at the time of his grandfather's funeral. He envied the black child his apparent self-sufficiency. Latchmer at eleven had been shy, anxious, and unwilling to cope with the world.

As he opened his mind to memory, he began to think of that time surrounding his grandfather's funeral and especially the night of the barn fire when he woke to find his room full of flames. At first he had been frightened that it was his fault, that he had caused the fire. Then he thought he was being punished because of the ring. He jumped from bed and at that moment he realized the flames were a reflection. Standing on the cold floor, he knew he had to tell his grandmother about the ring. He hurried into the hall and made his way to her bedroom. The door was wide open and she was gone. Latchmer stood by her bed. In her mirror, he could see the reflection of the burning barn.

Going to the window, he had looked out and there was his grandmother halfway up the hill, standing in the field and watching the fire. Maybe she was a hundred yards away. Her long white hair hung loose over her shoulders and she was wearing a light-colored bathrobe which reached the grass. As Latchmer watched, she raised both her arms, stretching them high above her head. The light from the fire surrounded her with an orange glow which seemed almost to flow out of her.

Latchmer had called to her. There was a lot of noise— the bawling of cattle and shouting of men, the noise of the fire engines and the crackle and rush of the flames which rose above the treetops. Then the barn roof gave way with a loud crashing and roaring and millions of sparks leaped into the night sky. The barn had been partly used to store hay and the hot wind of the fire carried the burning strands high up in a gigantic orange ball. Then they floated down: thousands of lights, thousands of little torches drifting out of the sky, brightening the whole field. In the center had been his grandmother and the bits of burning hay had fallen all around her. She didn't move but stood with her arms still raised. Some of the burning hay had started small fires in the grass and men came running to put them out. Other men stood staring up at the shimmering brightness which looked like thousands of birthday candles drifting down on little parachutes. Even though he could see the burning barn, it appeared to Latchmer that the fire and the sky full of light was connected to his grandmother, was part of her power, that she had made it happen and filled the air with flame.

Latchmer had been afraid to go outside and at last went to sleep on the floor by the window. His grandmother had found him there and got him into his own bed without waking him. When he woke in the morning, it was late. His grandmother had left for the funeral home. The casket was closed and it was too late to tell her anything.

Jean-Claude drew to a stop in a parking lot behind a five-story brick apartment building. A row of such buildings extended off in either direction. All the windows were dark and some were covered with sheets of plywood. It was two-thirty in the morning. The other cars in the parking lot were Cadillacs and Mercedes, a few Continentals and Chryslers, even a Rolls-Royce. A teenage boy sat on the back steps of the apartment house playing a mournful song on a reed flute. Above him rose a wooden fire escape and a series of wooden porches.

Jean-Claude blinked his headlights and the boy stuck the flute in his belt and trotted over to the car. "Tell Mama-san that Jinko has a nice fat dog for her," said Jean-Claude.

The boy was Oriental, perhaps Cambodian or Burmese. He nodded, then ran back to the building and up the steps of the fire escape. Latchmer watched him climb, then lost him around the fourth floor. "What kind of place is this?" he asked.

"You'll see," said Jean-Claude. "It's very clean."

Jasper was still in the back where the children had put

him and Latchmer found that he missed his comforting weight on his lap. Jean-Claude had turned on the top light and was peering into the rearview mirror, attacking his hair with a spikey comb to make it stand on end. It hadn't occurred to Latchmer that Jean-Claude's hair might look that way out of design. It resembled the polygraph test of a chronic liar: all ups and downs.

After about five minutes, the boy returned. "Mama-san says you bring dog," he said.

Jean-Claude winked at Latchmer. "What did I tell you, maybe we'll have good luck here. You carry Jasper."

They got out of the car and Latchmer retrieved the dog from the back seat. He seemed even heavier. Cradling Jasper in his arms, he followed the boy and Jean-Claude to the fire escape. Jean-Claude carried the leash and rubber mouse, twirling the one, squeaking the other. The parking lot was lit by a single arc light and much of the wooden fire escape was dark. Boards were loose and some were missing. Latchmer was forced to climb slowly and in no time Jean-Claude and the boy were way ahead. At one place there was no railing. Latchmer had reached out a hand to steady himself and nearly fell. Carrying Jasper made it hard to keep his balance and Latchmer imagined tumbling over the side. By the time he reached the third floor, he was telling himself that if he could fall on top of Jasper, then he might be all right, and he tried to hold the dog as one might hold a cushion. The floors of the porches and fire escape were slanted, which made him keep stumbling toward the edge. When he got to the fourth floor, he found Jean-Claude waiting.

"You should not dawdle," said Jean-Claude. "Mama-san is very busy and does not like to wait."

"Then you carry Jasper," said Latchmer, trying to catch his breath.

"He is your particular burden," said Jean-Claude. "I am only the agent, so I run on ahead." As he said this, he turned and hurried up the stairs to the fifth floor.

Latchmer followed. When he reached the fifth floor, he paused to look over the railing at the parking lot below. He didn't think that falling on Jasper could save him. Perhaps if he fell on top of Jasper on one of those parked cars. He had heard of people falling from great heights and hitting cars and surviving. Most likely he would bounce. If he bounced, then he should let go of the dog. He wondered if Cadillacs were softer than Mercedes. He glanced up to see Jean-Claude on the roof. He shifted Jasper's weight to his left arm and continued climbing.

When he reached the roof, he saw the boy waiting on the far side. It was a long, flat roof and covered with gravel. Jean-Claude was standing near the boy, waving at Latchmer to come along. At least the roof seemed safe. Latchmer looked up at the sky and again had the sensation that all the constellations were different. He could recognize nothing. Surely, the Big Dipper was there someplace. It was as if he had been popped over to another world, caught in a blank space between Saturday and Sunday lugging this dead dog. It reminded him of the poem about the guy with the dead bird around his neck. He too had told stories, Latchmer remembered. He saw a shooting star and wondered what to wish. Then he wished to be back in his own world again—safe and sound and fast asleep.

At the far edge of the roof where Jean-Claude was waiting was an open space of about eight feet between this apartment building and the next. A narrow board linked the two buildings. The boy stood in the middle of the board and bouncing slightly up and down. The board was about ten inches wide and rested on a low wall. Latchmer peered over the edge. Five stories below, he could see the twinkle of broken glass in a narrow alley.

"You next," said Jean-Claude.

"No," said Latchmer, still looking down into the alley.

"Why not?"

"I can't carry Jasper across that board. I'll fall."

"I've carried lots of dogs across this board. It's easy."

"Then you carry Jasper."

"I've already told you, he's your dog."

There was a hissing noise from the next building and Latchmer saw the boy motioning them to follow. Latchmer imagined himself falling. He knew it wouldn't help if he landed on Jasper. He looked up at the sky, trying to find another shooting star, but couldn't see one.

"I'll help you onto the board," said Jean-Claude. "The rest will be easy."

"Promise me that if I fall, you won't try to sell me," said Latchmer.

Jean-Claude laughed and Latchmer could see the white of his teeth. "Friends don't need to make promises," he said.

A cinder block was set against the wall. Latchmer climbed onto it, then slowly onto the wall itself. He put one foot on the board. Jean-Claude was holding him by the waist, guiding him forward. From the next building, the boy was hissing at them to hurry. Latchmer inched his way onto the board and very slightly it began to bounce. He was squeezing Jasper so tightly that part of him worried he might hurt the dog. Because of Jasper, he couldn't see his feet and he kept imagining he would step off into the black air. Jean-Claude let go of his waist. Latchmer tried to keep his eyes focused on the boy straight ahead of him, to not look down. The board began to bounce a little more. Far to his right, Latchmer could see the skyline of Manhattan, the lights of the George Washington Bridge. It was as if the city was enclosed in a glass dome and he was like a fly crawling up the outside unable to get in. He could imagine falling so clearly that it was almost as if he was already in the air. He squeezed Jasper a little tighter. When he reached the middle, the board began to bounce like the tip of a diving board, while also making a suspicious creaking noise. As Latchmer bounced, the skyline of Manhattan seemed to bounce with him. Behind him, Jean-Claude kept saying, "Don't stop, don't stop!"

Latchmer bent his knees and squinted down into the alley. It too was bouncing. He moved his right foot forward an inch, then another inch. The boy hopped up on the ledge and reached out to him. Latchmer began to fall forward. He took a running step and lunged toward the boy's hand. The boy grabbed his arm and part of the plastic bag and pulled. They all tumbled onto the roof of the next building: the boy on the bottom, Jasper in the middle, and Latchmer on top. The boy groaned.

Almost immediately, Jean-Claude jumped down beside Latchmer and helped him to his feet. Then he handed him the dog. The boy still lay on the roof groaning. Jean-Claude knelt beside him. Latchmer had had the wind knocked out of him but otherwise felt fine.

"He says his arm is broken," said Jean-Claude. "You must be more careful."

Latchmer looked at the board spanning the two buildings. He couldn't understand why he hadn't fallen. Jean-Claude helped the boy to his feet. He was still groaning and holding his arm. Glaring at Latchmer, he chattered out an unintelligible rush of Oriental words. Clearly, he was angry that Latchmer had landed on top of him. But Latchmer thought that was foolish. If the boy had to blame anyone, then he should blame the laws of gravity. He might as well get angry at the moon. Latchmer tried to feel grateful to the boy for saving his life but didn't feel much of anything except surprise. By all rights, he should be dead, yet here he was ready to continue with the work of the evening. The boy shook himself, then turned and led the way across the roof.

At the far side was a wooden fire escape like the one

they had originally climbed. Latchmer felt exhausted. Despite the cold, he was sweating heavily. They descended to the fourth floor. The boy was still groaning. Jean-Claude paused to brush bits of gravel off Latchmer's brown corduroy suit coat, then he knocked at a door.

Moments later it was opened by a thin Oriental in a black silk pajama suit with red birds embroidered on the chest. He wore a black beanie and when he saw Jean-Claude, he bowed.

"Jinko," he said, "Mama-san will be pleased."

The boy said something rapidly to the man and held out his arm. The man had a gray pigtail and looked about seventy. Hardly glancing at the boy, he reached out and slapped his face. Then he motioned Latchmer and Jean-Claude to enter, shutting the door behind them.

"There are many boys," he said, "and they all have problems."

They stood in a narrow hall. The Oriental crossed to another door, opened it, then stood aside. The hot smell of cooking food washed over them. Latchmer felt himself beginning to salivate. He was very hungry. Still clutching Jasper, he passed through the door into a bright kitchen with long stainless steel tables, immaculate white walls, and large black pots on a huge black stove. About ten men were working in the kitchen. All wore long white coats and white chef's hats.

It seemed they were in the kitchen of a large restaurant. The man closest to Latchmer had his back to him and was working with a cleaver at one of the long tables. As Latchmer approached, the man stepped aside. Lying on the table was the head of a dog, a blond cocker spaniel. The man turned again and Latchmer saw that he was in the process of skinning the dog's body, working the blond fur down off its front legs. The head lay on its side with its eyes open and stared gloomily at its body about two feet away. The man was whistling as he worked. Noticing

Latchmer and Jean-Claude, he smiled cheerfully and pinched part of the flesh of the cocker spaniel.

"Nice fat dog," he said. He too was Oriental, as was everyone else in the kitchen. Latchmer didn't think they were Chinese. Maybe Tibetan or Laotian. He could never tell.

Studying the room more closely, Latchmer saw six other blond and very fat cocker spaniels hanging from a bar by their hind legs. Their long pink tongues dangled from their mouths while their droopy ears fluttered in the breeze from a ceiling fan. Other men at other tables were cutting up haunches and shoulders. At the stove a proud-looking fat man who Latchmer guessed was the head chef was tasting something in a black pot. From a clothesline behind the stove dangled about thirty little blond ears.

A waiter entered through a swinging door on the far side and briefly there was the sound of people laughing and talking, the clatter of plates, and the click of chop sticks. Setting down a tray stacked high with dirty dishes and little piles of bones, the waiter began joking with one of the cooks. Everybody seemed to be having a good time.

The Oriental in the black pajamas led Latchmer and Jean-Claude through the kitchen to another door, opened it, then stood back to let them pass. The next room was full of barking. It too was a large room and stacked to the ceiling on four sides were cages containing dogs. Most were cocker spaniels, but Latchmer recognized some chows. All were very fat. The dogs whined or barked at them. Many wagged their tails and looked playful. One stuck its nose between the bars and Latchmer scratched it gently.

The Oriental made a clucking noise. "It is not allowed to tease the dogs," he said. He led the way across the room to another door, opened it, and again stood aside.

Latchmer and Jean-Claude entered.

It was a small room and three of the walls were covered with red silk hangings embroidered with dragons and eight-armed creatures holding flaming torches. Latchmer wondered if these were the dragons he was supposed to watch out for, but he felt no sense of threat. The floor of the room was covered with fur rugs, blond fur rugs, and Latchmer realized they were the skins of the cocker spaniels. Sitting on the floor facing them was a huge and ancient Oriental woman whose actual size was concealed by her dress, a massive blue garment resembling an Indian teepee. It flowed away on all sides while her head rose above it like the cone of a volcano. More exactly, her head made Latchmer think of a bowling ball made out of yellowish bread dough. Her eyes were two black currants and her nose hardly more than a bump. When she saw Jean-Claude, she began to smile. She had no teeth and her bare pink gums made her mouth look like a serious injury.

"What did you bring me, Jinko?" asked the old woman.

"Something very special," said Jean-Claude, and he signaled to Latchmer to put down the bag.

But Latchmer wasn't paying attention. The room's fourth wall was a sheet of one-way glass looking onto the restaurant. Through it, Latchmer saw about forty people happily eating. Most were Orientals, but there were some whites and even blacks. Latchmer was struck by their eager faces and the gusto of their appetites.

"Hey," said Jean-Claude, "put down the bag."

Latchmer placed the bag in front of Mama-san. Her teepee-like garment was embroidered with flowers, butterflies, and little green frogs. Her white hair was pulled straight back across her scalp into a thick braid which hung down her back. Lying in her lap, her fat hands looked like lumps of pastry.

Latchmer and Jean-Claude stepped away from the bag.

Latchmer kept staring out at the restaurant. Everyone seemed to be eating very fast. He was starving. Mama-san slowly reached forward and folded the bag away from Jasper until he lay fully uncovered on the pile of cocker spaniel rugs. He still had the chain of red flowers around his neck and tufts of his fur were gathered up with little bows of colored ribbon. His eyes had come open again. They looked glazed and unfocused as if he was trying to remember something: a phone number or somebody's birthday.

"But he's already dead," said Mama-san. "You know I don't like to buy dead dogs."

"It was an accidental death," said Jean-Claude. "He tried to bite me and I hit him too hard. When I saw what I had done, I thought immediately of you. He died as good as if I was a butcher. And he's still fresh, good fresh meat."

Mama-san leaned forward and began to poke Jasper's body, feeling a shoulder, squeezing a haunch. "He is cold and hard," she said.

"He's been outside," said Jean-Claude. "It's just the weather." He stood with his back to the one-way window. A foot away on the other side a chubby Oriental in a three-piece suit was cheerfully gnawing a bone.

Mama-san lifted the chain of red flowers. "What is this," she asked, "what is this foolishness?"

"He'd been at a party," said Jean-Claude.

"And the ribbons," asked Mama-san, "they too are from a party?"

"I wouldn't sell you a dog that hadn't been loved," said Jean-Claude.

Mama-san plucked off one of the ribbons and inspected it. "Food, Jinko, not love. I do not care about love. No more dead dogs. I have told you this before. In the beginning, yes, but now I have my own kennel. I do not need dead dogs and it is not fair to my customers."

"You could use him for soup," said Jean-Claude. "A nice bowl of cold dog soup with some watercress and sprinkled with white pepper and a few scallions."

Mama-san pushed Jasper away on the rug so he flopped over onto his other side. "This dog is old. If he were not so old, then maybe I would take him for soup. After a dog is eight or nine, he develops a sour taste. My customers would recognize it immediately. Mama-san is serving us old dog, they would say. A few bad words in a business like mine and it is all over."

"You could grind him up for meat and feed him to your cocker spaniels," suggested Jean-Claude.

"Not even the cocker spaniels would eat him," said Mama-san. "They are very proud. They only eat horse meat, horse meat and special dog cakes. This is no greasy spoon."

"You don't want a little taste just to make sure?" asked Jean-Claude. "Maybe a bit of the flank or a slice from the heart?"

"All would be sour," she said. Then, reaching forward, she began to fondle Jasper's ears. "But I tell you, these ears are very fine. I will buy the ears."

"How much?" asked Jean-Claude.

"Ten dollars. Ears like this can be very sweet."

"I don't want to sell just the ears," said Latchmer.

"Fifteen dollars," said Mama-san. "You take ears like this and fry them in a little butter. They are very special."

"I don't want to sell them," said Latchmer. "Jasper would look stupid without his ears."

"Fifteen bucks is not bad," said Jean-Claude.

"It's the principle of the thing," said Latchmer. "It wouldn't be fair to the dog."

Mama-san let go of Jasper's ear and sat back on her cushions. "I respect your decision," she said, "so I won't offer you more. But, Jinko, if you could get me a dozen dogs like this, I would pay a lot for the ears. The ears of cocker spaniels have an unpleasant, waxy taste."

Jean-Claude and Latchmer had begun putting Jasper back in the plastic bag. "Perhaps you would like to buy something else," said Jean-Claude. "I have this very good leash and there is a little rubber mouse that squeaks." He put them on the rug for Mama-san's inspection.

She picked up the mouse and squeaked it several times. It was a pink mouse with large pink ears. It seemed in pretty good condition. "This mouse is very nice," she said.

"I thought you would like it," said Jean-Claude.

"I will give you five dollars for the mouse."

"Eight."

"Six and no more," said Mama-san. "I can see it has been chewed."

"That shows it's the real thing," said Jean-Claude, "but we will accept six."

Mama-san took a roll of bills from underneath her robe and counted out six dollars. "Sometimes we serve mice," she told Latchmer. "We roast a nice cat and then arrange it on a platter surrounded by twenty little mice. They look like potatoes. This rubber squeaky mouse will make an amusing place setting."

"Are you sure you don't want the leash?" asked Jean-Claude. "You could boil it for bouillon."

"I do not need a leash."

"The mouse hardly pays for gas."

"I am sorry you drove all this way for so little," said Mama-san. "Perhaps you would like a sandwich."

Latchmer thought of the cocker spaniels hanging in the kitchen. "We had a couple of chili dogs right before coming," he said.

"Chili dogs?"

"You know, hot dogs with chili on them. And if you

want, you can get them with sauerkraut and onions, even melted cheese."

"I have never eaten a hot dog," said Mama-san. "What is in them?"

"Chickens and pigs and turkeys and cows, you name it. Cornmeal and sugar and smoked hickory flavoring. It's a big business."

"Let me get you a real sandwich," said Mama-san. "You like mayonnaise? A little lettuce and tomato?" She moved one of the cocker spaniel rugs to uncover a small intercom into which she spoke rapidly, then she turned back to Latchmer. "This will be my treat."

As they waited for the sandwiches, Latchmer watched the people in the restaurant. Seeing them eat so eagerly made him feel he hadn't eaten in six weeks. Waiters in white jackets hurried between tables carrying plates with round silver covers.

"You want to hear a story?" Jean-Claude asked Mama-san. "My friend here has wonderful stories. Tell her a story about a dog, Latchmer."

"I don't know," said Latchmer, "maybe I shouldn't."

"I like stories," said Mama-san. She leaned forward and grinned, showing her pink gums. "And I like dog stories a lot, we all do."

"Go ahead," said Jean-Claude. "Just while we're waiting for the sandwiches. He has a great story about a dog in a loaf of bread," he told Mama-san.

"I don't think it's a good idea," said Latchmer.

"Wait," said Mama-san. "Some of my people in the kitchen like dog stories. Let me get them." She again spoke into the intercom. "They are coming," she said. "How fortunate for us."

Even as she stopped speaking, the door opened and half a dozen men wearing chef's hats filed into the small room. There was a brief barking of dogs, then the door was shut. The men sat down cross-legged on the floor around Mama-san, chattering among themselves and glancing expectantly at Latchmer. The youngest seemed about fifteen, the oldest could have been in his nineties. When they were all comfortable and sitting quietly, Mama-san nodded to Latchmer to begin.

Latchmer leaned back against some cushions and stroked Jasper's head. Here I go again, he thought. He had no idea what he would say, but he knew that as he uttered the first sentence the story would take over. It was as if the story just grew out of his bones, erupted from his stomach. He wondered if that was what it was to be an artist, an artist of disorder, because he knew they wouldn't like his story, that these cheerful Oriental souls would turn against him. He guessed that was life, which mostly seemed a matter of frustrating others and disappointing oneself. He yawned and covered his mouth. He was getting sleepy. If he listened hard, he could just hear the faint clatter of plates and happy talk from the restaurant.

"There was a young man who went to college," he said. "He was from a city in the north where his father was a doctor. He knew nobody at the college and because of his terrible shyness it was hard to meet people. His only friend was his roommate, who was a wealthy young man from a nearby town. Well, after the young man had been at college for about two months and still didn't know anybody, his roommate invited him to his parents' house for the weekend. It was his parents' twenty-fifth wedding anniversary and all sorts of people would be there. Best of all, the roommate had a sister who was a senior in high school and very beautiful. So on a Friday night, they drove out to the roommate's house where there was to be a big party. It was a very rich house with white columns out in front and servants and everything very proper. The young man was so shy that he hardly said a word, but he had good manners and used his knife and fork correctly and stood aside to let older people pass and stuff like that. The whole family liked the young man and the sister seemed to like him too. At the party there was a twelve-piece band and the young man and the sister danced together about half a dozen times. He could tell that she liked him and she even agreed to come over to the college some weekend for a football game. That night the young man went to bed happy."

"What about the dog?" asked Jean-Claude.

"I'm coming to that," said Latchmer. "The next afternoon there was a formal tea. About thirty of the neighbors came and even a bishop. They were all sitting around on chairs in front of some big French windows looking out on the garden where two dogs were playing. It was early November but there were still a few flowers, marigolds mostly but even some bleeding hearts and irises. There was a lot of talk about how to grow flowers and about horse shows and whether a Mercedes was better than a Continental. At one point, the young man got up to go to the bathroom. When he came back, they were all talking about the ballet. He was sitting next to the sister and his roommate was sitting across from him. The parents and bishop and their friends sat around them in sort of a circle. It was all very cozy and there was a fire in the fireplace.

"Then, after a moment, the young man saw his roommate raising his eyebrows and trying to signal to him. The young man didn't understand until he saw his roommate pointing as subtly as possible to his own crotch. Glancing down, he saw that his fly was wide open. He had forgotten to close it when he went to the bathroom. Naturally, he was mortified, but he felt he couldn't just yank up the zipper. That would attract too much attention and be even more mortifying. He could feel his face getting hot. He was sitting with his hands over his crotch, but he couldn't sit like that forever. Some people were getting ready to leave and at any moment he would have to get up and shake someone's hand and then everybody would see that his fly was wide open. He was terrified. He knew that no matter what, he would have to fix his zipper. Then he got an idea. He pointed to the window and said, 'Oh my gosh, will you look at that.' And when everybody turned to look, he zipped up his fly. Nobody saw him. What a relief. He himself hadn't looked out the window and planned to say that he had seen a red-breasted woodpecker or something like that.

"But when he glanced around him, he saw his room-mate was staring at him in disgust, that the sister had gotten up and was quickly leaving the room, that the parents looked sick, the guests looked embarrassed, and the bishop looked angry. And staring out the window himself for the first time, the young man saw that the two dogs which had been playing were now fucking. Two fat black Boston terriers. And not only were they fucking, but the male dog had gotten himself stuck inside the female and couldn't get loose so that she was dragging him by his swollen prick back and forth across the terrace while he yelped and tried to pull himself free. The room-mate, the parents, the bishop, and all the neighbors tried not to look, but the plight of the little dog was so pitiful to watch as he was dragged down a flight of stone steps, then across a bed of dwarf marigolds, that nobody was able to tear himself away or could do so only for a moment or two which they used to turn and glare furiously at the young man.

"At last the father jumped to his feet, ran out into the garden, and kicked the male terrier, kicking him loose from the female and kicking him so hard that he sailed over a clump of sea lavender and disappeared. And in that moment, the young man hurried away from the tea party and ran upstairs to his room. When it got dark, he took his bag and hitchhiked back to the college. He never saw the family again and a few days later his roommate moved out and moved in with somebody else. For the next four years, the young man often saw his ex-roommate driving around town in a little red sportscar, but he never spoke to him. If anything, he became even shyer, never had any friends, and at last decided to major in police administration."

Latchmer stopped talking and stretched. He was pleased with the story, pleased with its shape, its roundness. It was like a whole completed object, something he could almost hold in his hands. As he had been telling the story, the elderly Oriental in the black pajamas had entered with a tray containing several covered dishes. These he had put down on the rug between Latchmer and Jean-Claude. Latchmer lifted off one of the covers. Underneath were little piles of sandwiches on thick white bread with thick slices of firm white meat. Latchmer took a sandwich, then glanced around him.

The half dozen men wearing chef's hats were all getting to their feet. They didn't look at Latchmer or even seem to know he was there. They appeared depressed. Quietly, they made their way past him and out of the room. Jean-Claude was staring down at one of the cocker spaniel rugs, idly tugging at a tuft of blond fur. The only person looking at Latchmer was Mama-san. She didn't seem happy.

"Why don't you take these sandwiches, put them in your pockets, and go," she said.

Latchmer took a little bite of sandwich. It was sweet. He took a bigger bite. He was amazed at how sweet it tasted. "These are wonderful sandwiches," he said.

"I want you to go," said Mama-san.

Latchmer took another bite, trying to get as much of the sandwich into his mouth as possible. He was sorry that Mama-san hadn't liked the story. He wanted to apologize, but his mouth was too full and when he tried to speak, he spat crumbs and little bits of meat onto the blond fur rugs. So he nodded and stood up. Jean-Claude was also eating as fast as possible, jamming the little sandwiches into his mouth. The elderly Oriental in the black pajamas held the door open for them.

"If I'd known you were going to tell that story," said Mama-san, "I wouldn't have given you sandwiches. Here I invite you into my room, feed you the best that my establishment has to offer, and this is how you treat me. My people were very disappointed."

Latchmer nodded and began shoving some of the sandwiches into his side pockets. He couldn't believe how sweet and juicy the meat was. It tasted a little like roast pork but with a sweet fruit flavor, maybe apple or plum. He swallowed, started to speak, then took another sandwich instead. After all, he could speak anytime. He began shoving the sandwich into his mouth. The elderly Oriental at the door cleared his throat. Mama-san was staring into the restaurant as if they no longer existed.

Latchmer swung the bag with Jasper over his shoulder. He again tried to thank Mama-san, but his mouth was too full. He passed through the doorway into the room full of dog cages. All the spaniels and chows began barking at him. Latchmer tried to say, "Good dogs," but instead he spat crumbs and bits of meat into their cages. He wished he had something to drink, just orange juice would be fine. The man in the pajamas held open the door to the kitchen and Jean-Claude prodded Latchmer to hurry.

They crossed the kitchen quickly. No one would look at them. As they went through the back door, Latchmer managed to swallow. "Do we have to go back over the roof?" he asked.

The elderly Oriental made a little bow. "It is the only way," he said. Then he shut the door.

Jean-Claude went up the fire escape and Latchmer

followed. When they reached the roof, Jean-Claude asked, "Did you have to tell that story?"

"You said you wanted a dog story," said Latchmer. It was difficult to hold Jasper and also fish the little sandwiches out of his pockets.

"I liked your other stories, but I did not like that one. It made Mama-san very unhappy."

"I just tell them," said Latchmer. "Other than that I have nothing to do with them. I'm like a radio. You ask for a story and a story comes out. Do you get angry at the radio for playing a particular song? Of course not. If you asked for a cat story, for instance, you'd get something entirely different. This is a skill I didn't know I had. It's like being an artist."

"What kind of artist?" asked Jean-Claude.

"I don't know, a kind of dog-story artist."

When they reached the board spanning the two buildings, Latchmer felt a little braver. Jean-Claude went first and steadied the board from the other side. Then Latchmer followed, inch by inch. The bag containing Jasper was slung over his shoulder. In his right hand, he held a fat sandwich.

The only dangerous moment came when Latchmer reached the middle and the board began to bounce. He was sure he would fall. In his panic, he let go of the sandwich. It tumbled through the air like a little white star, then plopped against a trash can five stories below. Latchmer found the loss so upsetting that he crossed the rest of the board without thinking of the danger.

"Do all the people in the restaurant cross that board?" asked Latchmer.

Jean-Claude seemed scornful. "Not the customers," he said, "they're too valuable. Not the cooks, not even the dogs. Maybe the bus boys and the old women who wash the dishes. People like that."

By the time they reached the parking lot, Latchmer

had finished his sandwiches and was picking the crumbs out of his pockets. He felt exhausted but content. "Are you going to drive me home now?" he asked. "I've still got to bury Jasper."

"Do you joke with me?" asked Jean-Claude. "Right now someone in this city is in need of a dead dog. He is holding his hand like a visor over his eyes and looking this way and that. Get in the car. We would have sold the ears if you were not so proud."

They were driving back downtown. Latchmer sat in the front seat with Jasper half in his lap. Jean-Claude had bought another pint of rum with the money that Mamasan had paid for the rubber mouse and they were both feeling better. Latchmer was scratching Jasper's ears. He found it soothing.

"When I was a little boy," said Jean-Claude, "we had a lot of trouble with magic. For the tourists we called it voodoo and they paid good money to see it, but for us it was just a nuisance. I mean, one day you would have a cousin who was your best friend and the next day he would be a bird. So what if he was a wonderful bird with a golden voice, you did not want a bird, you wanted your cousin. And another day all the furniture would start to jiggle and shake and you would have to run from the house while the walls went bang-bang and later when it was quiet you would go back and the furniture would be in many pieces and no good for anything. And sometimes it would rain lizards and the whole village would be full of lizards or it would rain frogs and the whole village would be full of frogs. You would find them in your bed and in your clothes. And sometimes it would rain snakes and they were the devil to catch. Yes, when I found that in the United States there was none of this voodoo, then I said, that is the place for me. Because if at any minute something can become something else, then you never feel comfortable or trust anything. How do you know if this is a chair or a pot of beans? That is why whenever I hear people complain against the United States, I always praise it because here a chair is a chair and a lizard, no matter how long you look at it, two-three months it doesn't matter, a lizard will always be a lizard."

"I never thought of it that way," said Latchmer, wary of yet another philosophical discussion. No matter how general they started, they always ended up personal, even accusing. Why do you do this, why do you do that? That kind of thinking only meant trouble. In fact, any thinking could wind up dangerous. If a news team ever stopped him on the street, he would say that a life unexamined was the only way to go. This night he had engaged in enough self-study to last a lifetime.

"Did you have an easy time when you were growing up?" asked Jean-Claude.

Here it comes, thought Latchmer, taking another sip of rum. "I guess so. My parents bought a TV when I was eight. We lived in Rochester and in the summer we visited my grandparents. The air was always soft there."

"Was there much sickness?"

"Chicken pox, measles. My sister had the mumps, but I never caught them. Colds, of course, we always had colds. But we were never sick in the town where my grandfather lived. Perhaps it was the water."

"I remember only one grampa," said Jean-Claude. "He collected bugs from under rocks and mashed them and made a paste and if you had a sore place he would smear the paste all over it and sometimes you would get better. What did your grampa do?"

"He was a doctor in a little town."

"What a coincidence," said Jean-Claude, "that both our

grampas should do the same work but so different and so far apart. Finally a bad man turned my grampa into a little white goat and the last I ever saw of him he was scampering into the jungle. What happened to your grampa?"

"Oh, he just died," said Latchmer, "but I guess he was with a woman when it happened."

The morning of his grandfather's funeral had been a bright July morning. When he awoke and found himself in his own bed instead of on the floor of his grandmother's room, Latchmer peered from the window to look for any trace of the barn fire. He was sure he had dreamed it. But there on the hill was a thin column of smoke. Latchmer quickly put on his clothes and hurried to tell his grandmother about the ring. Once downstairs, however, he discovered she was already gone.

He had started to tell his parents but realized they wouldn't understand. They might even get angry. He went into the kitchen and poured himself a bowl of Shredded Ralston. Then he peeled a peach. In fact, he peeled four peaches, trying to remove the skin in one long spiral. Each time it broke. At last his father stopped him and asked what the hell he was doing peeling all those peaches if he wasn't going to eat them.

The funeral was at 10:00. At 9:30, a black Cadillac from the funeral home arrived to take them to church. Latchmer rode with his parents, his sister, and his aunt, but felt very detached from them, as if he was really by himself. He tried to think of nothing that lay ahead and nothing that lay behind. Even so, he worried about the ring in his grandfather's pocket and how he would soon see Miss Mitchell. He wore a dark blue suit that his parents had bought for the occasion. It was too tight and Latchmer kept thinking how it would make it hard to run.

The church was a small, white, wooden building on a hill. It had narrow pointed windows and a green steeple. All the cars were parked facing downhill with their tires turned toward the curb. Latchmer entered the church with his parents, and the usher led them up to the front pew where their grandmother was already in place. Latchmer's mother gave him a little push, sending him in to sit next to his grandmother, who appeared to be praying. Although Latchmer had kept his eyes on the floor, he was pretty certain that Miss Mitchell hadn't arrived. The word *whore* kept repeating itself in his head and part of him was excited and part was ashamed, not of anything sexual but because he was thinking about Miss Mitchell and he knew his grandmother wouldn't like it.

The casket appeared big enough for several people. It was made of shiny dark wood and had lots of brass. Although beautiful, it was not pretty and Latchmer remembered how pretty his grandfather's cherry-wood coffin had been. Surrounding the casket were dozens of funeral wreaths, as if the casket were a luxury liner in a sea of flowers. Even though his grandmother knelt with her eyes shut, Latchmer knew that her attention was on the entire church.

Just as the service was about to begin, Latchmer felt his grandmother stiffen. There was an increasing murmur from the people behind them that sounded like wind blowing through the leaves of a tree. Turning his head, Latchmer saw Miss Mitchell entering a pew on the other side of the church. Even though the church was packed, she had a space around her.

Latchmer's grandmother poked him in the ribs. "It's her, isn't it?" she asked.

He began to pretend ignorance, then just nodded.

His grandmother stood up. To Latchmer it seemed that she popped to her feet as suddenly as a piece of toast is popped from a toaster. He stared at her with a mixture of admiration and terror. But whether she intended to shout or make some scene, he never knew. Before she could act, his father reached across and took her arm. For a moment, it seemed that she might defy him and Latchmer imagined his grandmother physically attacking Miss Mitchell, hurling herself across the crowded church to fasten her hands in Miss Mitchell's hair. Instead, she sank back into her seat and began to mutter. Almost unconsciously, Latchmer began to stroke her arm. He believed if his grandmother again jumped from her seat, he would be trampled. He imagined the casket knocked from its sawhorses and the mountain of flowers destroyed.

The minister began the service and everyone started to whisper. It took a second for Latchmer to realize that they were praying. In his anxiety he had thought they were whispering about his grandmother. She continued to mutter and Latchmer continued to stroke her arm. Glancing behind him, he saw Miss Mitchell staring at the casket. She wore a dark blue dress with a white scarf. Her small blue hat had a veil that partly covered her forehead. His grandmother's muttering grew louder.

After the prayer, the minister began talking about Latchmer's grandfather, saying what a good man he had been and how much he had done for the community. He had come down to the front of the church and stood next to the casket, less than five feet from Latchmer and his grandmother. The minister was a shy young man who was going prematurely bald. He couldn't talk without constantly swallowing and every time he swallowed his large Adam's apple bobbed up and down like a yo-yo. He was thin, wore glasses with silver frames, and had a small inconclusive smile that showed crooked teeth.

The muttering grew louder. While people had been rustling in their seats and then praying, the general noise had concealed whatever his grandmother had been saying. Now certain words began to emerge.

"Bitch," said his grandmother.

The minister stopped as if stuck with a pin. He stared down at where Latchmer's grandmother was sitting.

"Whore," said his grandmother.

People began to stir in their seats.

The minister grew red in the face, then tried raising his voice to cover the sound of the cursing. He had been saying that his grandfather was a kind and gentle man, a doctor who considered his patients before all else.

"Cunt," said his grandmother.

The minister had been talking in mild and slightly melancholic tones, but as he began to talk louder his voice changed. When he called the doctor a good man, it was as if he didn't quite believe it. When he spoke of the doctor's sense of social responsibility, he seemed to be laughing up his sleeve. When he described how the doctor would leave his bed at four in the morning to tend a sick child, he seemed clearly lying.

"Bitch, whore," said his grandmother.

It might have been all right if Latchmer's grandmother had continued in the same low mutter, but as the minister raised his voice, so did she, punctuating the minister's sentences with terms like "scarlet Jezebel" and "round-heeled slut," until the minister's voice rose toward a shout, as if furiously detailing the doctor's hypocrisy and barely concealed sexual crimes. He stood in front of the casket, slamming his fist repeatedly into his palm as people looked around and raised their eyebrows until at last the minister realized that his attempts to solve the problem had created a worse one.

Latchmer's grandfather had loved Negro spirituals and it had been arranged that the choir would sing several when the minister finished his eulogy. Turning suddenly to the organist, the minister signaled him to begin. Then he lifted his arms to lead the choir. He was breathing heavily and his back twitched in a nervous and spasmodic manner.

The first spiritual was "Deep River," perhaps one of the world's slowest pieces of music. But the minister was still so upset that he waved his arms not so much to conduct the choir but in general agitation. The result was to greatly increase the tempo, giving the spiritual a devil-may-care and even jaunty flavor.

> Deep river, my home is over Jordon;
> Deep river, Lord, I want to cross over into
>   campground.

During the singing, Latchmer's grandmother contin-ued to curse so that not only did the choir considerably jazz up the spiritual, they also sang loud.

> Oh, don't you want to go to that gospel place,
> That promised land where all is peace?
> Oh, deep river, Lord, I want to cross over
>   into campground.

In the midst of the second verse, Latchmer's father grabbed his arm and forcibly changed places with him. Then he began speaking rapidly into the old woman's ear. Latchmer looked back at Miss Mitchell, but she was still staring at the casket. The rest of the people, however, wore a variety of expressions ranging from amazement to glee. Abruptly, his grandmother stopped muttering.

For the minister and choir it was as if their backbones had been removed. The minister stopped waving his arms and buried his face in his hands. One by one the members of the choir fell silent. The organist struggled on for a few phrases, then he too threw in the towel. The church was quiet except for the minister's sobbing. It was a long moment and Latchmer dug his fingernails into his palms. At last the minister looked up and announced he would lead the congregation in the 23rd psalm.

The rest of the service was a confusion for Latchmer. He felt an almost impossible desire to contribute to the scandal by standing up and confessing that his grandfather was about to carry off Miss Mitchell's ring into all eternity. He knew that his grandmother would throw open the casket and search the pockets of the corpse. Why did he want to tell? Perhaps because he knew he must not. Perhaps in protest against knowing too much, against being pulled in two opposing directions. Despite his love for his grandfather, he knew that to keep silent was a betrayal. But it was too late, too late to do anything except make trouble, so he kept quiet and felt he'd done his grandmother a bad turn. At some point, his father got his grandmother out of the pew and they disappeared up the side aisle into a small room at the front of the church. There had been a few more prayers. Latchmer knelt with his head bowed and stayed that way until his mother poked him to indicate the service was over.

It seemed to Latchmer that Jean-Claude was driving too fast. They were roaring down Park Avenue and at every intersection the station wagon swooped into the air, then crashed back to the street, sometimes scraping its muffler or tailpipe. With each bump, Jasper took a little bounce on Latchmer's leg. Jean-Claude was slouched down behind the wheel. His head was nodding forward and his glasses had fallen into his lap. He appeared to be asleep. Latchmer leaned over to look at the speedometer and saw they were doing a steady sixty-five.

Latchmer had no wish to tell Jean-Claude his business. It seemed pushy to ask Jean-Claude to take responsibility for his own car, yet neither did Latchmer want to have an accident. He reached over and touched Jean-Claude's shoulder. "Were you disappointed when you came to this country?" he asked.

Jean-Claude jerked up his head and the station wagon made a little swoop toward the curb. He straightened the wheel, then found his glasses and put them back on. "The village where I grew up was very noisy, very violent," he said. "Even my dreams were noisy and all night in my sleep people would be running or climbing or jumping up and down and many times I would wake up even more tired than when I went to bed. And so I saw this country as a place where I would have only restful dreams, dreams about people sleeping or at least sitting very still. In those areas, I have been satisfied."

"But you're not completely satisfied?" asked Latchmer.

Jean-Claude took a deep breath, puffed out his cheeks, then let the air whistle through his pursed lips. "You know, sometimes you meet a very beautiful woman and she agrees to go out with you, then she agrees to come back to where you live and you are amazed at your good fortune and just when you have her all undressed she tells you that she has some disease that will make your whole body rot if you make love to her. That is what this country is like."

"I think that's a little excessive," said Latchmer. "I've had a pretty good life here."

"Me too," said Jean-Claude, "me too, but still there is something which is not quite right. When I first came to this country, I stayed with my cousin who lived in a bad part of Brooklyn. I had known him all my life and so I was happy to see him and I listened carefully to all that he told me. One day he said that when he had first come to this country, he had lived in a very dirty place where there were many rats. He would hear them in the walls. He would hear them in the kitchen and, at night when he was trying to sleep, they would run back and forth across his bed. But his very worst time with a rat was one day in the bathroom. He said that just as he had been about to settle himself on the toilet, he heard a splashing underneath him and suddenly a rat jumped up and bit him. It bit him on the loose foreskin of his pecker. But it didn't just bite him and let go, it bit him and held on. My cousin, he straightened up and looked to see what was happening and there was this little gray rat hanging from his pecker. All this happened very fast and at first the shock and surprise kept him from feeling any pain. Anyway, he stared down at the rat and the rat stared up at him and their eyes met. And my cousin said that between them there passed a look. But it was more than just a look, it was a kind of recognition, as if he knew what was passing in the rat's heart and the rat knew what was passing in his. Like when you are rushing down the street and you bump into a man or he bumps into you and you look at each other and shrug and rush on. In that shrug you are saying, This is what I have to do in my life and it is stupid but still I have to do it, and I am sorry that it has made me bump into you but I can't change it and it won't keep me from bumping into you again if I have to. My cousin stared down at the rat hanging onto his pecker and the rat stared up at him and the look they exchanged was that kind of look. Then my cousin felt the pain and screamed and the rat let go and rushed around the bathroom and for some moments everything was terror and commotion until my cousin stamped down on the rat's back and killed it. Well, when I first came to this country and asked him what kind of place it was, that was the story he told me. I asked him again, and again he told me about the rat biting his pecker, and for a long time I did not know what he was talking about, but now I am getting a better idea and each day I think I know a little more."

"Doesn't make sense to me," said Latchmer. "Where I live they have a kind of grate that covers the pipes. It lets out the sewerage but keeps the rats from swimming up into the toilets."

"I am not just telling you a story about rats," said Jean-Claude.

He was still driving fast and had run three red lights. Although there was very little traffic, Latchmer felt unhappy. Ahead of them, the octagonal mass of the Pan Am building loomed larger and larger.

"Do you have to drive so fast?" asked Latchmer. The swoops and dips at the intersections were beginning to make him seasick.

"It keeps me from getting too sleepy," said Jean-Claude. "Besides that, it is like my story. The world keeps a little pressure against you and you keep a little pressure against the world. Right now this pressure means driving sixty-five miles an hour down Park Avenue at three o'clock in the morning."

"You'd get arrested if you drove like this in Rochester," said Latchmer. He pulled Jasper more firmly onto his lap so the dog could act as a buffer between him and the dashboard.

"Latchmer, my friend, you are like a little river. You flow steadily in one direction. If someone does something to change your course, then you flow steadily in another direction. If something else happens, then you change again. Where you go or how you go, all that is determined by things outside you. Don't you ever make up your mind for yourself? You need to say, Yes, I will do this or No, I won't do that. You need to take charge of yourself." Jean-Claude crossed Forty-fifth Street and began skirting the right-hand side of the Pan Am Building and Grand Central Station. He passed two other cabs, then slid into the left-hand curve above Forty-second Street on two wheels. The screech of the tires echoed in the enclosed space. Latchmer was thrown against the door. He held on tightly to Jasper. Jean-Claude slammed down on the brakes and whipped the wheel to the right. The Plymouth slid around another curve, then plunged into a tunnel. Jean-Claude pressed down on the accelerator.

"Are you trying to insult me?" asked Latchmer. He didn't feel insulted but thought that might be because he was tired.

"No, I am just describing," said Jean-Claude. "Here in New York people are very tolerant about how someone lives his life. He wants to spend his night making love to a sheep, they say, Hey, who does it hurt? So they let him make love to a sheep. He can do anything as long as he does not wake the baby. This is very kind of people."

"So what's wrong with it?" asked Latchmer. He was aware that Jean-Claude was echoing the very argument he had earlier made to Sarah's mother about his roommate and his fondness for rubber clothing. Irritatingly enough, Jean-Claude had trapped him in a philosophical discussion. Worse, it was a personal philosophical discussion and it was bound to make him look bad. Latchmer slouched down further in his seat and put his feet on the dashboard. Jasper was balanced on his lap. The Plymouth rocked back and forth as it shot through the tunnel. It was like a subway tunnel and outside the car window everything was either rusty or gray. Jean-Claude had increased his speed to seventy-five. At the far end of the tunnel was a green light. Even as Latchmer looked, the light turned red.

Latchmer repeated his question, "So what's wrong with people doing what they want as long as they don't hurt anyone?"

"I haven't decided," said Jean-Claude. "But it means they don't choose, they just let things happen. It also means there are many ways for a man to make money. But I don't think people like what is happening, they just pretend they don't care and go on about their business. But you know what that kind of response does? It leaves a mark. It makes that little up-and-down crease right above your eyes. This bad thing happens or that bad things happens and you never complain, but the crease gets deeper. Every year it gets deeper. Next time you're walking around, just look at how many people have that crease. Half tolerance, half frustration, because they put up with it but don't like it. Even you have that crease and right now it is very deep. It is deep because I am driving very fast but even so you do not say anything. You know what that crease is? When it is time for you to die, Mr. Death will come and that is where he will deposit his nickel—not even a real nickel but one made from squashed tin cans. That's where he will pay you for all your trouble. Then he will take you away."

"Do you have to drive so fast?" asked Latchmer.

Jean-Claude appeared to ignore him. "This is my favorite place in New York. You see that light which is now red? That is where we come out of the tunnel. If that light is red when we reach it, then we'll probably be killed. Maybe a big street cleaner will slowly cross the street and we will hurry right into it. But if the light turns green, then we'll be safe. Every few months I come here to review my life. Does the world want Jean-Claude to live or is it time to say goodbye?"

"But what about me?" asked Latchmer.

"You are a river," said Jean-Claude, "and this is the way you are flowing."

"I wish you wouldn't drive like this." said Latchmer.

"If you want me to go slower, then say, 'Hey, you, go slower.' After all, I am the cab driver and you are my passenger. It is like you are my boss." The light was fifteen yards away and still red.

"It's not my car," said Latchmer. "I don't want to interfere in your business."

They were nearly at the end of the tunnel. At the last possible moment, the light turned green. Latchmer let the air escape from his lungs. The station wagon shot out of the tunnel, rose up off the pavement, then crashed back down. Jean-Claude straightened the wheel but slowed only a little. A delivery truck had been waiting at the light.

"A river," said Jean-Claude, "you are just like a river."

There was more traffic. Jean-Claude swerved to the left to avoid another cab. He was just making the tail end of the lights and didn't want to slow down.

"Have you ever had an accident?" asked Latchmer.

"Oh yes, many times. You Americans, you like to live ninety-nine percent safe. That is very hard. You spend many, many hours on those last few points. In Haiti, people live ninety-five percent safe and have more time for everything. Maybe I live ninety percent safe and so I have the most time of all. You want me always looking over my shoulder? Only people with money can do that. We poor people, we just barrel along."

"Watch out!" shouted Latchmer.

Several cars were waiting for the light at Seventeenth Street at the edge of Union Square. Latchmer had been expecting the light to turn green but it stayed red. A taxi and some other car, maybe a Chevie, were occupying the two lanes. There was a space of about three feet between them. Jean-Claude was aiming for that space, presumably thinking it would widen when the light changed. He was going about sixty. They were less than twenty yards away and the light was still red.

Jean-Claude pumped his brakes and blew the horn. The taxi driver saw them and began to pull forward, giving them a little more space. Consequently, when Jean-Claude smashed through the gap between the two cars, it had widened to five feet and he had slowed to about forty.

He hit the gap so perfectly that he seemed to rip an equal amount of metal from each car. It was like a karate chop. The taxi was knocked onto the traffic island while the Chevie was rammed into a line of parked cars. The station wagon slowed but did not stop. Although Jean-Claude was pumping his brakes, they appeared not to work. He bounced over the curb by Union Square and smashed into a trash barrel, hurling it into the street. They rushed along the sidewalk, knocking down bus-stop and no-parking signs. Latchmer squeezed Jasper more tightly. About a dozen people had been strung out along the sidewalk and all leaped up onto the ledge bordering the park. Jean-Claude yanked the wheel to the right and shot up some steps into the park as well. At the top, the Plymouth flew a few feet through the air, then crashed down on top of a concrete bench. For a moment, Latchmer and Jean-Claude sat motionless, as if waiting for more to happen. The Plymouth tilted forward, half on the bench, half on the sidewalk. Everything seemed very quiet.

"Don't say I didn't warn you," said Latchmer.

Jean-Claude seemed unperturbed. Taking pencil and paper from his pocket, he began writing something. He handed the paper to Latchmer. Printed in a small neat hand was an address near Canal Street.

"Take Jasper to that address," said Jean-Claude. "Ring the bell and say you have a dog for Jojo. They will understand."

"What kind of place is this?"

"A regular place. You will see. Ask for Jojo and say that Jaycee has sent him a nice red dog. Remember, we split the profits fifty-fifty."

"But what if I don't want to go all the way over there?"

Jean-Claude put a hand on Latchmer's shoulder. "You have no choice. I am telling you to do it. Remember? You are a river."

"What are you going to do now?" asked Latchmer. He decided he'd take a look at the place, just out of curiosity.

"I will have to talk to the police. They do not like it if you crash down on park benches. It means the bums have no place to sleep. Here, don't forget the leash. Make sure you get a good price for it."

Latchmer got out of the car. It was cold and the wind cut through his corduroy suit. Both the Plymouth's front fenders were missing. Without Jean-Claude, he felt oddly adrift. He pulled Jasper out of the car, put the leash in the bag, and swung the bag over his shoulder. Looking back, Latchmer saw a patrol car stopping at the inter-section where they had had the accident. He saw the taxi driver pointing in their direction. The patrol car's blue lights began to flash menacingly.

"Hurry," said Jean-Claude, "the police won't like you carrying Jasper in a black bag. They won't understand."

"How long will you be?" asked Latchmer.

"I don't know, but wait for me. Otherwise, I will find you and I will be angry."

Latchmer nodded and set off across the square toward the subway stop. His shoulders ached from carrying Jasper. It felt like he'd been carrying Jasper for his entire life. Even so, he didn't want another cab. He reached the entrance to the subway and hurried down the stairs. A warm wind blew toward him out of the subway. It felt comforting, almost soothing.

Latchmer had to wait ten minutes for a train. Then he climbed into the last car, which was empty except for a sleeping Chinaman and four black kids at the other end listening to rap music on a tape deck. Latchmer sat down and put Jasper on the seat beside him. The black kids kept looking at the plastic bag as if deciding whether to steal it. Earlier in the evening Latchmer would have tried to protect Jasper. He might even have put up a fight. Now he kept looking into the bag and patting it as if it contained something valuable. He imagined the black kids grabbing the bag and rushing off into the night. The inside of the subway car was so covered by graffiti that its original color was hidden. It was like traveling inside an angry message, a curse, as if someone had shouted, "Fuck you!" and then made a subway car out of it and invited you inside.

When Latchmer got off at Canal Street, the black kids stayed on the train. The address he wanted was over on the west side near the Holland Tunnel. He decided to walk. He passed several men wrapped in newspaper who were sleeping in doorways. A police car shot by him going east. A middle-aged woman in a ragged fur coat asked Latchmer if he wanted to have a good time and he said No.

The address was a four-story brick warehouse. A blue light shone over the door. Latchmer knocked, then waited. There was no sign or anything to indicate what was inside. The air felt damp from the river. After a minute, the door opened and a fat, bald man wearing jeans and a sheepskin vest over his bare chest raised his eyebrows at Latchmer. Hanging from his left ear was a tiny red Swiss army knife. On each arm he had black leather wristlets with short silver spikes.

"I've got a nice red dog for Jojo," said Latchmer. "Jaycee sent me."

"Great," said the man with the Swiss army knife in his ear, "we're all outta dogs."

He stood back to let Latchmer enter. Inside was a long narrow bar with flickering blue lights. The juke box was playing an old song called "Steam Heat." The singer was maybe Doris Day or Patti Page or Peggy Lee. Latchmer wasn't sure which. A dozen men were sitting at the bar. They all appeared to be waiting for something.

"I'll go tell Jojo about the dog," said the man. "Why don't you make yourself comfortable."

"Thanks," said Latchmer. It seemed that all night he'd been meeting nice people.

He wandered over to the bar. A shiny brass rail ran along the edge just even with the counter. The bartender smiled at Latchmer. He wore tight denim shorts and a jean jacket unbuttoned to his navel. Hanging over his shoulder was a pulp hook—the short iron hook used to heave around cord wood or packing cases. The man must have worn the pulp hook often because his jacket was faded at that spot and the point of the hook had made a small tear.

"Take your order?" said the man cheerfully.

"Just a beer, and some pretzels if you have any."

"Imported?"

"Why not."

Latchmer let his glance travel down the bar and as he did so he realized that the dozen men were all handcuffed to the brass rail. The man sitting closest to Latchmer signaled to him to come over. He was about Latchmer's age, wore a dark-colored suit, and had a small beard and mustache like the ones worn by Prince Albert on a box of Prince Albert cigars. Latchmer heaved the dog up onto the bar and Jasper's head lolled out of the bag. Then Latchmer walked over to see what the man wanted. The juke box began to play "Shrimp boats is a-comin'."

"See this place right here on my cheek?" asked the man. His face was pale and puffy, as if made from the same kind of bread dough that is used to make hot rolls.

"What about it?" asked Latchmer. The bartender had brought him a St. Pauli Girl dark and Latchmer took a sip. It was nice and cold.

"Make a fist," said the man.

Latchmer made a fist. The man was handcuffed to the brass rail by his left wrist. He was drinking some cream-colored drink in a brandy snifter. The blinking blue lights over the bar made everything blurry.

"That's a nice big fist," said the man. "May I touch it?"

"Sure," said Latchmer. He held out the fist and the man felt it gently while Latchmer opened the bag of pretzels with his teeth. He was very hungry. He'd been hungry all night.

"Do me a favor," asked the man.

"Sure, what is it?"

"I want you to take your fist and hit this place on my cheek very hard."

Latchmer ate a pretzel. "I really don't want to," he said. He found himself thinking about that Italian who'd made a tour of Hell. He too had met a lot of peculiar people.

"Just once. I promise it won't hurt. Just haul off and belt me in the face."

"I don't want to," said Latchmer. "I mean, I just don't feel like it."

"What about insults," said the man. "Call me something really mean."

"Like what?"

"I don't know, something that makes me feel terrible."

"You're silly," said Latchmer.

"No, no, something worse than that, something really terrible."

"You're really silly," said Latchmer.

The man sighed. "What's in the bag?" he asked.

"A dog."

"Can he bite me?"

"No, he's dead."

"Too bad," said the man. "Maybe you can hit me with him."

"I'm trying to sell him," said Latchmer.

"I was into dogs last year," said the man. "I liked it, but you just can't go back."

The man with the Swiss army knife in his ear walked up and put his arm on the other man's shoulder. "How're you doin', sweetie?" he asked.

"Things are a little slow."

Turning quickly, the man with the Swiss army knife slapped him twice across the face. Latchmer jumped out of the way.

"Love it," said the man. "Love it."

"Jojo says to come back and bring the dog," said the man with the Swiss army knife in his ear.

Latchmer shoved the rest of the pretzels into his mouth, gulped down his beer, and grabbed Jasper.

"Don't say goodbye," said the man handcuffed to the rail.

"Goodbye," said Latchmer.

"Oh, damn," said the man.

Latchmer followed the other man back through the bar and down a long hall until they came to a room that looked like a doctor's waiting room. Sitting at the desk was a woman in a white nurse's uniform. She had wavy blond hair that curled over her shoulders just like Dolly Parton's. In front of her, a bank of twelve black and white TVs had been set into the wall. The nurse was watching the screens and eating a banana. Her collar was turned up and she looked quite chic.

"Jojo will be here in a minute," said the man with the Swiss army knife in his ear. "Read a magazine."

Latchmer sat down in the middle of a couch and put Jasper on the cushion beside him. He began leafing through an old copy of *Boy's Life*, then turned his attention to the television screens where people were wrestling. He decided it must be some sort of closed circuit TV system. The screens were about fifteen feet away and quite small, but after a moment Latchmer realized the people were not wrestling but engaged in a wide variety of sexual acts either singly, in couples, or in crowds, both men and women, and in one screen Latchmer caught a glimpse of something dark with four legs. He glanced at the nurse in surprise. She was very pretty. She had large breasts and the top three buttons of her uniform were open. As she finished her banana, she looked at Latchmer and pouted her lips. After a moment, she got up, came over, and sat down beside him.

"Hi," she said. "I'm Dallas." She had a thick husky voice.

"I'm Michael Latchmer," said Latchmer. "What's happening on the TV?"

"Oh, just the usual stuff," said Dallas. "I've just got to make sure that no one pops an aorta." She looked at Latchmer appraisingly. "You're the man with the dog, aren't you. I like big men with dogs."

"My dog is dead," said Latchmer.

"I don't care," said Dallas.

"A lot of people would," said Latchmer. He looked at Dallas's fingernails, which were very long and dark red.

"I'm different," said Dallas. "You want me to blow you?"

"Pardon me?"

"I said, would you like a blow job? I could do it right here."

"No, thanks," said Latchmer, "I've got to meet Jojo." He remembered that in the story about the Italian wandering through Hell, he'd been led by some kind of poet, and it made Latchmer wonder if Jean-Claude ever wrote poetry.

"Jojo won't mind," said Dallas. "That's the kind of guy he is, just a great guy to work for." She wore a lot of black eye make-up and had long black lashes. "Come on, unzip."

"I just don't feel like it," said Latchmer.

"It'll only take a second."

"I guess I'm not in the mood."

"You can tell, can't you?"

"Pardon me?"

"You can tell I'm not a girl," said Dallas. "What was

it that gave me away, was it my voice?"

Latchmer looked at Dallas more closely. Her teeth were perfect and she had a rich smell like cinnamon. "No, really," he said, "you had me completely fooled."

"Maybe my make-up wasn't right. You know, men have bigger pores than women. I have big fat pores." She took a lacy handkerchief from her sleeve and touched the corner to one eye.

"I mean it," said Latchmer, "I never noticed. I could have sworn you were a girl."

"You're sweet," said Dallas. "It was my smell, wasn't it? Men have a special smell. Sissy, that's my roommate, she says I smell just like a man."

"I had no idea," said Latchmer. "Really, you look just like a girl. You've done a great job."

"Then why didn't you want to have some fun?"

"I don't know," said Latchmer, "it's three-thirty in the morning and I'm just trying to sell this dog. I guess I didn't feel scheduled for it, that's all."

"You're kind," said Dallas. "Most guys when they find out get a little aggressive. But I think you sensed it. I mean, something tipped you off. Maybe I really have to go all the way. I mean like Sissy and have it surgically removed. I can't just tie it back between my legs. It probably makes me walk funny. I bet that's what you saw, that I've got a kind of limp. It's a big decision. I mean, every year I go back and see my folks. They're sweet, you know. Just like you. If I had it cut off, it'd be hard on them. 'Hard on,' what a funny thing to say."

"They'd probably get used to it," said Latchmer. He had folded back the top of the black plastic bag and was holding Jasper's head on his lap. He wondered if he was really kind.

"That's what Sissy says, that they'd love me anyway. They always wanted a daughter. What would you do if you were me?" asked Dallas. "Would you cut it off?"

"That's a hard decision to make for somebody else," said Latchmer.

"There," said Dallas, "now you're saying it."

"Saying what?"

"'Hard.'"

"It's just a word," said Latchmer. Probably he wasn't kind, probably he just didn't feel very strongly. But wasn't he supposed to feel strongly?

Dallas leaned across Latchmer to look at Jasper. "My, what a pretty red dog," she said. "Too bad he's dead."

"It's not the inconvenience you might think," said Latchmer. "Dead dogs don't eat. They don't need to be taken for walks. They don't whine or bark or bite or scratch. They never have to go to the bathroom."

"I go to the bathroom all the time, " said Dallas. "I love it."

"Tell me something," said Latchmer, still wondering about his possible weakness of feeling, "let's say you were given a warning that you couldn't make any sense of, what would you do?"

"Gee," said Dallas, "I get warnings all the time, but usually they're pretty clear. What was it?"

"Well, I was told to watch out for a dragon. I mean, it was a skywriter and it warned a lot of people, but somehow I thought it had to do with me."

"And you haven't seen any dragons?"

"Not so I could recognize. At first I thought it might be this dog, but he doesn't seem much like a dragon."

Both Latchmer and Dallas looked thoughtfully at Jasper. One eye had come open again and Latchmer shut it. "No," said Dallas, "he doesn't look much like a dragon. But maybe it's not a real dragon, maybe it's a person or even a thing. Or maybe it's something you're not supposed to do or maybe it's even warning you against something inside your own head. I mean, all you know for certain is that it's something different."

"What do you mean?" asked Latchmer. He hoped the conversation wasn't taking a philosophical turn.

"Like falling in love or suddenly being afraid of something or being jealous or envious or suddenly hating something or thinking some new thing or desiring something you've never desired before. That's my big problem, I get all these funny desires. Have you been doing anything out of the ordinary, I mean, in your head?"

Latchmer tugged at one of Jasper's ears. How silly the dog would have looked without them. He was glad he hadn't sold them to Mama-san. "Well," said Latchmer, "I've been having a lot of memories. Mostly I don't remember anything, but tonight I've been going hog-wild."

"Are they nice memories?"

"Not particularly, and they seem to be getting worse."

"Then why don't you stop?"

"I can't really control them. It's like falling downstairs. They just keep going and going."

"Lack of control," said Dallas, "that's my problem too. Sometimes I'm afraid I'll eat until I burst."

Jojo arrived a few minutes later. He was an energetic red-haired man in a three-piece gray tweed suit. He wore thick glasses in thick black frames and had a little red goatee. Right away Latchmer felt warmly toward him.

Jojo stuck out his hand and Latchmer stood up and shook it. His hand felt rubbery, like a soft rubber toy. "Glad to meet you, Mr. Latchmer," said Jojo. "Any friend of Jaycee's has a friend here as well. Has Dallas been treating you okay?"

"Great," said Latchmer. He thought Jojo was about fifty. He had a large, open face with lots of freckles.

"So what's Jaycee been up to?" asked Jojo. "I haven't seen him since just before New Year's."

"He wanted to be here tonight," said Latchmer, "but he cracked up his cab. Maybe he'll get here later."

Jojo rubbed his hands as if warming them. "That's the kind of guy he is: always pushing himself to the limit." He glanced down at Jasper and smiled. "So this is the dog, is it? What a nice red color. What's his name?"

"Jasper."

"What a nice name for a dog," said Jojo. He bent down and patted Jasper's head. "Some people don't like dead dogs, but I don't know, living or dead, he's still a dog. Right? I mean, you can't take that away from him. You can kick him or beat him or kill him, but he's still a dog. Just like people. Even after a man's dead, he's still a man. He's just dead, that's all—*The Big Sleep, The Long Goodbye, The Far Side of the Dollar.* You like mystery novels?"

"I guess I never thought of it," said Latchmer.

"As far as I'm concerned," said Jojo, "it's all a mystery novel. I mean, how often d'you know why somebody does something. It's a mystery, right? Like here you are with this nice dead dog. Who knows why you're here? Maybe you're a tormented soul, maybe you're just a nut. Maybe you're something else altogether. In any case, something urged you to come to us; something made you bring this nice red dog down to Jojo's. Well, we like death here. Some people discriminate, but not us. The dead are the great underprivileged class. They're the untouchables—worse than the wops, the kikes, the niggers, the chinks. But here with us the dead have a friend. Just because a man's dead doesn't mean his life is over. Necromancy, necrophagia, necrophilia—we've had some of our people when they pass over to the other side, we've had them bequeath their bodies right here to Jojo's. Later, if there's time, I'll show you our morgue, We say, 'He's not dead, he's just shy.'"

"What's that stuff on the TV screens?" asked Latchmer.

Jojo looked with pride at the bank of consoles. "Isn't that great," he said. "Isn't that wonderful. You know,

New York has its gay bars, its leather bars, its sex bars, but this is the one place where you can run from vibrator follies right through to the jolly geriatrics in the space of ten minutes. That's why they call Jojo's 'The One-Stop Sex Shop.' Take you, for instance, what interests you most in terms of sex?"

"I don't know," said Latchmer, "just girls, I guess."

"But what do you like, what drives you crazy?"

"You mean like French kissing?"

"No, no, what makes you maniacal?"

Latchmer thought a moment. Even with ice cream he preferred vanilla. "I've got a friend who offered to show me the pressure cooker," he said.

Jojo snapped his fingers in disappointment. "Old hat. They even do that in Vermont. You should be careful, you're at a dangerous age. You must watch out for sexual fascism. Here at Jojo's we try everything. You know the great French philosopher Rousseau? All his life he wanted to be spanked by a pretty girl, but he never got up the nerve to ask. Here he could have been spanked to his heart's content."

"I don't like philosophy," said Latchmer. "It tends to get too personal."

"That's not the point," said Jojo. "I'm talking about sexual fulfillment."

"You mean you really do everything?" asked Latchmer.

Jojo winced. "No kids. We do referrals, but that's it. Personally, my motto is 'Sex by eight or else it's too late,' and if you can swing it, we've got some midgets that look like five-year-olds in a dim light. There's one little lady that if you put her in a pink polka-dot dress and get her singing 'Little Miss Lollipop,' you wouldn't know the difference. Also we don't go in for a lot of pain. Slapping, sure. Spanking, sure. But no knives, no fire. This is a wholesome place. More like McDonald's or Disneyland. You know, something for everybody."

"So what about Jasper?" asked Latchmer.

"Well, the only trouble is we had a National Dog Week back in February where we did a lot of dogs. It's like eating candy—you eat till you get sick, then you can't look at it for a while. But I'll tell you what, we're having an auction at five a.m. I'll put Jasper on the block. That'll just give me time to make him pretty."

"An auction?"

"That's right. Once a week we have an auction for the folks, introduce them to some of life's wrinkles. I usually take thirty percent, but because you're a friend of Jaycee's I'll take only twenty. You got anything else except the dog?"

"His leash." Latchmer reached into the bag and took out Jasper's leash. It was dark brown leather and looked fairly new.

"Fantastic," said Jojo, "we always need leashes here. Let's go to my office, then I'll take Jasper and fix him up. Would you like coffee, beer, whiskey, some poppers, maybe a reefer?"

"I'll just rest a bit. I'm not used to these late nights."

Jojo led the way through the door and down a short hall. "You want to rest with anybody else or just yourself?"

"By myself, I guess."

"You want a love doll or vibrator? I got a love doll that looks exactly like Winston Churchill."

"Just a pillow would be fine."

"I like a man of simple tastes," said Jojo. He opened another door, then stood back to let Latchmer enter. "Here we are."

The walls of Jojo's office were covered with mammoth black and white photographs showing fragments of a face. Occupying all of one wall was part of a forehead and hairline, right ear and eye. On another wall was the chin, goatee, and part of the mouth. Latchmer realized the pictures were of Jojo himself. Behind the desk was a picture of Jojo's nose and the lower part of his eyes. Latchmer recognized the glasses. Along the wall to the right was a black leather couch. Covering the floor were several zebra-skin rugs.

Jojo went to a closet, took out a pillow and a bright red blanket, and tossed them on the couch. "Make yourself at home," he said. "You want to brush your teeth or anything like that?"

"No, I'm fine."

"Then I'll be back a little later." Jojo gave a wave of his hand and left the room. Latchmer sat down on the couch and took off his loafers. On the ceiling was a photograph showing the back of Jojo's head with a small bald spot. Latchmer spread the blanket over his legs. From far away, he could hear the song "Ding, Dong, the Witch Is Dead."

Latchmer hoped he could sleep. No more thinking, he told himself. No more memories. He knew they only meant trouble. Surely, they were taking him to a place where he didn't want to go. Maybe that's what the dragon was. Maybe it was just memory, a huge dragon made up of the memory of his grandparents and Miss Mitchell and some failure of his own. He scrunched his eyes shut and tried to make himself sleep but even the word *memory* was enough to defeat him. Immediately, he saw the small white church with its green steeple, could see the ornate casket and mounds of white flowers.

When the service had ended, Latchmer had been afraid to leave the pew. He sat as if praying, but actually he was picking loose threads off his new blue suit. He was very conscious of Miss Mitchell sitting across the aisle to his right and three pews behind. He remembered his promise to her, two promises really: not to tell about the ring and not to treat her as invisible. He knew if he spoke to her, then everyone would see them and his grandmother would hear of it and she would be furious.

Latchmer's aunt and sister were already leaving. His mother gave him another poke. Latchmer bent his head a little farther and continued to pretend to pray. His mother looked at him suspiciously, then left the pew. As she entered the middle aisle, Latchmer scooted over to the side. He glanced back and saw Miss Mitchell staring directly at him. He pretended not to see her. He tried to look confused and stared vaguely around the church as if he was having some sort of amnesia attack and didn't know where he was. He had every intention of speaking to her, of walking up to her and saying Hello, but he just wasn't ready. Hurriedly, he walked up the side aisle to the little room where his father had taken his grandmother.

The room was empty except for the minister, who was changing out of his vestments. He looked angrily at Latchmer. "You just think it's funny," he said. "A crazy woman like that and you just laugh."

Latchmer hurried around him toward the farther door. Without his vestments, the minister looked unnaturally thin. He was wearing a white sleeveless T-shirt and Latchmer felt embarrassed to have caught him in his underwear. Again he felt that too much was being asked of him. This was supposed to be his summer vacation and in the fall he would enter sixth grade and go on learning about fractions, which he despised.

"Why didn't you make her shut up?" the minister called after him. "Why didn't you do something?"

Latchmer escaped out a side door, then ran around to the front of the church. He wanted to get into one of the big black cars before Miss Mitchell came out of the church.

The funeral procession was parked at the curb. Latchmer ran toward the first car. As he reached it, he saw Miss Mitchell at the top of the church steps. She was glancing around and he knew she was looking for him. Then she saw him and Latchmer felt his eyes locked onto hers. Like the time when he had passed her house on his bike, their exchanged look was like a bridge and he felt himself falling toward her. He imagined being sucked into her body and forced to do her will. Maybe he even took a step in her direction. Then he jerked his head away and yanked open the back door of the limousine. Quickly, he climbed inside and found himself face to face with his grandmother.

She looked at him as if she'd never seen him before. Her black hat was crooked and the mesh veil had slipped over one ear. She had been putting on lipstick but it was all wrong. Her mouth was a bright red X. Slowly, she lifted her hands and took hold of Latchmer's cheeks, pinching them until they hurt.

"Round-heeled slut," she said.

Her eyes were so peculiar and unfocused that Latchmer wanted to get out of the car. Then he saw Miss Mitchell standing only fifteen feet away. His grandmother saw her at the same moment and lunged across Latchmer's lap, making a grab for the door handle and pushing open the door.

"Bitch-slut," she shouted.

Latchmer pulled her back. He knew that if she got out she would start screaming and might even attack Miss Mitchell. The sidewalk was crowded with people preparing to go to the cemetery. Latchmer felt that if his grandmother made a scene, he would be blamed. He imagined the two women fighting and ripping off their clothes until they were both naked. He kept thinking of them naked until he felt his face getting hot.

"Traitor," said his grandmother, "you're on her side."

She tried to pull herself free but Latchmer held on, wrapping his arms around her waist and burying his head beneath her mammoth bosom. She began hammering on his back. Latchmer told himself he would never let go, never, never.

Moments later his father and the driver got into the limousine and they left for the cemetery. Gently, his father separated him from his grandmother. She began to cry and touched Latchmer's cheek where she had pinched it. Then she turned to his father and put her head on his shoulder.

Latchmer looked out the rear window of the limousine and saw Miss Mitchell staring after them, standing perfectly straight in her dark blue dress. Latchmer felt he had let her down and let his grandmother down as well. No, it was worse than letting them down. He hoped that Miss Mitchell wouldn't go to the cemetery. He was afraid of what might happen. He wished he could just jump out of the limousine and sneak home. Out behind his grandfather's house, he had built a tree fort at the top of a tall pine that always covered his hands with resin. He wanted to climb to the tree fort and sit and not let anyone else come up. From the very top he could see half the town, see how it was laid out in neat little blocks, and he liked how the distance made everything far away and manageable.

There was a knocking on the door. Latchmer started up and realized he had been asleep. At first all he saw were the huge pictures of Jojo's face and it seemed he might be trapped inside Jojo's head like a forgotten thought.

The door opened and Dallas entered. Even though Latchmer knew that Dallas was a man, he could see nothing to suggest it. Hanging from the collar of her nurse's uniform was a shiny stethoscope.

"The auction's about to start," said Dallas. "Jojo told me to take you to the showroom. You want to pee first or maybe have a cup of coffee?"

"No, I'm fine," said Latchmer. It was just five o'clock. He was surprised he wasn't sleepier. Putting on his loafers and brown corduroy suit coat, he followed Dallas out of the office and down a hall hung with oversize posters of old movie stars—Bogart, Clark Gable, George Raft.

"Did you sleep?" asked Dallas, "or did you have more of those nasty memories?"

"I guess I did both," said Latchmer. "The funny thing is, I'm remembering stuff I'd completely forgotten. I never have memories and now I remember every detail."

"Are they dirty?" asked Dallas.

"No, I guess they're just regular memories."

"That's the worst kind," said Dallas. "All work and no play."

At the end of the hall were two swinging doors covered with padded red vinyl. Dallas pushed them open. Inside was a small theater with about eighty seats covered with some purple material. In front was a stage. At the four corners of the ceiling hung little naked cherubs pressing long horns to their lips. About thirty people were in the theater. At first Latchmer thought they were both men and women, but then it seemed that some were men dressed as women and some were women dressed as men. Possibly they were all men. Possibly they were all women. Their clothes ranged from conventional blue serge suits to one person who wore only a series of red bandannas tied together at strategic spots. From speakers in the ceiling came some very muted disco.

"This is where we have our theatricals," said Dallas, "and also the auctions and any activity where a lot of people get together. These seats come right out. Let's go down to the front row."

Dallas led the way. Now and then she gave a little wave to someone she knew. It seemed to be a friendly place and if it hadn't been five o'clock in the morning,

Latchmer would have liked it better.

After another minute a woman dressed as an airline stewardess wheeled a metal cart about the size of a stretcher onto the stage. The cart was covered with a piece of blue cloth. The woman was tall, black-haired, and very pretty. There were several wolf whistles from the audience and the woman pouted and blew a kiss to someone in the back row. Then she left, only to return seconds later wheeling another cart of the same size. This one was covered with a red cloth. Then she left again and returned pushing a square structure surrounded with green curtains decorated with black silhouettes of dogs sitting with their noses pointed upward. The stewardess wore very tall high heels and took very small steps. This time she remained on stage, smiling and nodding to people in the audience.

Dallas nudged Latchmer in the ribs. "That's my roommate, Sissy. Isn't he great?"

"Wonderful," said Latchmer.

The dark red curtains at the back of the stage were pulled aside and Jojo swept through them. He wore a black tuxedo with a red paisley cummerbund and was smoking a cigarette in a black holder like the one once used by President Franklin D. Roosevelt. He too waved to people in the audience and when he saw Latchmer he winked. As people quieted down, Jojo stepped to the front of the stage.

"Friends," he said, "I have some very special items for you this morning. Is your life a little slow? Do you feel sluggish in bed or too tired to get up from the TV? What I have for you today are a few small pick-me-ups, a little nudge from the realms of the strange, the boudoir of the peculiar. Just remember, there's no pleasure you can imagine that hasn't delighted hundreds of others. So relax, loosen up. Do you like cake? This morning I'll offer you the whipped cream and frosting. I'll even sell you the candles."

Dallas again poked Latchmer. "Isn't he terrific?"

"He's got a real flair," said Latchmer. The auditorium had become crowded and people were sitting in the aisles. Everyone seemed eager. Some people were already holding money in their hands. Latchmer still expected Jean-Claude and kept glancing back toward the doors.

"Let's see what we have first, ladies and gentlemen," said Jojo. Sissy swept the blue cloth off the metal table. "Chains, vibrators, erotic paraphernalia, a pair of rubber boots, a box of diapers, a straitjacket, rubber molds of male and female genitals to make ice sculptures for your favorite drinks, a cattle prod." Jojo held up a pair of gold handcuffs which were spotted with rhinestones. There was an appreciative ooo-ing noise from the audience. "What am I given for this pair of love-cuffs? Don't be shy, ladies and gentlemen, every indiscretion must begin with a willing heart."

A man in the back bid $5 for the handcuffs. This was raised to $6, then $10. Dallas leaned over and put her mouth to Latchmer's ear. "Those can be a lot of trouble," she said. "I once had to wear a pair for nearly a week because I'd accidentally swallowed the key."

"All that stuff seems a little artificial," said Latchmer.

"Oh, I don't know," said Dallas, "cattle prods can be a lot of fun."

The love-cuffs sold for $20. Jojo followed this up with the straitjacket, which went for $75. Bidding was brisk. As Jojo sold the articles from the table, some people left and others arrived to take their place. Latchmer was struck by how the people were all different ages, dressed differently, and were clearly from all different social classes and backgrounds. Near the door was a policeman but maybe it was just somebody dressed up to look like a policeman. A man on the other side of Latchmer bought a black rubber bikini. He was an ordinary looking fellow who resembled his parents' plumber in Rochester.

"It's not for me," he told Latchmer. "It's a present."

Dallas leaned over and patted the man on the leg. "If you've got it, flaunt it," she said.

Jojo sold the diapers and some branding irons and some rabbit fur mittens. He sold a set of a dozen vibrators each in the shape of a famous writer: Hemingway, Rimbaud, Norman Mailer. He sold a box of edible underwear made from spun sugar and various salves and creams guaranteed to alter the length of one's orgasm. The last item on the table was Jasper's leash. He held it up.

"My friends," he asked, "do you have trouble with straying? Does your dear one wander into the street? Or perhaps you'd like to walk your doggie in the privacy of your home. . . ."

Although the bidding started at only a dollar, it quickly increased until a man in a black leather suit nailed down the leash for twenty-five bucks. As soon as he got it, he attached the clasp to the gold earring of the man seated beside him and led him from the auditorium. Jojo caught Latchmer's eye and winked again. Then he turned to the next table as Sissy swept away the red cloth. Beneath the table was a cage of four geese. As soon as they were lit up by the spotlights, they began honking and sticking their long necks between the bars of their cage. There was an excited muttering from the audience. On top of the table were various other creatures. From where he sat, Latchmer could make out a cage of white mice, a bowl of goldfish, and a turtle. Jojo picked up what appeared to be a bucket of dirt and lifted it over his head.

"On this table, ladies and gentlemen, we have those small residents of God's kingdom that can give that last soupçon of pleasure to an almost perfect night. Yes, my friends, what I have here is the ultimate in the full body massage. Don't be deceived, don't turn away your heads. This is no ordinary bucket of night crawlers. What I'm offering is a million magic fingers to soothe away the night fears, the pain, the harsh words, to make you ready for tomorrow with all the interest and curiosity needed for a healthy life of experimentation."

The night crawlers started at $10 and finally went for $25. The mice went for $10, the turtle for $15. A twelve-foot king snake went for $75. Jojo pulled out the cage of geese. Bidding was eager and the first one went for $60.

Dallas was scornful. "I was into geese last year. Their main problem is that they bite. I mean, I don't mind being bitten when I want, but I didn't like being bitten when they wanted and they wanted to bite all the time. Rude, noisy birds."

Everyone was curious about what was under the tall structure surrounded by green curtains. Jojo seemed to be saving it for last. Latchmer kept looking around for Jean-Claude. Part of him hoped that Jean-Claude would arrive, part hoped never to see him again. When Jojo finished selling the animals, the auditorium was still full even though the only thing left was whatever was hidden by the green curtains. Sissy kept peeking behind it, then looking back at the audience and rolling her eyes.

Dallas tugged at Latchmer's sleeve. "Aren't you excited?" she asked.

Jojo raised his hands, signaling for silence. His cigarette had gone out, but he still held the black holder between his teeth.

"Ladies and gentlemen," he said, "I have a little extra treat tonight, a little taste of the past, a little sign that what is gone need not be forgotten. Those of you who like cold cuts, who like your meat rare, who like that brisk winter feeling of cold flesh, well, one of you will thank me this morning. One of you will look back on this morning as the time you discovered that Charon's

raft traveled a two-way street, the time you put aside
your fear of the unknown and took your first step across
the great divide only to discover that you need not aban-
don all hope or fear that the great metal door will slam
and lock behind you. No, ladies and gentlemen, what I
have behind this curtain can be your first taste of the
resurrection that awaits you if you take the wise step of
putting a special paragraph in your last will and testa-
ment. I am speaking of course about that full life of sexual
experimentation that lies beyond the grave. But no more
words, ladies and gentlemen, no more prevaricating. Here
at last is the most special, the most important, and most
valuable of all the items I have shown you this evening.
My friends, let me introduce you to Jasper!"

Jojo pulled back the green curtains. Behind them was
a boxlike structure made of chrome-plated tubes. Jasper
appeared to be standing within it but actually he was
supported by several belts. Both his head and tail were
held up by wires. His eyes had been propped open and
he looked eager and engaging. His head was tilted to one
side as if he were listening to something far away. The
tail appeared to be wagging. He had been carefully
brushed and looked wonderful. A blue bow had been
tied around his neck and he even appeared to be wearing
a trace of lipstick.

"Isn't this the nicest little dead red dog you've ever
seen?" asked Jojo. "Who'll start the bidding at fifty dollars?"

But the audience wasn't pleased. There was a general
groaning. "For cryin' out loud, Jojo," said a man in the
third row, "we just did a whole mess of dead dogs in
February. We're sick to death of dead dogs."

"This isn't your run-of-the-mill dead dog," said Jojo,
laying his hand on Jasper's head. "This dog had a full
life, was surrounded by love and attention, and is still
practically warm. Besides, look at his color, where've you

ever seen a nice red dog like this one? Okay, who'll start us out at forty."

Dallas leaned over toward Latchmer. "The only trouble with dead dogs," she said, "is that once you've had one dead dog, you've had them all."

People were leaving. Latchmer found himself feeling sorry for Jasper. After a lifetime of love, Jasper would have found this lack of interest humiliating. The man who had bought the rubber bikini shook his head and stood up to go.

"One time they had a live seal," he told Latchmer. "That was really something. It could balance all sorts of stuff on its nose. But dead dogs, who needs 'em?"

"My good friends," said Jojo, extending his arms to the audience and lowering his voice so it sounded confiding and intimate, "would I introduce you to another dead dog if there was nothing special about this one? Whoever takes this dog for thirty dollars, gets to use the frame entirely free. Makes it a lot easier. No struggling, no wrestling holds."

More people left. Jojo's smile was as bright as ever, but there seemed something strained about him, something unhappy. His black bowtie was crooked and his white shirt front bulged out above his cummerbund. Latchmer sensed his disappointment.

"What about dead sheep?" someone shouted.

People laughed. Jojo refused to acknowledge the heckler. He stood with his hand still on Jasper's head.

A young man in the front row jumped to his feet. "I'll bid two dollars," he said. He was very thin and wore white pants and a white shirt. Around his waist instead of a belt was a red scarf. He seemed excited and turned to the man sitting beside him. "You know, I've never fucked a dog for two dollars before. It'd be a first." The two men began whispering and giggling.

Jojo took out a cigarette and put it in the black holder.

"Two dollars is what I'm bid," he said. "Do I hear four, four?" He lit the cigarette and blew a series of smoke rings out into the audience. The young man with the red scarf around his waist could hardly contain his excitement. He kept bouncing on the balls of his feet. "Two dollars," said Jojo. "This is a mighty nice dog that's going for that price. Do I hear three? No? All right, two dollars going once, two dollars going twice—"

"Wait!" said Latchmer, jumping to his feet.

"What's wrong," said Jojo.

"I don't want to sell Jasper for two dollars." He had stood up without thinking, and now he wasn't sure what to say.

"Why not?"

"It seems disrespectful."

"What about ten dollars," asked Jojo, "would you accept ten?"

"Maybe."

"What's the difference between two and ten?"

Latchmer felt everyone staring at him. "It doesn't seem fair to Jasper to sell him for two dollars. I mean, he was a good dog. Even his collar went for four. A dog should be worth more than his collar, even if he's dead."

The young man with the red scarf around his waist clapped his hands several times to get their attention. "I'm not going to pay ten dollars for that old has-been," he said. "Two dollars, yes, it would've been a treat. But ten dollars, that's ridiculous, I can get nice living dogs for ten dollars."

Jojo dropped his cigarette on the floor and stepped on it. Then he drew the green curtains back around Jasper, hiding him from view. "There you have it, ladies and gentlemen, once again scruples raise their ugly head." A telephone began to ring backstage and Sissy went to answer it. "This is what happens in an overpermissive society," Jojo continued. "This is what happens when the will of the few is allowed to trample and beat down the will of the many; when scruples, conscience, and second thoughts are allowed to intrude themselves into the affairs of adults above the age of consent. No, my friends, it seems that no nice red dog will be sold here tonight."

Sissy came back carrying a white telephone. "It's for you," she said. Jojo took the phone and began talking into it with his back to the audience.

Dallas tapped Latchmer on the knee. "I admire a man with scruples," she said, "but if that boy was silly enough to buy Jasper for two dollars, then you should have done it. After all, you could have gotten him back later. Two dollars here, two dollars there. It adds up."

"The dog came from a good family," said Latchmer. "He was surrounded with love for his entire life. He deserves better treatment."

"You're a sentimentalist," said Dallas. "I think that's cute."

Jojo hung up the phone and gave it back to Sissy. He was grinning and all trace of disappointment was gone. "Ladies and gentlemen, before you go I believe I have an extra treat for you this morning. Something not for your bodies but for your hearts and minds. Mr. Latchmer, will you step up here, please?"

Latchmer felt suspicious. "What for?"

Jojo shook a finger at him. "Don't be modest. Here at Jojo's every talent is appreciated."

"I don't have any talents," said Latchmer. "I'm just a normal sort of person."

"Will you come up here?" repeated Jojo, still smiling.

"Oh, go on," said Dallas, "you'll be great."

Latchmer stood up and walked to the stage. Part of him had no idea what Jojo wanted, but another part knew that he would end up telling another story. People were sitting down again. Latchmer climbed the steps until he stood beside Jojo. It was strange being higher than everyone else.

"I have just spoken to a close friend of Mr. Latchmer's," said Jojo, "and he was kind enough to tell me that the man now standing beside me is a tremendous storyteller."

"That's not true," said Latchmer. "I'm terrible at it." But maybe it wasn't the stories which were awful, maybe he just told them to the wrong people. For instance, if he had told Mama-san the story of the dog baked in the loaf of bread, maybe she would have liked it. And this group, they'd probably like the story about the little dogs fucking. But he wouldn't tell that story, he'd tell another, and they would hate it. Not that it was his fault. He just opened his mouth and the story took over. If anyone was blamed, it should be the story itself.

"Protests will do no good," said Jojo, patting Latchmer's shoulder. "A story we want and a story we shall have."

"No, really," said Latchmer, "my stories get me in a lot of hot water. People find them offensive."

"At Jojo's *offensive* is a word without meaning." Jojo then turned to the audience. "Normally, since this is auction time, I'd auction off Mr. Latchmer's story to the highest bidder, but since you found poor Jasper so disappointing, I'll give you the story for free. What do you say? Do you want a story this morning?"

There was a smattering of applause. Latchmer felt he had no choice. In fact, part of him was eager. People were nodding and smiling at him. Dallas gave a little wave. "What kind of story?" he asked.

"Jaycee said it had to be a dog story."

Latchmer wondered why Jean-Claude would call up and insist he tell a story. "That's the kind of story that gets me into trouble. Where is he, anyway?"

"At the police station, but he said he'd be here by six-thirty. Are you all set?" He gave Latchmer a little pat on the back. "It'll be the hit of the evening." Jojo and Sissy descended the steps and sat down beside Dallas.

Latchmer looked out at the crowd of people. He had never felt at ease speaking in public and kept shifting his weight from one foot to the other. He was sorry that Jasper was covered up, because he had come to take comfort in his company. Still, he could feel his presence behind the curtain, only a few feet away. He wondered if Jean-Claude would really get out of the police station and if it mattered. He wondered what Jean-Claude had meant by calling him a river. Was he really so feckless and unable to take charge of his life? Even this story was going to control him; he knew he had only to speak the first sentence and the rest would take over his brain.

"There was a young man," said Latchmer. "He was just eighteen and a freshman in college. He had gone away to school to the other side of the country. He felt lonely being so far from home, but his parents had saved all their money to help him so he knew he couldn't complain. He had an uncle and aunt in a town about fifty miles from the college and around the beginning of October the uncle died unexpectedly. The young man's family couldn't afford to come all the way for the funeral so the young man went as the family's representative, even though he had some big tests coming up and had only met this uncle, Uncle Jack, once about seven years before when his uncle and his family came through on a camping trip.

"Well, the young man took a bus to his aunt's house and arrived the day before the funeral. The coffin was in the living room and many people came to pay their respects. Uncle Jack had been the town pharmacist and had a million friends. He also had a big family with seven kids and they were all pretty much broken up. Uncle Jack had only been in his fifties so his death was a surprise to everyone.

"Uncle Jack and Aunt Minnie had had a dog, a little Pekinese by the name of Woofie, and along with the whole family Woofie also seemed upset and sat in the living room just beneath the coffin and whimpered quietly or barked if anyone got too close to his master. And every time one of the cousins started to remove Woofie, someone would say, No, let him stay, he's got his grief too. The uncle was a handsome man and looked very distinguished in his coffin and some people thought he looked so good that they took snapshots just so they could remember him.

"The funeral was to be held the next morning. The young man had a bedroom on the first floor and didn't sleep very well. Around seven, he got up and dressed in his dark blue suit. Although he was hungry, it was too early to bother anyone about breakfast and so he went into the living room because he remembered there had been some little bowls of green mints and he hoped they would take the edge off his hunger. He tried not to look at his Uncle Jack because to tell the truth he had never seen a dead body before and it made him nervous to have his uncle just lying there in plain sight. He grabbed a handful of mints and started to leave. Soon, he knew, the men from the funeral home would come to close the coffin and take it to the church. As he walked toward the door, he glanced back at his Uncle Jack and immediately saw there was something dreadfully wrong with his face and that instead of lying straight in his coffin, he was all crooked as if someone had been wrestling with him. Feeling a little scared, the young man walked to the coffin. From outside, he heard the hearse pull up to the front of the house but he barely paid any attention because what he saw was so awful.

"It seemed that little Woofie had gotten inside the coffin, had jumped up on a chair, then a table, and then onto his Uncle Jack. And he had chewed Uncle Jack. He had chewed off most of Uncle Jack's nose and part of his left ear. Then he had torn his jacket and tie as if the dog had been playing a kind of tug of war. The face looked terrible without a nose and one of Uncle Jack's eyes had come open. It was a small town and the young man knew that something like this would be talked about by everybody. Just then he heard footsteps on the porch and the ring of the doorbell. Then he heard one of his cousins running downstairs to open the door. The young man knew he couldn't let anyone see Uncle Jack like this, and just as the men from the funeral home entered the living room with two of his cousins, the young man leaned forward, kissed Uncle Jack on the forehead, and closed the lid of the coffin. Then he turned to address his cousins, but he could hardly speak because of what he had just seen. He'd made a hideous mistake and now could do nothing but hide it. 'My father,' he said to his cousins, 'asked that I be the last one to say goodbye to Uncle Jack and so I have closed the coffin. I hope you don't mind.'

"The young man's voice was trembling so badly and he was so obviously upset that his cousins said of course they didn't mind, and the men from the funeral home hurried to screw down the lid. But what upset the young man was not this last farewell or any pledge to his parents, it was not that his uncle's nose had been chewed from his face or that his clothes were twisted and torn. Rather, he was upset because just as he closed the lid, he had seen that little Woofie was still inside the coffin, sleeping peacefully beneath the knees of his old master. He was upset because there was no chance to drag him out and now little Woofie would have to stay with Uncle Jack forever.

"At the church the young man sat in the front row

next to Aunt Minnie. When little Woofie began to bark, nobody realized it was coming from inside the coffin. It sounded muted and far away. 'Little Woofie loved him so much,' said Aunt Millie. The young man thought of how his Uncle Jack had looked without his nose and he tried to cough or clear his throat whenever the dog began to bark, and so throughout the service he kept coughing until everyone was looking at him and at last one of the ushers brought him a glass of water.

"At the cemetery little Woofie's bark seemed more distant. He was running out of air. Aunt Minnie looked to the left and right, searching for her dog. She even sent her children to hunt for him throughout the cemetery so that while the minister was saying a last few words one could hear the children calling, 'Little Woofie, Little Woofie!' The coffin was lowered into the ground and each of the mourners filed by and tossed in a handful of dirt. When it came to be the young man's turn, the barking was louder and clearly rose from the grave itself. But either nobody heard or it was just too fantastic because nobody said, 'There's something funny going on here,' or 'Hey, there's a dog in that coffin!'

"After the funeral the young man returned to his aunt's house where a great search was in progress. Little Woofie was missing and his aunt had gone to bed saying she wouldn't get up until little Woofie was found. The state police had been called and the sheriff's department as well. The young man said he'd join the search, but instead he went and packed his bag. Then, when everyone was spread across town looking for little Woofie, he snuck out of the house and hitchhiked back to the college.

"During the months that followed, he occasionally saw reward posters for Woofie. At first the reward was $50, but then it kept getting higher and higher until it reached $5,000. The young man wondered if there was some way to get the money because he was poor, but he didn't see how he could get it without people discovering that little Woofie had chewed off Uncle Jack's face, and so he said nothing. Nor did he ever go back to visit Aunt Minnie and her family. From his parents he learned that Aunt Minnie remained a semi-invalid, rarely leaving her bed until finally she needed constant nursing care. Nor did Uncle Jack's children do well because two dropped out of school and another got pregnant, even though she was only twelve, and another broke his back in a motorcycle accident."

Latchmer stopped and looked up at the audience. About fifty people were still in the auditorium. Many were getting to their feet, putting on their coats or searching for a hat or a lost glove. No one would look at him. Dallas sat in the front row staring down at her white nursing shoes. Slowly Jojo stood up and climbed the steps to the stage.

"Why did you tell that story?" he asked.

"I don't know," said Latchmer. "It seemed interesting."

Jojo looked at Latchmer with a mixture of disgust and sadness. "Ever since I opened this place, I've tried to create the kind of atmosphere that would let people forget their inhibitions, their shortcomings; I tried to create a place where their craziest dreams might come true. Isn't that the best definition of a Home? I know it's my definition, and I've worked hard to make it happen. Then you come along. I don't care about your dog. I mean, dead dogs have a lot of potential and I was only too happy to help out. But your story's another matter. It made people anxious. It made them forget they were at Jojo's. The moment I saw what you were doing, I asked myself what sort of pervert would come into a person's home and take a dump on the living room rug. Because that's what you did, you know, you just shat on the floor."

"I just thought it was a funny story," said Latchmer. "The dog barking inside the coffin, I mean, it seemed amusing." Jojo shook his head. "Jaycee wanted me to keep you here. He wanted to make sure you'd be here when he arrived, but I want you to go. I just want you to take your dog and get out."

"What about the money from the leash?" asked Latchmer.

Jojo handed him twenty dollars. Only a few people were left in the auditorium. Dallas was still sitting in the front row. She was weeping and Sissy was comforting her. Jojo signaled to the man with the Swiss army knife in his ear. "Let's put this dog back in his bag and get this creep out of here."

They lifted Jasper out of the boxlike structure and slid him into the plastic bag. It was getting ragged and Latchmer thought it would soon have to be replaced. Jasper was pretty stiff and they had trouble bending his legs, which made him seem unfriendly. Latchmer stood to one side, thinking about the difficulties of language and how hard it was to be understood. Had he really meant to insult these people? To him it seemed like a pretty good story. How odd that it partly resembled what he remembered of his grandfather's funeral, and he wondered if that was significant.

The man with the Swiss army knife in his ear picked up the bag and led the way out of the auditorium. Latchmer hurried after him. He glanced back at Jojo and Dallas, but they pretended not to see him. At the front door the man returned the bag to Latchmer. Then he pulled open the door and jabbed his thumb toward the street. The little Swiss army knife swung back and forth.

"I'm sorry," said Latchmer.

The man refused to meet his eye. "You ruined our evening," he said.

Latchmer stepped through the doorway and the man gave him a shove, sending him stumbling onto the sidewalk. It was now daylight. The sky was bright pink and the sun was cresting the tops of the nearby warehouses.

Latchmer hoisted the bag over his shoulder and wondered if he should wait for Jean-Claude. A Checker cab drew up beside him and a pleasant-looking black man rolled down the window. "Need a cab?" he asked.

"Sure," said Latchmer, opening the back door.

CHAPTER SIX

The cab was very comfortable. The heater was on and warm air blew into the back seat. The driver—whose hack license identified him as Billy Specials—had decorated the dashboard with pictures of his wife and four kids, as well as glittering 3-D reflecting stickers saying, "Peace," "God is Love," and "Coke Is Where It's At." There was a smell of disinfectant, so Latchmer knew the cab was clean.

"Where to?" asked Billy Specials, looking at Latchmer in the rearview mirror. His eyes twinkled with friendly good nature.

"I don't know," said Latchmer. "What would you do if you had a dead dog?"

"Shit, I'd bury it," said Billy Specials. "No question at all, I'd stick it right in the ground."

Latchmer was struck by the novelty of the thought. "Where would you take it?" he asked.

"I'd take it to where there's the most ground."

"You mean Central Park?"

"Sure, why not? They got lots of dirt there."

"You know where I can buy a shovel?"

"There's an all-night hardware store over on Canal Street."

"Let's go there first," said Latchmer. He leaned back

and shut his eyes as the yellow Checker made a U-turn. It was nice to be in a real taxi. There was lots of room in the backseat and he could stretch his legs.

"You look like you've had a hard night," said Billy Specials.

"I guess I just never knew how hard it was to get rid of a dog in New York City."

"You mean a dead one?"

"Sure."

"That's no problem," said Billy Specials. "There's a taxidermy school out in Brooklyn. They're always looking for dead animals. 'Nothin's too big or too small,' that's their motto. And they got a night drop as well. You want me to whiz you over there? It's a great way to bury your pet and then always have him with you."

It seemed to Latchmer like a fine idea. He tried to calculate the surprise of Sarah and her mother when he returned with Jasper stuffed. However, it was now past six in the morning. It had been a long night and Latchmer had had his share of disappointments. At the moment all he wanted was to see Jasper into the ground. "Maybe my next pet," he said. "This one I think I'll just bury."

The shovel at the all-night hardware was expensive and took every penny of the twenty dollars that Latchmer had gotten from Jojo for the leash. The only other customers were two young men in leather suits buying a pair of vise grips. The store smelled of oil and cold metal. A clerk with an ill-fitting blond hairpiece was making a four-story card house, which collapsed as Latchmer opened the door to leave.

Jasper had been left in the taxi with Billy Specials. When Latchmer came back with the shovel, Billy Specials said, "That's a nice-looking red dog. Too bad he's dead."

"Death puts a crimp in one's life all right," said Latchmer.

"You sure you don't want to try the taxidermy school? They could make this dog as right as rain."

"No," said Latchmer, "I think Central Park's the best bet. Take me up near the Tavern on the Green. Maybe I can bury Jasper in the Sheep Meadow. He'd like that."

"You're the boss," said Billy Specials, heading uptown.

Latchmer linked his fingers behind his head and leaned back in the seat. For a moment, he worried that Jean-Claude might find out he was trying to bury Jasper and become angry. Maybe Latchmer would have waited if Billy Specials hadn't arrived. It was almost as if the appearance of a friendly cab had made up his mind for him. If Jean-Claude became angry at anyone, then it should be at Billy Specials.

As it was, Jean-Claude was slowly fading into the past. He was becoming as far away as Sarah and her mother, as far away as all the people he had known in Rochester, as far away as his parents, his childhood, even the funeral of his grandfather. Just as Latchmer had seen his grandfather into the ground, so he would see Jasper into the ground. He began to think of Miss Mitchell as he had last seen her outside the church—tall, white-haired, and full of grief as she had stared after the limousine carrying him to the cemetery. Was that the last time he had seen her? At first he thought it was, then he remembered she had gone to the cemetery as well.

His grandfather had been buried in a family plot. Latchmer's great-grandparents, great-uncles and -aunts, even his great-great-grandparents were also buried there. All had little rectangular stones while up at the front, like a teacher at the front of a class, stood a huge stone angel with a beautiful hawklike face and its wings folded around it like a cape.

Over a hundred people had come to the service in the cemetery. The day was intensely blue and the tall oaks were full of jays. The casket rested on a pair of canvas straps over the grave. Latchmer and his grandmother stood next to it, while the minister, red-eyed and embarrassed, waited for everyone to arrive. His grandmother had seemed restless. She kept shrugging, jerking around, muttering to herself. Her black hat kept slipping down over one eye, which made her seem mad and piratical. Latchmer was certain she felt the presence of Miss Mitchell's silver ring in his grandfather's vest pocket only a few feet away. He imagined it burning her mind like a hot spark can burn a piece of fabric.

When the crowd had settled itself next to the grave and the minister began his last words of farewell, his grandmother abruptly looked up and peered around her. Latchmer thought she might have heard a baby crying. His grandmother hated babies. Then he too looked and there at the edge of the crowd was Miss Mitchell, staring at his grandfather's casket and apparently unaware of everything else. Her height and the white scarf around her neck made her stand out from the rest of the mourners. Latchmer moved a little to his left to block his grandmother's view. His only hope was that the minister might finish quickly so they could go home. But the minister was attempting to make up for the display of sarcasm he had shown in the church. He went on at length about his grandfather's goodness, how well he had treated the poor, the unfortunate, and the rejected, how he had once even bandaged the paw of the minister's own cocker spaniel.

Then, as luck would have it, his grandmother realized that Latchmer purposefully was blocking her view and she pushed him aside. There was Miss Mitchell. "I see her," shouted his grandmother, "I see the shameless creature herself!"

Latchmer made a grab for her arm, but she dodged away and began to trot briskly toward where Miss Mitchell was standing. The crowd was made up mostly of townspeople. Latchmer recognized the barber, the high school principal, and Mr. Green from Green's Newsstand where Latchmer bought his "Tales from the Crypt" comic books. No one had any doubt as to what was happening, but instead of stopping his grandmother, people stood aside as if wanting to see the two old women wrestle on the ground. Mr. Green was even smiling, and the bald-headed barber had an eager look.

Latchmer sprinted after his grandmother. Looking ahead, he tried to locate Miss Mitchell, but didn't see her. The minister had broken off his story about his poor cocker spaniel and signaled to some workers to lower the casket. Latchmer glanced around for his father but couldn't spot him. Most of the crowd had turned away from the minister and was staring after Latchmer's grandmother, who was hurrying into the open cemetery shouting, "Bitch, bitch!" There was no sign of Miss Mitchell.

His grandmother disappeared around the end of a tall hedge. Latchmer could hear her still shouting. Looking back, he saw that people were beginning to leave. He wondered what he should do and stopped near a large concrete crypt.

"Michael," said a voice.

Turning, he saw Miss Mitchell leaning against the wall of the crypt. Near her feet was a mound of dead flowers. There were tears in her eyes and she wiped them away with a white handkerchief.

Latchmer turned, then turned back again, as if he had looked and seen nothing, as if there was nothing there but wall. The white scarf around her neck was fluttering in the breeze. She said his name a second time but he ignored it. For a moment he tried to stand very still as if he just might disappear into the ground, might sink down to China. About a hundred yards across the cemetery, he saw his grandmother rounding the far side of the tall hedge. She ran by taking very small steps so that she seemed to be running on tiptoe. It made her look frail and foolish.

Miss Mitchell took another step toward Latchmer. "Michael," she said again.

Without looking at Miss Mitchell, Latchmer turned and ran after his grandmother. He still heard her shouting "Bitch" and "Whore" but so far away that it was like a distant barking. She ran zig-zagging among the tombstones, pausing to look behind a tree or a crypt, then hurrying off again. She had lost her hat and had only one shoe. At last Latchmer had trapped her in a fenced-in corner of the graveyard. Her eyes were shiny with anger.

"Come on back, grandmother," he said.

"Round-heeled slut," she answered.

"There's nobody here. Come on back. We're going to have lunch soon. Don't you want lunch?"

"Red bitch!"

"She's gone, grandmother. Let's just go home." Latchmer was depressed that no one had come to help him, that he was stuck with his grandmother on the far side of the cemetery. He could see some cars driving away. "Aren't you hungry, grandmother? Everybody brought pies. You know you like pie. Don't you want fresh strawberry pie? Let's go home, grandmother."

After about fifteen minutes, he persuaded her to let him walk her back across the graveyard. They found her shoe but not her hat. She sat on a tombstone and let Latchmer put the shoe on her foot. The toe and heel of her stocking were torn and he tucked them in as best he could. She wouldn't speak or even look at him, but as they walked she leaned a little on his shoulder. Now and then she stopped to peer behind a tree. There was no sign of Miss Mitchell. When they neared his grandfather's grave, Latchmer saw his father. He was a portly, balding man who walked with a cane. He was angry with Latchmer. Where had they been? Didn't they know that everyone was looking for them? Neither Latchmer nor his grandmother said anything. His father said he'd give them a ride back to the house but Latchmer wanted to walk. He felt like being by himself for a bit.

After they had left, Latchmer wandered over to his grandfather's grave. The dirt had been filled in. Latchmer picked up a handful and broke it apart with his fingers, letting it fall back to the ground. It was so soft that Latchmer thought he could probably dig it up with his bare hands, dig into it like a dog, clear it away from his grandfather's casket, then get some people to help him and they could lift the casket onto the ground. He could take out his grandfather and stretch him out on the grass. He would put his head in his lap and try to wake him. Perhaps he could sing to him, perhaps he would tell stories.

But most likely his grandfather would be furious. "Why have you betrayed Miss Mitchell?" he would say. "I asked you to look out for her." Latchmer felt himself misunderstood. He had tried to do the best for everyone. He wished his grandfather was in the cherry-wood coffin he had made for himself. He wished he could come downstairs the next morning and find his grandfather in the kitchen. He would be standing at the sink peeling the skin from a peach, peeling it in one long strand so it hung down like a thin necktie. His grandfather would hold it up for Latchmer to see, then he would slice the peach onto Latchmer's Shredded Ralston. Latchmer would take the bowl and add cream and a little sugar. Then he and his grandfather would eat, not talking much, maybe saying something about the weather or how loudly the birds sang.

But none of that would take place. That time was over and done with, and what was the point of nice things happening if bad things came along to wipe them out?

* * *

The taxicab had been moving along very smoothly. If there were prizes given for the careful driving of a cab, then Billy Specials would be a hot contender. He looked both ways at intersections. He never went through a yellow light, much less a red one. He stayed in one lane and drove uptown quickly but not hastily. Cutting over to Columbus Circle, he continued up Central Park West. There was hardly any traffic and, had he wished, Billy Specials could have really ripped. But he chose not to. At last he turned into the parking lot at Tavern on the Green and stopped. Latchmer got out with the shovel. Then he pulled out the black plastic bag and let it plop down to the curb. He gave Billy Specials fifteen dollars and told him to keep the change.

"It's been a pleasure," said the cab driver. "I hope you find a first rate spot for the dog. A nice dog like that deserves a nice grave."

Latchmer thanked him, then picked up the bag and slung it over his shoulder. As Billy Specials drove away, Latchmer waved the shovel in farewell. Billy Specials tooted his horn. The sky was blue and lots of robins were out hunting for worms. Latchmer crossed West Drive and entered the woods just above the Sheep Meadow. A gray squirrel clucked at him from a branch. The trees were budding nicely and it seemed that spring was at last taking hold. Latchmer looked around at all this beauty but he felt so disoriented that he could hardly enjoy it. Cheer up, he told himself, once Jasper is buried, everything will be okay. He felt that Jasper and Miss Mitchell were somehow linked, and his big hope was that once Jasper was underground, then he could stop this unpleasant brooding and return to the eternal present of his normal life.

Latchmer walked along the border of the Meadow until he could hear no more sounds from the city. Then he found an open spot about ten feet from the path and protected from sight by a few bushes. He put Jasper down on the grass, took off his brown corduroy jacket, and spat on his hands. Above the trees he saw the skyscrapers ranged along Central Park South starting with the Plaza Hotel. The ground was soft. Latchmer liked digging; it seemed like good exercise. He decided to give Jasper a nice big hole with lots of room to stretch out. Soon he began to feel warm but not uncomfortable.

When the hole was three feet deep and three feet across, Latchmer began to think he had dug enough. He had been at it for thirty minutes and had made a substantial mound of black dirt, which, when he stood in the hole, he couldn't see over. He was developing a blister on his palm. It would be a shame to pull a muscle. Still, he thought he owed it to Jasper to go another foot. He paused to take off his vest and roll up the sleeves of his shirt. He had begun to sweat and dark half moons had formed on the fabric beneath his arms.

It was just past seven by the time he finished. He looked for some green leaves with which to line the bottom but could find only buds. Instead, he gathered some dandelions and a few small blue flowers and tossed them into the hole. In front of the Tavern on the Green he had seen tulips, but he didn't feel like walking back. Carefully, Latchmer lifted the plastic bag and set it within the grave. Jasper just fit. At first he had thought of taking Jasper out of the bag but then decided that the plastic would offer protection from the elements. He looked down at the plastic and tried to think of something to say, some solemn goodbye, but all he could think of were phrases like "See ya," or "Take it easy." He also felt rather guilty. He felt bad about abandoning Jasper, as if their journey together was not yet over. But what was there left to do? Then in his mind he again saw Miss Mitchell as he had seen her standing by the wall of the crypt near the little heap of dead flowers. She appeared to be blaming him for not speaking. But couldn't she see he had been forced to help his grandmother, that it would have been wrong to let her run crazily through the cemetery? Why couldn't anyone see it from his point of view?

But best forget it. Best pile in the dirt and just walk away. Latchmer again tried to achieve a solemn moment and for a good thirty seconds he stood quietly above the grave and looked serious. Then he picked up the shovel and threw in the first shovelful of dirt. It made a splashing-rattling noise on the black plastic. Just as he was about to throw in the second shovelful, he heard a voice behind him.

"Hey, Bowser, guess what we found. Somebody's burying a baby."

Latchmer turned to see two New York City patrolmen pushing through the bushes. One was holding a gun.

"Hands up, buddy. Drop the shovel."

Latchmer tossed the shovel onto the mound of dirt. "It's not a baby," he said. "It's my dog." He felt oddly relieved.

"Sure, sure, mister. Take the bag out of the hole and do it pretty slow."

The patrolman named Bowser was a middle-aged man whose uniform looked too tight for him. He seemed tired and kept sighing. The other patrolman was young, blond, and ready. He was the one with the revolver and he seemed eager for Latchmer to make a mistake so he could put a little hole in him.

Latchmer bent down and lifted Jasper out of the grave. A shower of dirt slid off the black plastic. He put Jasper on the ground, then pulled back the top of the bag so they could see Jasper's head.

"Hey," said the young cop, "it's a dog. Look at that red dog, Bowser."

"Oldest trick in the book," said Bowser, "you don't

want anyone to know you're burying a baby so you bury it inside a dog first, just like Jonah and the whale. Take the dog outta the bag, buster, so we can see the baby."

Latchmer took Jasper out of the bag, then picked him up from behind, wrapping his arms around his chest. The dog was stiff and his four legs stuck straight out. The plastic bag was clearly empty.

"Where's the baby, Bowser?" asked the young cop.

"Shut up," said Bowser. He walked over to Jasper and began prodding him. "Sometimes they sew the dog up again."

"This is all dog," said Latchmer.

"Shut up,"said Bowser. His face was so round that it could have been drawn with a compass. A thick black curl protruded from his cap and seemed stuck to the center of his forehead.

"You kill this dog?" asked the young cop.

"No," said Latchmer, "he had an attack. He'd been eating too many anchovies." He set Jasper back down on the ground.

"Are there any marks on its body?" asked the young cop.

Bowser poked at the dog with his foot. "Maybe he strangled it or even poisoned it."

"You poison that dog?" asked the young cop.

"He died a natural death," said Latchmer. He was getting chilled and again put on his vest and jacket.

"It looks like a pretty old dog," said Bowser. "I gotta pretty old dog at home and he looks a lot like this dog 'cept my dog's not red. What're you doing digging this hole?" he asked Latchmer.

"I was burying the dog."

"How come?"

"He was dead. I don't know, I'm from Rochester. In Rochester when we have a dead dog, we bury it."

"I gotta aunt in Rochester," said the young cop. He

put his revolver back in its holster, then fished a cigarette out of his breast pocket and lit it with a Zippo lighter.

"We can't let you bury this dog in the park, mister," said Bowser. "There're city services for stuff like that. We're gonna have to slap your ass in jail."

"How come?" asked Latchmer. He stared down at Jasper. The dog looked happy and peaceful in the new grass.

"You know what would happen if we let you bury this dog in the park?" asked Bowser. "Why, then everybody'd be trying to bury their dogs in the park. You know how many dogs there are in New York City? Hundreds of thousands. You know what would happen to the park if we let all those dogs get buried here? It'd fuck up the park, that's what. How could little kids roller skate and play with their hoops if there was dead dogs all over the place? Shit, we'd be up to our necks in dead dogs."

"Who has to know?" said Latchmer. "I mean, I already got the hole. I can just put the dog back in the hole, cover it up and nobody will know anything about it."

"But we'll know," said the young cop. "I mean, it's even against the law to dig a *hole* in this park. That dirt is New York City property. Tax dollars have paid for that dirt, my tax dollars as well as your tax dollars. And now you want to stick a dead dog in it? I hope you got yourself a good lawyer 'cause you're going to need it."

"If you arrest me," asked Latchmer, "then what's going to happen to the dog?"

"We'll keep him in the morgue till you get out," said the young cop. "He'll be fresh as a daisy."

"Nah," said Bowser, "we won't arrest you as long as you give me the shovel."

"The shovel?" asked Latchmer.

"What do you want a shovel for?" asked the young cop.

"It's spring," said Bowser. "The flowers are coming

up and I gotta little garden. I gotta hoe and a rake and a trowel, but I don't have a shovel. Just give me the shovel and I'll see to it you stay outta jail."

"What about the dog?" asked Latchmer. "Can I bury the dog?"

"No way," said Bowser, "that'd be breaking the law. You just give me the shovel, pick up the dog, and get out of the park, and we'll let bygones be bygones."

"What if I don't want to give up the shovel?" said Latchmer. "It's a brand-new shovel."

"Sure," said Bowser, "you think I'd want an old shovel? If you don't give me the shovel, then you'll go to jail. Shit, you might even get shot resisting arrest, like shot in the leg, you know, or maybe a little crease in the fat part of your belly."

"Here's the shovel," said Latchmer.

"Fill up the hole first," said Bowser. "We can't leave a hole like that lying around. Just be careful not to scratch up my shovel."

Latchmer began shoveling the dirt back into the hole. There seemed more of it somehow. The two cops stood by and watched, smoking cigarettes and discussing how the Yankees had botched spring training. Jasper's eyes were open and Latchmer kept thinking that the dog was staring at him. It was as if Jasper wanted him to do something. As Latchmer shoveled the dirt back into the hole, he developed two more blisters and pulled a muscle in the small of his back. When the hole was full, he flattened the dirt down on top with the back of the shovel.

"What about the dog?" asked Latchmer, breathing heavily.

"Put him back in the bag and get him outta here," said the young cop. "You're not even supposed to be in the park with a dog unless it's on a leash."

"But he's dead," said Latchmer.

"I don't care. That's the law. All dogs must be on

leashes. Doesn't say whether they have to be alive or not. You gotta gripe, take it to the mayor."

Latchmer put Jasper back in the black plastic bag. He was so stiff that he tore the plastic and one red paw stuck out the side like the branch of a small tree. "But what can I do with him?" asked Latchmer.

"You'll have to keep him till Monday, then call the Pound," said Bowser.

"You know," said the young cop, "there's a taxidermy school over in Brooklyn that'd give good money for that dog."

"I don't want to sell him," said Latchmer. "He was my pet."

"My sentiments exactly," said Bowser. "He may be dead, but he still deserves respect."

Latchmer hoisted the bag over his shoulder and began to push his way through the bushes to the path.

"Wait a second," said Bowser, "we'll walk you down to our cruiser. Here, you carry the shovel."

Latchmer took the shovel. The two cops walked along on either side of him. Bowser began whistling "Home on the Range."

"You're lucky some pervert didn't find you instead of us," said the young cop. "This park can be real trouble."

"I guess I'm fortunate you fellows happened along," said Latchmer. It was hard to hold the bag with his blistered hand, and he kept having to stop and shift its weight. The shovel was a nuisance.

"You know," said the young cop, "I heard a joke yesterday about a dog. It seems there was this guy who wanted to move a grand piano up to his fifth floor apartment so he asked a buddy to help him. The piano was supposed to be delivered at three and the buddy said he'd be there. Well, the buddy was late by two hours but when he got there, the grand piano was already up on the fifth floor. 'Shit,' said the buddy, 'how'd you get the piano up the stairs?' 'Well,' said the guy, 'I had my dog drag it up,' and he pointed to a tiny little dog lying under the piano. 'Shit,' said the buddy, 'you mean that little dog dragged that piano up here by himself?' 'No,' said the guy, 'not all by himself. I had to use the whip.'"

Bowser grunted. Latchmer remained silent. They walked about ten more feet without anybody saying anything. Way off to the other side of the Sheep Meadow, Latchmer saw two men throwing a yellow Frisbee.

"That was an awful joke," said Bowser. "You want to hear a dog joke, then listen to this. There was this guy, see, and every Saturday night he goes to a whore house. Well, one Saturday night he tells the Madame, 'Hey, I'm sick of girls, don't you have something different?' And the Madame says, 'I gotta dog you can fuck for two bucks.' 'How come so cheap?' says the guy. 'Special this week,' says the Madame. So the guy fucks the dog and he's satisfied. Well, the next week the guy comes back and he says to the Madame, 'Hey, I'm sick of sex altogether, what can you do for me?' 'What about just watching,' says the Madame, 'we have a special room with a one-way sheet of glass and it costs only ten bucks.' 'Okay,' says the guy, and he goes in. Well, inside are all these guys sitting in theater seats watching a guy in the next room jack off. The guy sits down and he watches for a while, then he turns to the guy next to him and says, 'Hey, is this all there is, it's pretty dull.' 'Yeah,' says the other guy, 'you shoulda been here last week—there was a bozo fucking a dog.'"

The young cop made no response. Latchmer shifted Jasper's weight to his other hand. He started to make a laughing noise, then thought: Why bother? They walked a little way in silence. At last, Bowser reached over and gave Latchmer a poke on the arm. "If you're so critical," he said, "why don't you tell your own joke?"

"I don't want to," said Latchmer.

"Why not?" asked Bowser.

"I don't know, I just don't feel like it."

"I hate snobs like you," said the young cop.

"I can still toss you in the can," said Bowser, "shovel or no shovel."

The two cops stood facing Latchmer. They looked sullen and ready to cause trouble. "You really want a story?" he asked.

"Not any kind of story," said Bowser. "It has to be a dog story."

"And make it funny," said the young cop.

Latchmer thought of the five other stories he had told that night. Mrs. Hughes had believed it was the story about the rubber dog mess which had caused Jasper's heart attack. She hadn't directly accused him, but Latchmer knew it was true. All the stories, it seemed, had been told to the wrong people. These two cops, for instance, would probably like the story about the accidental burial of little Woofie. After all, they had interrupted Latchmer while burying a dog and so that story would seem appropriate. But Latchmer couldn't tell that story. Again, he wouldn't know what the story would be until he spoke the first sentence. It amazed him how the stories seemed connected to Jasper and also to the memories of his grandparents. It was almost as if Jasper was giving him the power, because, as he often thought, he was usually terrible at telling stories and could never think of anything.

"There was a young man," said Latchmer, "he was eighteen and trying to work his way through college. He was also very shy and it was hard for him to meet girls. Well, one weekend in November, his roommate set him up with his cousin who is not only beautiful but has the reputation for being promiscuous. The only problem is that all fall the young man has been working for an old lady who lives in a small house near the campus. He takes care of her yard and does her shopping and takes care of her dog, which is a little Yorkshire terrier with a fine bluish-gray coat that the old woman washes every day. He likes this old lady and she pays him well. She's got some kind of cancer and every so often she has to go to the next town for chemotherapy treatments. And whenever she goes, the young man has to stay in the house and take care of the dog, which means staying all night.

"Well, as bad luck would have it, the day before this young man's big date, the old lady calls him and says she needs another treatment and can he stay with the dog the next night. Because she pays him well and because she's a little eccentric, he's afraid to say that he's already busy because he might lose the job with her altogether. Instead, he figures he can take the job, then go out with the girl anyway. Not only that, but he can take her back to the old lady's house after they have dinner or go to a movie or whatever. The only trouble is the old lady has two rules. The first is that he stay in the house the entire time and not go out because the dog might get lonely and upset. And the second rule is that he can't have any visitors. The young man feels bad about breaking these rules, but his roommate's cousin is very beautiful and it's clear she likes him.

"Anyway, the young man takes the job, goes to the old lady's house, and she tells him what to feed the dog, whose name is Ralphie, then she leaves, saying she'll be back about noon the next day, which is a Saturday. That evening, the young man goes and picks up the girl and takes her to a Chinese restaurant. Afterward, they go back to the old lady's house. But right away he knows there's going to be trouble because when he opens the door he hears the telephone ringing and the dog whining. He runs to the phone and it's the old lady. 'Where have you been?' she asks. And the young man says, 'I was taking a bath.' 'A bath?' says the old lady, 'this is the fifth time I've called.' 'Well, I was in the back yard,' says the young man. 'You didn't take Ralphie outside, did you?' asks the old lady. 'Oh no,' says the young man, 'he's been right here in the house the whole time.' 'And you're sure you haven't left the house?' asks the old lady. 'Oh, no,' says the young man. 'I don't even want you to go into the back yard,' says the old lady. 'I won't do it again,' says the young man.

"Well, when she hangs up, the young man goes into the living room where his date has flicked on the TV. He sits down on the couch beside her and puts his arm around her and she snuggles up to him and then he looks around the room and says, 'Where's the dog?' 'Oh,' says his date, 'he was scratching at the door so I let him out.' Right away, the young man is out of the room like a shot. He goes tearing out of the house just in time to see Ralphie disappearing around the corner. The young man has never run so fast. But Ralphie is also pretty fast and he leads the young man through one alley after another, through back yards and trash cans and mud puddles and a small river and finally, when the young man traps the dog in the corner of a fence and picks him up, he sees that Ralphie is all muddy and has burrs in his coat and a big dollop of tar on his right ear. The young man carries the dog all the way home even though Ralphie is squirming to get loose. Finally, he approaches the house and sees his date waiting on the front porch. But when Ralphie realizes where he's being taken, he gets frantic and bites the young man, which makes the young man drop him. And again the dog takes off. The street where the old lady lives is a big busy street and Ralphie is so stupid that he immediately rushes into the traffic and before the young man can even shout, 'Stop!' a huge semi-truck rolls over Ralphie and squashes him flat.

"The young man looks down at Ralphie lying as dead

as a doornail in the middle of the street and he feels terrible. I mean, the old lady has had this dog for ten years and it's her only friend and companion and the young man had promised to guard it with his life and here he's gone and killed it. His date comes up and puts a hand on his shoulder. 'It's not so bad,' she says. 'I'm finished,' says the young man. 'No,' says the girl, 'I know a place downtown where they specialize in Yorkshire terriers and you can replace this one in the morning.' 'It won't work,' says the young man. 'It might,' says the girl, 'besides, what choice do you have?' 'You're right,' says the young man, 'I'll give it a try.' 'By the way,' says the girl, 'while you were gone the telephone rang and I answered it. It was some old woman. She got rude so I got rude right back. Is that all right?' 'Oh no,' says the young man, 'that was the lady who owns the dog.' 'Well, she certainly was rude,' says the girl.

"After that, the young man feels too depressed to be with the girl, so a few minutes later she goes home. The young man then scrapes Ralphie off the street and buries him in the back yard. When he gets back in the house, the phone is ringing. It's the old lady. 'I know you've got a girl in there,' she says. 'If I wasn't so sick I'd come home right now.' Then she says, 'Don't let anything happen to Ralphie, you hear me?' 'I won't,' says the young man, and he hangs up.

"Well, the young man is terrified. He can't sleep all night. He just tosses and turns and worries. The next morning he figures all he can do is look at one of these Yorkshire terriers and maybe he can find one that looks like Ralphie and when the old lady gets home maybe she won't know the difference. Just before the young man leaves the house, the old lady calls him again. 'How's Ralphie?' she asks. 'Just fine,' says the young man. 'I'll be home in an hour,' she says. 'We'll be waiting,' says the young man. The moment he hangs up he runs as fast as he can to the pet store. It's a cold November morning and beginning to rain.

"As it so happens, the young man can't believe his luck. His date was right. The store has five Yorkshire terriers and one of them looks a lot like Ralphie. The dog is expensive but the young man pays for it nonetheless. Then he grabs the dog and runs back to the old lady's house. All the way back, he says, 'Ralphie, Ralphie.' Over and over he says it, 'Ralphie, Ralphie,' hoping the dog will get used to the name before the old lady arrives.

"When the young man gets back to the house, he realizes there's just one problem. This new dog is a lot darker than the other dog. By now it's about ten minutes before the old lady is due home. The young man is frantic. He rushes with the dog into the kitchen where he finds a bag of flour. Quickly, he sprinkles flour all over the dog's fur. 'Ralphie, Ralphie,' he keeps saying, 'Ralphie, Ralphie.' Like he's still trying to get the dog used to the name. The flour seems to work. The dog gets a lot lighter and the young man shakes him over the sink to get rid of the excess. Just as he finishes cleaning up, he hears the front door open. He grabs the dog and runs to meet the old lady. 'Ralphie, Ralphie,' he says, 'Ralphie, Ralphie.'

"Well, the old lady comes in. She's obviously tired but when she sees the dog her eyes light up. 'Ralphie,' she cries. The dog wags his tail. He's a friendly little dog and the young man hopes he can get out of the house. He doesn't care if he never works for the old lady again. 'I told you not to let anyone in here,' says the old lady. 'I'm sorry,' says the young man, 'it was an old friend from high school who just dropped in to say hello.' 'I'll forgive you this once,' says the old lady. 'Great,' says the young man. All this time he is working his way toward the front door. He wants to get out of there fast. The old lady follows him. 'Just as long as Ralphie is all right,' she says, 'but if anything ever happened to this dog I'd never forgive you. He was the last thing my husband gave me before he died. Ralphie loved my husband and still remembers him well.' 'He's a fine little dog,' says the young man.

"He gets to the door, opens it, and goes out onto the front steps. The old lady follows him. It's now raining harder but the young man doesn't think of it, all he wants is to get out of there. 'Every time that Ralphie sees my husband's picture he barks a little greeting,' says the old lady. 'This little dog is the only thing I love.' She's standing on the steps and the young man is standing on the sidewalk. There's rain splashing off the roof and a few drops are splashing onto the old lady and the dog. She's so glad that Ralphie is all right that she doesn't notice the water. But the young man notices and a few seconds later he sees that a terrible thing is beginning to happen— all the water that's falling on the dog is making the flour run and leaving great dark streaks on the dog's fur. Then the old lady looks at the dog and she sees how the flour is running off the dog's nose and falling in little globlets to the sidewalk while the dog just gets streakier and streakier. She stares at the dog, then she stares at the young man. All at once she hurls the dog away from her. 'This isn't Ralphie,' she cries, 'you've betrayed me. . . .'"

"Stop!" said Bowser, "I don't want to hear anymore."

They had been walking down West Drive and were approaching Columbus Circle. Both cops had moved well away from Latchmer so it wouldn't appear they were together.

"What an awful story," said the young cop. He took off his hat and wiped his brow with his sleeve. He looked upset.

Latchmer put Jasper down on the sidewalk. "You don't want to hear the end?" he asked.

"You'd only make it worse," said the young cop. "I mean, what could happen? The new dog could get hit by a car, the old lady could have a stroke and die, and the kid's life could be ruined. And you expect us to listen to it. Hey, I'm a family man, I don't like sadness and hard times. Being a cop is bad enough."

"Guys like you," said Bowser, "you're sadness freaks. You go along with a bunch of unhappy stories and whenever you feel like changing your life you drag out one of these stories and it convinces you not to do anything. I mean, why do anything when the world's so sad?"

Latchmer picked up the bag and they began walking again toward Columbus Circle. "I sort of saw it as a funny story," he said. He thought the cops had probably disliked the story because the young man broke so many rules.

"Jesus," said the young cop, "what would you call a sad story?"

"Don't even ask," said Bowser. "Sadness freaks prey on questions like that."

Latchmer wondered if he was a sadness freak and if he wanted to change his life. He looked down at his brown corduroy suit and saw that it was torn in several places and spotted with mud and chili dog stains. He wondered if changing one's life was like putting on a new suit of clothes, or if it was like getting old clothes dirty, or dirty clothes clean.

"And betrayal," said Bowser. "Sadness freaks are always into betrayal. They're always doing somebody a bad turn, getting somebody to trust them and then giving them the double whammy. Give me my shovel and get lost."

"You really didn't think it was a funny story?" asked Latchmer, handing him the shovel.

But the patrolmen had no further interest in talking. Their cruiser was parked about fifteen yards away. Bowser took the shovel without looking at Latchmer. "I'll put this in the trunk," he said.

Latchmer stood on the sidewalk next to the black plastic bag and watched the cops get into the front seat. The sun was in his eyes and he kept blinking. The young cop started the car and when they drove past Latchmer, both cops gave him a vague look of partial recognition, as if he was someone out of their past, their childhood, a face they couldn't quite put a name to.

Latchmer picked up the bag and balanced it on one shoulder. As he watched the cruiser disappear up Central Park West, he realized he could easily go back to the park, dig the loose dirt out of the grave with his bare hands, and bury Jasper as he had originally intended. But that seemed no longer possible, something had changed. Jasper would have to have some other end.

He crossed Central Park South and began walking down Broadway. Although tired and hungry, he felt surprisingly strong, as if he could carry Jasper all the way down to the tip of Manhattan, all the way down to Battery Park. He again asked himself what he was going to do with Jasper. Maybe he could take him to the taxidermy school after all. Maybe from Battery Park he could take the Staten Island Ferry or take Jasper out to the Statue of Liberty. Maybe he could take Jasper up to the top of the World Trade Center and drop him over the side. Then the wind could deal with him; the wind could take responsibility.

But no, those plans were wrong. Maybe he could just carry him, and Latchmer imagined himself carrying Jasper year after year, carrying him to the office in the morning and the health club in the afternoon, and on dates with him at night. He would carry him to football games, baseball games, carry him to Rochester to see the relatives, carry him to that small town where his grandparents were buried and where Miss Mitchell was probably buried as well.

But those plans were also wrong. He had to find the right spot for Jasper, something like a home. Where had he taken him so far? He had taken him to the scientists, the specialists of the mind, and they did not want him. He had taken him to the furriers, the ones who protect people from wind and rain, and they told him to move on. He had taken him to the cooks, the specialists of the belly, the ones who save people from starvation, and they told him to get lost. He had taken him to the sex shops, the specialists of lust and desire, and they had sent him on his way. He had even buried him, had seen him into the ground, and it was as if the ground had spat him up again. What was left?

Near Fiftieth Street he sat down on a bench to rest. It was eight o'clock Sunday morning. At a newsstand by the entrance to the subway people were buying copies of the Sunday *Times*. Latchmer held the bag partly on his lap. Rolling back the black plastic, he looked at Jasper's face. In the bright light of morning, the face seemed hard and undoglike. The skin appeared stretched. Latchmer reached down and covered the dog's muzzle so that only the top part of the face was visible. It made the dog look almost human. Latchmer even found the face familiar. Perhaps the dog looked like Mrs. Hughes, Jasper's owner. Maybe that was what happened when you had a pet for a dozen years—either you grew to look like it or it grew to look like you, just like an old married couple.

If Jasper had grown to look like his owner, then he must also look like Miss Mitchell, whom Mrs. Hughes resembled. Latchmer stared down at the dog and pushed the ears back out of the way, trying to recreate Miss Mitchell's face as he had last seen it.

He had been leaving the cemetery. He had wanted to be by himself and was walking back to his grandparents' house. At the entrance to the cemetery were two brick pillars and on top of each was a marble statue of an eagle perched as if on a mountain crag. The wrought iron gates stood open and Latchmer passed between them. When he reached the street, he saw Miss Mitchell was waiting for him. His impulse was to turn and run. Instead, he forced himself to keep walking as if she wasn't there. She stood in the middle of the sidewalk as he approached. To her left was the red brick wall of the cemetery. Latchmer began to move around her but she also moved, blocking his path. She was a foot taller than he and stared down at him.

He had no choice but to stop and look at her. He felt unhappy and scared because it seemed she was crazy. She wore no make-up and her face was very pale. It was a narrow face with high cheek bones and a long straight nose. Her light blue eyes seemed to poke and dig into him. She looked at him for a long time and it seemed her face went through many changes, many expressions from sadness to disappointment to grief, but finally she began to smile.

When Latchmer saw her smile, he started to feel relieved. But then he realized there was no warmth in her smile. She was mocking him. It seemed she was looking into him as if through a window or down a deep well, down into a dark place where there were only a couple of skinny creatures quarreling with each other and fighting over a bone. She stood above him and stared down to the very bottom of himself, and what she saw, he saw as well: saw the dark place and the meanness there. Then she pulled back and it was like a door being slammed shut. But instead of being on the outside, Latchmer had been left in that dark place along with his meanness, pettiness, his trivial fears.

Miss Mitchell reached out, took hold of Latchmer's chin, and lifted it slightly. "You broke your promise to me," she said.

"I didn't tell about the ring."

"No, but you wanted to. Why didn't you do as I asked?"

Latchmer tried to look away from her eyes. "I don't know, my grandmother was acting strange and I knew I had to help her. I didn't have the chance to talk to you—"

"That's not good enough," interrupted Miss Mitchell. "You were scared. You were afraid your grandmother would get angry. Your grandfather said you were stronger than that. You know, if I was a witch, I would curse you."

"How would you curse me?" asked Latchmer, frightened.

"Maybe I'd make you a toad."

Latchmer was so scared he wanted to cry. He tried to imagine life as a toad. "Not that," he managed to say.

Miss Mitchell smiled, but again it was without warmth. "No, not a toad. I would curse you with human things. Unhappiness, stupidity, superficiality, the inability to love. But I don't need to. You'll end up cursing yourself."

"What would I curse myself with?" He couldn't tell if she was serious.

Miss Mitchell let go of his chin, actually giving it a little push. "You'll find out," she said. Then she turned and walked away.

Latchmer sat on the bench with Jasper's head on his lap. He felt dreadful, and again he wondered how much was true and how much invented. But no, it was all true. Wasn't this the dragon memory? Looking down at Jasper's face, Latchmer took his fingers and prized up the edges of Jasper's lips so the dog seemed to be smiling. By pushing up at the corners and pulling down the front of the mouth, Latchmer tried to recreate the smile he had seen on Miss Mitchell's face nearly twenty-five years before. Then he looked at it, looked at Jasper staring at him with a mocking grin, and again he had a sense of that dark place within himself where the small creatures were quarreling, where he was again confronted with his meanness and triviality. And having seen that part of himself, he was stuck with it as he had never been as a child. This time there would be no forgetting. Whatever he did with Jasper, the memory would stay with him.

But did the face really look like Miss Mitchell's? Staring at it again, he thought it didn't. Still, it seemed familiar. Perhaps it was Sarah's face. After all, she resembled both women: a narrow face with high cheek bones. No, said Latchmer to himself, it's none of those faces. It's my face. Seeing it without the snout or ears was like looking into a mirror. It wasn't a nice face. It reflected pettiness and superficiality.

This is my own face, thought Latchmer. This dog is me. And it struck Latchmer that the dog represented his own guilty feelings, guilt he had never admitted but which was still poisoning his life until memory had made him aware of it: guilt for the betrayal of Miss Mitchell, for his grandparents, and even for himself. No wonder I don't like philosophy, thought Latchmer, if it gets me into pickles like this one.

And instead of accepting his guilt, he had tried to foist it off. He had tried to give the dog to the scientists and furriers and cooks and sex specialists and each time he had failed. As for the dog stories, maybe he hadn't even told them. Maybe Jasper had told them in order to turn people against him. He had been possessed. Wasn't he normally a terrible storyteller? Jasper had taken over his tongue.

Then he stopped himself. Here again he was putting the blame someplace else. He had told those stories all by himself and had done it only to upset people. Why had he ever thought that Mrs. Hughes would like a story about rubber dog turds on a carpet? If he didn't try to understand what he was doing, he was destined to repeat the same actions over and over, like taking Jasper to place after place and never getting rid of him. It was only by saying, Yes, this is my life, that he could move forward.

But what could he do with this guilt? He thought of how Miss Mitchell had said he would end up cursing himself and he wondered if this was it and he imagined hanging Jasper around his neck just like the guy with the bird. But no, there were other solutions. He could acknowledge the guilt, take it inside himself. After all, how could he live unless he took charge of his life? Jean-Claude was right, he had to take charge. It was only by believing this that he could free himself of Jasper.

As Latchmer leaned back on the bench wondering what to do, he saw a garbage truck pull up to the corner of Broadway and Fifty-first Street. Two men in blue coveralls jumped off the side, picked up a trash container, and emptied it into the back. Then one of the men gave a sharp whistle and the truck moved slowly forward along Broadway. From the cab came the sound of rock and roll music: the J. Geils Band declaiming that after all love, too, stunk. The garbage truck stopped again at Fiftieth Street and again the men emptied a trash container into the back. Then, instead of driving away, the two men and the driver hurried across Broadway to a small coffee shop.

Latchmer sat looking at the garbage truck. Way deep inside him, he heard a voice frantically urging him forward. At first he hardly understood. What should he do? Just dump the dog in the back? But if Jasper was so connected to him, if the dog existed as an image of his own guilt, then surely he couldn't just throw him away. Something else was needed first. Quickly, he stripped the plastic bags from Jasper and sat him up on his lap. The dog was hard and rigid, all four legs stuck straight out and the head pointed upward. His black lips were still shiny with lipstick from Jojo's One-Stop Sex Shop. Latchmer squeezed his hands against Jasper's ribs. Although dead, the dog seemed full of life. Latchmer even thought he saw him move, a twitch of an eyebrow, a jerk of the tail. Latchmer opened his mouth and drew Jasper to him, pressing the dog's mouth to his own, trying to suck the dog into his own body. At first there was nothing, only resistance. Then, very slowly, he felt as if Jasper was passing across his lips, filling his mouth and throat. He felt like a boa constrictor eating a small pig. Bit by bit Jasper slid into his body, down into his lungs and stomach and legs, filling his body as water fills a riverbed. And there, deep inside him, Latchmer felt the dog begin to move, stirring slightly as if just waking up, sliding his paws down Latchmer's arms and legs, positioning his chest inside Latchmer's chest, sliding his head up Latchmer's throat so Jasper's black nose lay at the very back of Latchmer's mouth.

When it was done, only a few moments had gone by. Latchmer glanced at the dead dog on his lap. It was nothing, just a corpse, all that was important had been joined together inside him. Clumsily, he got to his feet and gathered the dead dog in his arms, cradling him like a bag of laundry. He took a step forward, then another. His own body felt heavy and his legs tingled as if asleep. Across the street, he could see the men from the garbage truck waiting at the cash register. Latchmer took another step. He felt he was climbing a steep hill. Inside him, the real Jasper was just coming to his senses and stretching his legs. He was surprised by his surroundings and perhaps a little frightened. As yet he didn't have his movements coordinated with Latchmer's and so Latchmer stumbled and could hardly walk. The men from the garbage truck were paying their bill and already opening the door. Latchmer knew if he didn't get rid of the corpse immediately, he might be stuck with it forever. But then it seemed Jasper himself finally understood and helped guide Latchmer's feet. He did more than just guide, he helped Latchmer to run. With a burst of energy, Latchmer sprinted the last few yards across the sidewalk, hurled the body of the dog into the back of the garbage truck, then ran back to the bench and sat down as if nothing had happened.

Seconds later the three men came out of the coffee shop carrying small brown paper bags and white Styrofoam cups. One of the men looked at Latchmer. Maybe he was Puerto Rican. He had a thin handsome face and his blue coveralls appeared brand-new. He nodded to Latchmer as if he recognized him. Latchmer nodded back. The three men got into the cab of the truck and slowly drove off. Sticking out of the back was the tip of a red tail. Latchmer watched it as the dog inside of him, turning this way and that, tried to get comfortable. Is there really a dog inside me? he asked. And it seemed there was—something cumbersome and furry and with a tail of its own, something that would guide and direct him with little barks, growls, and perhaps a nip or two.

Suddenly there was a honking from the curb. Latchmer looked up to see a half-demolished station wagon without hood or front fenders. The sides were scraped so badly that one could hardly see its original green color. Jean-Claude was sitting behind the wheel. He waved at Latchmer to come over.

Latchmer walked across the sidewalk to the car, sort of bouncing on his toes in a way that made Jean-Claude stare at him. He now knew what it meant to be a river and knew that he was a river no longer. "What is it?" he asked.

"I am very angry," said Jean-Claude.

"Why?"

"You cheated me."

"I didn't cheat you," said Latchmer. "What are you talking about?"

"Where's Jasper?" asked Jean-Claude. In the light of day, the Haitian's round black face looked rough and pock-marked. The frames of his Buddy Holly glasses had been broken and repaired with Scotch tape. The style of his hair, the way it stood up at different levels, seemed not a matter of design but caused by scalp disease.

Latchmer pointed down Broadway toward the garbage truck. "You see that little sticklike thing pointing up from the back?" he asked. "That's Jasper's tail." He didn't mind lying, the occasion seemed to require it. In truth, Jasper was curled up warm and comfortable inside his own body.

"You mean he's in the garbage truck?"

"That's right."

"What did they give you for him?"

"Nothing. I just tossed him in the back."

"You mean you let them have Jasper for free?"

"That's right," said Latchmer.

"But we can sell him, no trouble. Just because we have had one or two disappointments is no reason to give up."

"You sell him," said Latchmer. He felt strong and confident. "If you want Jasper, then go get him. It's not too late. You can have my share of the profits."

"But we're partners," said Jean-Claude. He was leaning across the front seat of the station wagon with his head out the window. He looked up at Latchmer and spoke quickly. "I know a school where they teach young people how to stuff animals. It's over in Brooklyn. They would give good money for a dog like that. It is a fine opportunity. In Haiti, yes, when we have a dead dog, we just throw him away. But here, a dog that is dead is not really dead. It changes from being one kind of commodity to another. We could take that dog to dozens of places and one day we would find a person who wanted him. We would find a person who would think Jasper was important. There is always somebody who wants things. But beyond that, the dog does not matter. He is nothing. Dogs, dogs, who needs them? What is important is that we are partners. We are in this together. Since I have not seen you, I have been very worried. I visited Jojo and he said he asked you to leave because of some story you told. But I like your stories, I like all your stories. They show a great sympathy for what it is like to be a dog. And I have been driving all over this morning, searching for you and poor Jasper, because the three of us, we are in this together, right? We are in this for the long haul."

Latchmer felt sorry for Jean-Claude but knew he couldn't help him. Whatever the dog symbolized for the Haitian, it was different from what he meant to Latchmer. Jean-Claude would have to work out his fate by himself. Perhaps someday Jean-Claude would also take part of Jasper inside him, then he and Latchmer might meet and talk about it and perhaps grow to be friends.

"You better go rescue that dog," said Latchmer, "before he disappears into the truck."

"And you'll wait here?"

"Sure. We're partners, aren't we?" Latchmer felt guilty about lying, but then it was such a novelty to feel guilty that he almost enjoyed it.

"No tricks?" Jean-Claude looked up at him suspiciously. The garbage truck was now about three blocks away.

"Of course not," said Latchmer.

Jean-Claude jumped back behind the wheel and tromped down on the gas. The Plymouth hurtled forward with a sharp squealing noise. It was tilted to one side and the back bumper dragged on the pavement. The muffler was missing and the resulting roar reminded Latchmer of the stock car races he had loved as a teenager. With its dents and scrapes and crumpled doors, the station wagon seemed to be made entirely from scrap metal.

Latchmer watched it go. It seemed he had been given a new life and he thought of all the things he might do. He considered visiting Sarah, of waking her and telling her to teach him the pressure cooker. She would ask what had happened to Jasper and he would say he had buried Jasper in the best place in the world. Would she realize that he had buried Jasper in his own body? Perhaps she wouldn't understand. Perhaps he should have breakfast instead. He thought of two different restaurants. One made great omelets, the other made great French toast. Jean-Claude had started honking at the garbage truck. Even the horn seemed broken. It made a hoarse, gasping noise. Latchmer looked up at the sky. He couldn't remember when he had last seen it so blue. Then Latchmer thought of another restaurant famous for its fresh fruit salads. He could order fresh fruit and croissants and café au lait. He could sit at one of the outside tables under a green umbrella and contemplate the nature of his new life. The entrance to the subway was just at the corner. For a moment, he stared after Jean-Claude, who had now reached the garbage truck. He had gotten out of the station wagon and was arguing with the two men in blue coveralls. Latchmer could almost hear Jean-Claude's voice: high, complaining, and far away, so far away that it hardly existed at all.

Latchmer hurried toward the entrance of the subway. The stairs were littered with bits of paper, cigar butts, and a couple of beer bottles. He ran down them, his heels clicking on the cement. He could feel Jasper running inside him, as if running through a field of tall grass. He was sure the dog was happy. The air was dark and cool on Latchmer's face. Beneath him was the great cavern of the subway. He imagined it stretching thousands of miles under the city, like a person's nervous system or a network of veins and arteries. That's like me, thought Latchmer, and I'm going to learn all about it. Latchmer heard the rumbling and rattling of an approaching train. He ran faster. He was so happy that he felt like barking. He would jump the gate.

FOR THE BEST IN PAPERBACKS, LOOK FOR THE

In every corner of the world, on every subject under the sun, Penguin represents quality and variety—the very best in publishing today.

For complete information about books available from Penguin—including Pelicans, Puffins, Peregrines, and Penguin Classics—and how to order them, write to us at the appropriate address below. Please note that for copyright reasons the selection of books varies from country to country.

In the United Kingdom: For a complete list of books available from Penguin in the U.K., please write to *Dept E.P., Penguin Books Ltd, Harmondsworth, Middlesex, UB7 0DA.*

In the United States: For a complete list of books available from Penguin in the U.S., please write to *Dept BA, Penguin*, Box 120, Bergenfield, New Jersey 07621-0120.

In Canada: For a complete list of books available from Penguin in Canada, please write to *Penguin Books Ltd, 2801 John Street, Markham, Ontario L3R 1B4*.

In Australia: For a complete list of books available from Penguin in Australia, please write to the *Marketing Department, Penguin Books Ltd, P.O. Box 257, Ringwood, Victoria 3134.*

In New Zealand: For a complete list of books available from Penguin in New Zealand, please write to the *Marketing Department, Penguin Books (NZ) Ltd, Private Bag, Takapuna, Auckland 9.*

In India: For a complete list of books available from Penguin, please write to *Penguin Overseas Ltd, 706 Eros Apartments, 56 Nehru Place, New Delhi, 110019.*

In Holland: For a complete list of books available from Penguin in Holland, please write to *Penguin Books Nederland B.V., Postbus 195, NL-1380AD Weesp, Netherlands.*

In Germany: For a complete list of books available from Penguin, please write to *Penguin Books Ltd, Friedrichstrasse 10-12, D-6000 Frankfurt Main I, Federal Republic of Germany.*

In Spain: For a complete list of books available from Penguin in Spain, please write to *Longman, Penguin España, Calle San Nicolas 15, E-28013 Madrid, Spain.*

In Japan: For a complete list of books available from Penguin in Japan, please write to *Longman Penguin Japan Co Ltd, Yamaguchi Building, 2-12-9 Kanda Jimbocho, Chiyoda-Ku, Tokyo 101, Japan.*